Alien Blood Wars

BLOOD DANCE

SAMANTHA CAYTO

Blood Dance
ISBN # 978-1-78686-345-4
©Copyright Samantha Cayto 2018
Cover Art by Posh Gosh ©Copyright February 2018
Interior text design by Claire Siemaszkiewicz
Pride Publishing

BLOOD DANCE

Prologue

Southern Carpathian Mountains
1022

"Blow it." The captain gave the order in the same measured tone that he'd used throughout the long journey and the emergency landing. He had no choice. His crew depended on his staying calm and in control, even though his insides were quaking as much as theirs.

"You can't be serious!" His first officer dared to grab his arm and put his face in close. His furious expression was like a physical punch. "We'll be trapped here forever."

Shaking off the hold, the captain said, "We're already marooned, you fool. We cannot allow the indigenous population to see our craft, let alone claim it."

With a jerk of his head, he reiterated his order. The young engineer, who was forced to take on the mantle of chief, set off his series of well-placed charges. The great irony of their crash was that while most of their essentials were so much metallic junk, the explosives they'd carried to take core samples from planets had survived.

They did their adapted job admirably. The remnants of his very first ship as captain turned into a fiery ball that shot plumes of flame high into the night sky. *What will the natives think of such a sight? Who can say?* They were undoubtedly still pondering the meaning of the bright streak created by the crash, so one more unfathomable event hardly mattered.

The first officer bared his teeth, the glow of the fire shining off the white enamel. "You've doomed us! We're stranded here now."

"Our fates were sealed the moment we left the wormhole prematurely."

"A mistake made by *your* navigator."

"Yes, and he paid the ultimate penalty for it." The captain closed his eyes briefly against the pain of his loss. He'd hand-picked most of the crew and now over two-thirds of them were gone. He forced calm into his voice before he gave in to the temptation to shove his fist into his first officer's face. This bickering was useless — and dangerous. If they had any hope of surviving, they needed to work together.

"We were never going to be able to fix the ship. This primitive ball of dirt won't have what we need. The longer we left the wreck intact, the more likely local intelligent beings would get over their fear and come explore the goings-on here. You've already killed two of them," he added with a snarl because he still felt guilty.

The male scoffed. "They got too close. I did what had to be done, and what do you care? These creatures are far beneath our species. Their intelligence is less than that of a child. They spend their days watching other animals eat grass that they've just pissed and shit in."

"Exactly. In small numbers, they are no threat to us. There are less lethal ways to deal with them, but we can't afford to let others of their kind know we are on their planet. They will react out of fear and we number only thirty now. If enough of them attack, not even our weapons will save us."

The male's eyes flashed with glee. "Then we attack them first. If we have to live on this far-flung place, at least we can rule it as we see fit."

"No! We are warriors, trained and pledged to defend."

"Our *own* people — the hive."

"Everyone!" he roared, his patience at an end. There were more important and urgent matters. They needed to move on from this place and find somewhere to settle before the locals got bolder, an isolated spot until they could determine how to blend into this world. Thankfully, their species appeared outwardly similar enough to give them a fighting chance to do so.

As he stared his first officer, the others arranged themselves in an emerging pattern. Half of the surviving crew placed themselves behind the belligerent male, while the captain could feel others covering his back.

So, is this how it's going to be?

He tried for more patience and reason. "We must work together to forge some kind of life. Perhaps our people will find us one day. Maybe the highest of the creatures living on this planet will gain technology and wisdom to a point that we can reveal ourselves and find a way home."

He stared into the eyes of someone he'd thought of as a friend, someone else he'd picked for his crew. "We have a long time to discover a solution to our situation. This planet can support us. The sun may be too bright, but the night comes often enough. We can breathe the air and the lower gravity makes it easy for us to maneuver. Even the available food is palatable so far."

The officer flicked his tongue across his teeth. "The aliens do taste good. Sweet," he added with a heavy-lidded gaze.

Sometimes being captain meant putting aside personal disgust and doing what was best for the crew. "Yes, their blood can sustain us, but there are other things to consume. We will not kill sentient beings again unless we are given no choice. In time, we might find those who will be willing to feed us."

Although the officer raised his eyebrows at the word 'willing', he also inclined his head in subtle submission. "You heard the captain," he bellowed to those around them. "Pack what you have and be ready to move. This place holds nothing for us now."

His officer had said the right words, sending the crew scrambling to obey, yet when he turned back to nod once again, there was a look in his eye that told the captain all he needed to know.

The battle over the course their future would take was not finished.

Chapter One

Boston, Massachusetts
2017

Quinn blinked a few times to help adjust his vision to the dimness of the club. Compared to the bright, sunny day outside, the black walls, carpet and low-lit sconces gave the entryway a tunnel-like effect. The rapid eye movement caused his world to tilt a bit — or that might have been the gnawing hunger. He'd spent his last few dollars on a stale sandwich more than twenty-four hours ago and he was beginning to feel the drop in blood sugar. *God, if I don't get this job, I'm totally screwed.* He'd have to implement Plan B, and given that it meant selling his body on the street, he prayed that wouldn't happen.

The short hall led to a massive, two-story club room. For a second, Quinn stood and stared at the gorgeous opulence that was Lux, according to the sign on the door — a private gentlemen's club. The open floor plan contained a sunken dance floor surrounded by plush circular booths all along the edges. A shiny, dark wooden bar ran the length of the back wall and high-tops of the same material dotted the railings of the interior. Everything here was black, too, trimmed with silver and red.

What caught his attention the most, however, were the small, round stages at the four corners of the dance floor. Each one had a stripper pole imbedded in the middle. That was where he'd be working — *if* he got the job and *if* he didn't pass out from lack of food or an overload of adrenaline. *Why did I think coming to Boston would be a good idea?* He should have stayed in Michigan and found some low-paying work until he could afford to be bold. Right now, he felt like a lost kid in the big city. Thank God, he hadn't stopped in New York. The Big Apple would have eaten him alive in five seconds.

Instead of the two days that Beantown is threatening to take.

"Hey, kid, what's doing?"

Quinn jumped at the sudden question, issued in a booming voice to his left. Turning, he saw a huge man lounging at one of the plush tables against the wall. He had black hair in a Mohawk cut, pale skin and impressively large muscles bulging out of a tight, dark T-shirt. He had 'bouncer' written all over him, yet regarded Quinn with an appraising intelligence that made his empty belly quake even more.

The only thing breaking up the frightening façade was a red-headed twink curled in the guy's lap like a cat. The boy sported a half-shaved hairstyle where one side was stubble and the other had thick, straight strands curved against his jaw. Silver hoops twinkled around the shell of his ear. Quinn envied the edgy look and wondered if he could pull it off. That was, if he started making money, which wouldn't happen if he stood there with his mouth open.

Mustering the last of his courage, he answered, "An online ad said you were hiring go-go boys. I'm…ah, here to apply for the job." The fact that the club was advertising for boys, not girls, told him it was for gay patrons. The sight of the bouncer-guy with the twink confirmed it.

The hulk and his boy toy stared some more at Quinn. He tried not to shrink under the attention. He knew he had a scuzzy appearance, having traveled by bus for a couple of days and catching what sleep he could on a park bench the previous night. He'd at least gone to the nearby train station and washed in the men's room as best he could. He'd also put on the last of his clean jeans and a rumpled button-down that his grandmother had given him the previous Christmas — before he'd come out and turned into a wicked child undeserving of anything.

The man licked his lower lip. "How old are you?"

"Eighteen, sir." He knew he appeared younger and hoped that would earn him both a job and more tips. *God, it sucks counting on the world being populated by pervs in order to make a living.*

The man shot him a skeptical look. "You got ID.?"

"Yes, sir." Quinn walked to the table while he fished his wallet from his front pocket. He pulled out his driver's license and offered it.

The man reached over without having to move — his arm being that long — and plucked the plastic card from Quinn's trembling hand. He was so hungry and stressed that he felt like he was going to fly apart — or pass out. Face-planting on the thick carpet was a *definite* possibility.

"Relax, kid. I don't bite...much," the bouncer added with a flash of gleaming white teeth.

The redhead giggled and snuggled closer to the broad chest he curled against. Something predatory flashed in the boy's one visible eye. Quinn ignored it. He wouldn't mind putting up with some bitchiness if it meant earning a living without having to suck off strange men in alleys.

With a grunt, the man handed back the card. The action caused their fingers to touch and the bouncer's felt oddly cool. "Seems legit, although I'd swear you're no older than sixteen. I suppose the members will like that, though," he added with another blinding smile. "Go take him to the boss, Mackie."

The boy made a little mew with his pouty, full lips, but slipped off the man's lap, anyway. He looked incredibly slutty to Quinn, wearing a white sleeveless crop-top hanging off one shoulder and skinny jeans that hugged his thin body.

Cocking his hip, the boy raked his gaze up and down Quinn with his lips pursed. "You sure you can hack being a go-go boy? At a glance, I'd say you just got off the bus from get-me-the-fuck-out-of-here, Iowa, or something."

Quinn squared his shoulders. He wasn't going to let this kid get under his skin. "Close. It was Michigan, actually."

The twink opened his mouth and a yelp came out because the man had swatted his ass. "Be nice, Mackie, and do as you're told...or else."

Mackie gave a petulant sniff and glanced over his shoulder. "You'll punish me later?"

Jesus, the guy sounds eager for it.

The man gave him an indulgent smile. "Yeah, except it will be the kind you don't like."

"Humph." Mackie turned his gaze to Quinn. "Come on. Let's go see the boss. I suppose you'll be okay," he added with a flick of his wrist.

"Thank you, sir." Quinn gave the man a quick nod before falling into step beside Mackie.

They walked over to one end of the bar to a small elevator recessed into the wall.

Mackie pushed the call button. "Just an FYI, sweetheart, Val is all mine."

"Val?" The door swooshed open and they stepped inside.

Mackie pushed the top button for the fifth floor. "Yeah, the man I was recently and happily groping until you arrived. He's the head bouncer and the boss' right-hand man," he added with a flip of the long part of his hair. "They're also cousins or something. This is mostly a family-run business, except for a few outsiders like me. I've been here for over a year already," he added, as if proving his standing. "Val and I have been an exclusive item for most of that time. Neither of us is into sharing, either." He shot a warning at Quinn.

"Oh. No worries. I'm here for a job, not a boyfriend."

"Great, then we should get along famously."

The short ride caused sufficient movement to make Quinn lightheaded again. When they stepped into a small vestibule, he had to take a deep breath to steady himself. Mackie pushed a button on an intercom by a large door opposite the elevator. Like everything else in the place, the color scheme ran to black, red and silver and the lighting was muted.

"Yes?" A deep, rich voice floated out and right into Quinn's nervous system, causing goosebumps to rise on his arms and the back of his neck.

Mackie glanced up and following his gaze, Quinn saw a small camera mounted in the corner. "Val sent me for you to interview a dancer." The boy jerked his thumb in Quinn's direction.

There was no response for a few seconds, and once again, Quinn straightened his back to put on the best appearance. He could feel invisible eyes judging him. A clicking sound came from the door and Mackie twisted the handle to open it. Apparently, the boss was a man of few words.

The apartment they walked into followed the same décor as everything else. It was done in an open loft plan, yet it managed to convey a sense of coziness. *Probably the dim lighting.* Quinn felt as if he'd entered a cave—a lair, really—and its inhabitant didn't do anything to dispel that feeling as he strode toward them. Quinn's breath caught in his throat and his steps faltered.

If the bouncer, Val, had seemed big to him before, that was no longer true. While not as beefy, the boss gave the appearance of being at least taller and his shoulders were as broad as any linebacker. He had the same jet-black hair and pale skin as Val did, although he wore it swept back in a queue of unknown length. The style accentuated a sharp widow's peak. His untucked button-down shirt was a deep red, while his slacks were as black as his hair. He walked with a kind of grace powerful men often possessed and his amazingly violet eyes would have made Liz Taylor jealous.

The man stopped at the bottom of the three steps leading to a sunken living room and stuck one hand in a front pocket. "Who do we have here, Mackie?"

The boy shrugged. "Some kid from Minnesota who thinks he can dance."

"Michigan," Quinn corrected in a voice too hoarse to impress anyone.

Mackie shrugged again. "Same dif."

Because the other boy made no move to join the boss in the living room, Quinn planted himself in the entryway, too. He worked up some moisture for his dry mouth. "My name is Quinn Cooper, sir."

"Quinn," the man repeated, and this time, his voice held a hint of some kind of accent. "I'm Alexandru Stelalux. Everyone calls me Alex."

Okay, that explains the accent. He must be from somewhere in Europe. Quinn now had too much spit in his mouth, so he swallowed before speaking. "It's nice to meet you, sir. I hope you'll consider me for the job."

Mr. Stelalux — Alex — stared at him for a moment. His gaze made Val's perusal seem like a casual glance. "Do you have a resume?"

Quinn fixed his attention on his feet. "Um, no, sir. I'm sorry I didn't think of that. I've only ever worked at my family's hardware store, anyway. I have no dancing experience other than in school plays."

Mackie smirked at the confession and Alex chuckled, except it didn't sound like he was being contemptuous. "Well, that's all right. It's not like I'm considering you to tend bar or keep my accounting books. My clientele likes pretty boys to dance for their amusement. They don't even really care how skilled you are, either, so long as you look good doing it. The only real job requirement is having the right body."

He paced closer and cocked his head. "You've got a nice one from what I can see. All that shaggy blond hair and those bright blue eyes will certainly turn heads." He stepped to one side. "Yes, lovely profile. You'd make a nice contrast to the other boys. Don't you think so, Mackie?"

The other boy studied his nails. "I *suppose*."

Alex's expression became stern. "Don't be bitchy, Mackie. You know I can't abide that."

Mackie straightened and appeared contrite. "Yes, sir." He slanted his gaze toward Quinn. "He's very pretty, and we haven't had a blond since Blake left."

"Exactly. Come here, please." Alex stepped back and flung himself on the end of a large sectional sofa. Then he braced his arms on the back of it, slung an ankle over a knee and watched as Quinn entered the living room area. "I'm afraid I'm going to have to ask you to strip. Nothing fancy, just take everything off except your underwear. We're not a nude club—not on the dance floor, anyway."

Quinn's head really began to swim and his palms turned sweaty. He told himself it was no big deal as he placed his scruffy backpack on the carpet by a chair. He would have to get used to being mostly naked in front of a big crowd. *If I can't do it now with only two guys watching, what hope do I have of keeping the job?*

Silent and self-conscious, he toed off his sneakers, pulled off his socks and unbuttoned his shirt. He folded the clothing and placed it on top of his pack before unsnapping his jeans. His vision blurred and he took deep breaths to keep oxygen pumping into his lungs. The sound of the zipper of his worn jeans lowering rang in his ears at an exaggerated decibel. As he slid the cotton down his legs, the room tilted enough that he grabbed the arm of the nearby chair to keep from tipping over. When he'd stripped to his boxer-briefs, he stood with his arms behind his back and his gaze fixed on the floor. His cheeks felt as though they were on fire.

"Hmm, a bit on the skinny side." A sigh crossed the room. "Then again, some patrons do like that sort of thing. I think you could use a few good meals, though."

The mention of food made Quinn's stomach grumble in protest before it clenched in pain. Quinn couldn't hold back the gasp. He wrapped his arm around his waist and listed to one side. Once more, he grabbed the arm of the chair, except this time, it wasn't going to be enough to keep him from falling. His vision blurred then closed to an ever-smaller circle of light before going completely black.

The last thing he was aware of was a rush of movement and something strong catching him.

Keeping the boy from hitting the floor was the easy part. Doing it with a speed that was possible for a human to achieve was what had made the feat difficult. For all the time Mackie spent with Val, the human boy was not privy to their secrets. It was damn inconvenient sometimes, maintaining the façade, especially when in one's own home. Alex was going to have to have a talk with Val soon. Either the man committed to Mackie or he had to let him go.

The human weighed as little as expected, which bothered Alex. During the thousand years he'd spent with this species, he recognized when they were malnourished. Quinn's soft skin stretched too tightly over his delicate frame, a testament to not eating enough in recent days or even weeks. That didn't stop the thrum of his heartbeat from snaking its way into Alex's blood, turning him thirsty and hard.

As he carried his charge over to the sofa, he tossed Mackie an order. "Find Harry."

"Sure thing, boss."

The human's footsteps retreated, telling Alex that the boy had obeyed—not that he'd had any doubt. Commanding humans was all too easy. They responded to forceful tones. He expected Mackie would find Harry ensconced in his office, as the man usually was. Although Harry was trained in life sciences for exploration purposes, he'd managed to adapt as a physician for the crew. He'd also obtained a human degree in medicine and often aided the employees with minor problems.

He hoped there was nothing wrong with this one...Quinn. *A lovely name for a lovely boy. So soft and warm, the way humans typically are.* Alex felt the tug of those attributes as he always did. He hadn't indulged himself in human companionship for quite some time. Knowing his weakness for this species, he worked at abstaining as much as possible for fear of giving away too much of himself and of taking too much from the human.

But this boy was almost irresistible, the perfect embodiment of everything Alex loved in his unwitting planetary hosts — delicate, pale beauty. He was so unlike Alex's own species and his fair hair was both exotic and silky. The human smelled so sweet, too. Laying him down, Alex took in a deep breath and savored it. *Delectable.* Like a meadow after a spring rain.

He shook his head and chuckled low at his own flights of fancy. A poet he was not, but he was always a sucker for the needy and the beautiful. Put the two together and his protective instincts roared to the forefront. To that end, he covered the boy in a soft throw to keep him warm and give him back some modesty. Silly, given that Quinn would probably be stripping to a G-string that very night, if he felt ready. The sudden picture of other men slavering over him irritated the hell out of Alex for some reason. *Ridiculous. What's the matter with me?*

Knowing hydration would always help and needing to give himself something to do other than gazing at the boy, he sprinted over to the kitchen. He grabbed a bottle of water and a made a cold compress out of a dish towel. He returned to the sofa and found his would-be employee still out. So, he placed the cloth across the boy's forehead and knelt with the water to wait for Quinn to revive.

His gaze was drawn to the pulse at the base of the boy's throat. That steady throb mesmerized him. The sound of the blood racing through the veins called to him. He had a hard time keeping his biting canines inside the roof of his mouth. Saliva pooled, making him swallow convulsively. It would be so easy to bend and sink his teeth into that slender neck. He knew he could take a quick drink, lap the puncture wounds closed and blame the residual marks as somehow coming from the fall. Over the centuries, he and his men had learned well how to cover their tracks.

But, no. He'd followed a strict code of conduct for close to a thousand Earth years. Consent from human blood donors was critical. They were sentient beings deserving of a certain respect, which included not using them as a blood source without permission. He'd laid down that law for himself and his crew and had lost half of them because of that and other rules. He'd be the worst possible hypocrite if he gave in to this almost-overwhelming urge, notwithstanding that he couldn't remember ever being so tempted before.

The boy's long, thick lashes fluttered, pulling Alex out of his need and forcing him to concentrate on those of his guest. *Thank God*, as the humans would say. *Saved from my own weakness by the boy coming around.*

Quinn opened his eyes and moaned prettily. "Shit, did I pass out?"

Alex smiled at him to alleviate any concerns that he'd done something bad. "You certainly did. Here, have some water," he added, unscrewing the cap.

Cupping the back of Quinn's neck, he helped him raise his head enough to take a few sips. Alex allowed himself to touch that pulse with the pad of his thumb. Just the feel of it sent his cock into overdrive, hardening even more and pressing against his fly. He had to stifle the groan threatening to come out. It was a relief when the boy stopped drinking and dropped his head back.

"Better?" Alex fumbled with unsteady hands to get the cap back on and put the bottle on the floor.

Quinn licked his lush pink lips. "Yes, sir. Thank you."

"Alex. Everyone calls me Alex. Remember?"

The human's cheeks turned a dusky rose color in that delightful way they did when the creatures got embarrassed. "Yes, sir. Alex. I, ah, don't suppose I got the job."

Before Alex could answer, they were interrupted by Harry rushing in. "Mackie told me I have a patient?"

"Indeed." Alex stood, reluctantly giving Harry room to tend the boy. "This is Quinn, our new go-go boy," he added because he wanted that worry off the boy's mind. He was rewarded with a wan smile.

"Quinn, this is Horatiu Stelalux, my uncle."

They had long ago adopted human names from the region where they'd first settled. They'd also found the easiest thing to do was to pretend a familial relationship using human terms. After all, they did come from the same hive, so they were related, just not in a way that would make sense to someone like Quinn.

"Everyone just calls me Harry," the man added before pulling the coffee table closer to the sofa to use as a chair.

Alex winced inwardly. The furniture was too big and heavy for a human to move so easily, but it was hard to keep the pretense a hundred percent of the time. Poor Quinn was still too unfocused to notice it and Mackie hadn't returned with Harry. The healer went through the usual routine of checking heart rate, blood pressure and the like. Alex marveled at how at ease the guy was. If Alex had to muck about with a human's bloodstream he might go mad from keeping himself restrained.

Harry sat back. "You seem perfectly fine, young man, other than needing a good meal or two."

"Thank you, sir." The boy pushed himself to a sitting position. "I'm sorry for causing all the drama."

Alex found himself standing by the boy's head before he even registered his own movement. Good thing Quinn had been staring at his own feet and not Alex's rendition of The Flash. He laid a gentle, yet firm, hand on the boy's chest and once more savored the rhythm of the human's heartbeat.

"Don't rise until you've had more to drink and something to eat." He used his commanding tone in order to ward off any resistance. He also shoved a couple of pillows behind the boy to bolster his back.

Handing Quinn the bottle of water, Harry nodded in agreement. "Yes, those are the doctor's orders."

Quinn took the bottle and drank a healthy amount. "Thank you, Doctor." He flicked his gaze at Alex. "Sir. Alex," he amended, then frowned. "Sorry. I make you sound like a knight."

Alex chuckled, mostly because he found the boy adorable, but also because he had spent some time as Sir Alex back in medieval days. "Relax, Quinn. You're among friends. I'll order you some food from the club's kitchen."

"I already told Mackie to fetch something," Harry said, standing. "Ah, here he is now."

Alex had also heard the elevator opening but could see that Quinn's human ears hadn't detected the sound. He hoped the boy put that discrepancy down to his continued fogginess. Mackie tripped in with a tray in his hands and the usual saucy look. *Such a brat.* Val loved that about the boy—loved meting out punishment, as well. And, of course, Mackie loved most of the discipline he received from Val's hands. That was why he acted out so much, to get those spankings. Still, the boy had a good heart and was loyal to his friends. Alex hoped Quinn would become one of them.

With a seductive swish of his hips, Mackie brought the tray over and placed it on the spot Harry had just vacated. "I hope you like cream of tomato soup and grilled cheese sandwiches, 'cause that's what the chef sent. He said it was a safe bet in case you were like...vegetarian or something."

Quinn pushed himself up a bit more, his face still too pale. "Thanks so much. This is perfect." He reached for the tall mug containing the soup, but Mackie got there before him and passed it over. The expression on Quinn's face when he took his first sip was one of amazing gratitude and pleasure.

The sight tugged at Alex's heartstrings. He felt a sudden need to journey to Michigan and find whoever was responsible for this boy landing in such dire straits. He'd been on this planet plenty long enough to know how badly this species often treated even their own family. *Well, no matter...* Quinn was now in Alex's domain and he would be taken care of.

"Drink that slowly," he admonished in a light tone. "We don't want you to upset your stomach."

Having finished packing his physician gear, Harry gave him a gimlet eye. *Damn, nothing gets past the old man.* "Indeed." Heading for the door, he added, "I recommend sleep, as well, then more food. Don't work tonight unless you feel one hundred percent."

"Excellent advice, Uncle Harry," Alex chimed in. "Thank you."

"I'm sure I'll be fine to work later," Quinn said over the rim of his mug.

Alex smiled at him and watched with delighted fascination as the boy's cheeks pinked again. "We'll see." He frowned an instant later at a thought. "Do you have a place to stay?"

Quinn swallowed his mouthful. "No, sir. Alex." Averting his gaze, he took another sip of soup.

"Hmm." Alex didn't like the idea of sending the boy back out into the world. The idiot part of his brain latched onto the idea of having the boy remain in his loft. His dick seconded the motion but his rational side won the day…sort of.

"I have a guest room on the fourth floor that's currently unoccupied." He did a mental facepalm the second the words left his mouth. *As if having the boy one floor below is going to make any difference.* The offer having been made, there was no taking it back, however.

Quinn looked at him round-eyed. "Oh, thank you, but I couldn't impose."

"Nonsense. It's only temporary until you get back on your feet, financially speaking." *And, you'll be right where I can keep an eye on you.* That stray thought alarmed him enough to cause him to retreat.

Pulling his wallet out, he grabbed two one-hundred-dollar bills and slapped them on the table. "Here's an advancement on your pay, which is fifteen dollars an hour, by the way, plus you keep whatever tips you make." *Tips that will be shoved by sweaty hands into the boy's G-string.* Another stray thought that had him practically growling inside.

He backed up some more. "I'm sure I'm needed somewhere, so, Mackie, please show Quinn his room when he's finished eating and help him get settled. I'll, ah…see you later then?"

With that awkward finale to his flustered act, Alex turned and hot-footed out of his own home as if the hounds of hell were nipping at his heels.

Chapter Two

"This is your room—for the time being, anyway," Mackie added with a sniff.

Quinn looked at his new—albeit temporary—place with raised eyebrows. He'd expected something pretty basic, but this was gorgeous—all rich browns with green and cream-colored accents. A sitting area was arranged in one corner of the room and a bathroom was located at another. He couldn't believe his new boss wanted him to stay in what was clearly intended for important guests.

"Wow. This is amazing." Quinn walked over to the bed and sat on the edge. His ass sank into the fluffy duvet and landed on a firm mattress.

"Yeah, well, this floor is normally for family members," Mackie said as he leaned against the doorjamb. "There are a bunch of them, and sometimes they visit. Harry and his husband and son have a suite at the end of the hall and Val's room is across from this one." He studied his nails. "I'm there pretty much every night. It's almost not worth my keeping an apartment."

In the little more than an hour since he'd arrived and made a complete jackass out of himself by fainting into his boss's arms, Quinn had managed to take Mackie's measure. For all his bored air and bravado, the guy seemed insecure — and nice. He'd hovered over Quinn while he ate and made sure he was steady on his feet when they'd left the fifth floor. Quinn knew fake when he saw it, but Mackie's concern had struck him as being genuine. The least Quinn could do in return was reassure the boy that he had no designs on the bouncer whatsoever.

"Like I said, I'm not in the market for a boyfriend." If he were, there was a clear candidate, and it wasn't Val. A vision of Alex's violet eyes conveying a surprising amount of worry popped into his head, as did the memory of a bulge behind the man's tailored slacks. *Was that for me?* An intriguing — and disturbing — shiver ran down his spine.

He focused his attention back on Mackie. "I'm just grateful to have a job and a place to stay, even if it's temporary." He also had two hundred dollars in his wallet, more than he'd ever had in there at any one time. Knowing that he had the means to feed himself for a while relieved him of the anxiety he'd been living with since his parents had kicked him out of the house.

Standing, he slid his backpack off his shoulder and put it on the deep pile carpet. "I'd really like to start work tonight, but I don't have the appropriate clothes." He couldn't hold back the blush. *God, I need to get over my shyness if I'm going to be a go-go boy.*

Mackie sighed and pushed away from the jamb. "No worries. We have lots of stuff you can use. I suppose I should give you a tour. Come on."

Quinn followed the boy out of the room and to the elevator bank, although they didn't enter there. Instead, Mackie pushed an exit door that opened into a staircase. They went down one flight and into the third floor. A series of open doors lined the hallway.

"This is where we keep the playrooms."

Stretching his neck to peek inside the first one they passed, Quinn saw a plain bed and what appeared to be a padded wooden sawhorse with a bunch of cuffs — everywhere.

"What kind of games are played in there?" His voice kind of squeaked with the question.

Mackie giggled. "The sort that you probably couldn't handle."

"And you can?" Quinn couldn't resist taking a quick glance at each room during their journey.

Mackie flipped his hair out of his eyes and gave Quinn a mischievous grin. "Let's just say I'm a natural. But, don't worry. This floor is totally optional for employees, even the go-go boys."

They hit an open staircase that led to the second floor. The walls were lined with plush couches and the inside contained a rectangular balcony from which one could watch the dance floor below.

Mackie leaned against it, his slender hips jutting out in a provocative pose. "Patrons can come here and relax with a drink, get a lap dance."

Shoving his hands inside his front pockets, Quinn hunched his shoulders. "Oh, is that a thing? Lap dances?"

"Sure. You charge twenty bucks a song and you get to keep it all. Alex doesn't take a cut. He charges like a huge annual fee for membership and he's not exactly giving away the drinks, either." He looked away. "Any other deals you want to strike with the patrons are purely your choice. Alex doesn't want to know and doesn't care, so long as you're discreet."

A knot formed in his full stomach. "You mean I'm not just hired to dance? I'm supposed to whore, too?" *Shit, out of the frying pan and into the fire.* If that was the job, he'd have to give the money back and leave, except what difference did it make? He'd be back to Plan B, and at least here, he'd be safer.

Mackie grunted. "No, dummy. I said you make your own deals — or not. Some of the boys fuck for money. *I* don't. Val would redden my ass if I did, after he ripped out the guts of the other guy." The boy sounded quite smug in describing his boyfriend's jealousy. "A lot of the members bring their own dates or hook up with each other. The rooms on the higher floors do see a lot of action, regardless. Come on."

Quinn followed the boy down another staircase that led to the main floor. They walked the length of the bar. A tall, bald black man stood behind it, stocking bottles on the shelves.

"Hey, Kitty," Mackie called out in greeting.

Quinn was still trying to wrap his head around the idea that the guy was called Kitty when the bartender turned around and flashed them a smile. That was when Quinn started trying to wrap his head around the fact that Kitty *was* a woman.

"This is Quinn," Mackie said with a jerk of his thumb in his direction. "He's our new go-go boy."

Swallowing past his surprise, Quinn nodded at the bartender. "Ma'am."

Kitty's smiled widened. "What a nice, polite boy. So unlike some people," she added with a nod at Mackie. "I'm pleased to meet you, too, sweetie. Don't listen to everything this one has to say. He'll lead you to the wrong path, given half the chance." She blew a kiss toward the boy to show she was only teasing.

"Ugh," Mackie scoffed, but he blew a kiss back. The two of them were obviously fond of each other. "I'm only getting him settled, per the boss's orders. Quinn's going to start dancing tonight."

Kitty placed another bottle on the shelf behind her. "Well then, break a leg, as they say. And I'm going to assume you aren't twenty-one." She gave him a look that warned him not to even try lying.

"No, ma'am. Eighteen."

Kitty tsked. "Too young to be shaking your mostly naked ass in front of strange men, but I don't make the rules around here, except for the bar ones. If I catch you sneaking drinks, I'll have Val bounce you and that mostly naked ass out of here. Got that?"

"Yes, ma'am." Quinn put as much sincerity in his voice as he could because he wasn't going to lose this job that he desperately needed over something so stupid.

With a nod, Kitty went back to what she was doing. "Good. 'Cause that's what happened with the last one."

Mackie tugged at Quinn's arm. "Come on. I'll take you to the changing rooms. See you, Kitty." The bartender waved at them. "It wasn't just the booze," he added. "The kid was doing heroin and came into work high every night."

"God."

"Yeah," Mackie agreed with a heavy sigh. "It was a real mess." He stopped short. "Not surprising, though, given that lots of gay kids turn to drugs to ease their pain. It's tough being bullied in school and at home." Mackie appeared pensive and a flash of misery crossed his pretty face. "Alex tried to help him, paid for rehab and everything. But…" With a shrug, he kept walking.

He led him past the elevators and down a hallway. To the left was a large kitchen, already bustling with activity. Mackie pointed in that direction. "So, the kitchen is open almost twenty-four seven. A great perk as an employee is that all food is free."

"Really?" That sounded too good to be true. "There must be a cost."

"Not to us, and because you'll be living here for a while, you can eat all your meals. Just ask Emil and he'll set you up. He's the head chef and another cousin or something. The family connections are hard to keep straight."

Beyond the kitchen was a large dressing room, complete with a long mirror on the far wall with a narrow counter covered with brushes, curling irons and various beauty products. The rest of the room had a couch and a few overstuffed chairs. To the right was a bathroom with at least one shower.

Standing in the center with his hip cocked, Mackie flicked his hair and did the Vanna White thing with his hand. "And this is where the magic happens. We come in as ordinary boys and leave as sin personified." He blew Quinn a provocative kiss.

Quinn took in the room where he'd be spending a lot of time. He wandered over to the counter and poked at tubes and discs and bottles with a frown. "Do we have to wear make-up?" He wasn't sure how he felt about that. He'd known for a long time that he was gay, but he wasn't a drag queen or transgender. He wanted to look like a boy, not a girl.

"Only if you want to." Mackie wandered over and grabbed a tube of glittery blue stuff. "Sometimes a little sparkle adds to the allure. And the lights in the club can be kind of dim, so I like to use some liner and mascara to make my features stand out. Your choice," he added with another flip of his hair.

Mackie went over to a drawer at the end of the counter and opened it. "Here's where we keep extra thongs." He pulled out one and dangled it by his finger. It was very shiny and a red-orange color. "This would be fabulous with your blond hair."

Quinn took a few steps forward and reached out tentatively to take the offering, as if it could bite. The tag was still on, so that meant no one else had worn it. *Thank God. Because…ick.* "It's so small."

"Yeah, well, so's your ass, honey. And, the more the rest of what you've got struggles to stay in that thing, the better. Tips are the name of the game."

Quinn took a deep breath and let it out slowly. "You're right." He gave Mackie a determined look. "Will you show me how to put gunk on my face to — you know — accentuate my features?"

Mackie smiled. "Sure thing. Let me finish the rest of the tour first. Over here, we have a bathroom with a couple of showers, washer and dryer, toothbrushes and paste, razors — everything you need to stay fierce and fabulous all night long."

Quinn rubbed at his smooth face. "I don't really need to shave, unfortunately."

Mackie rolled his eyes. "The razors aren't just for your face." He flicked his gaze to Quinn's crotch. "You have to make sure there's no *hai*-er down *they*-re."

Once again, Quinn's cheeks flushed. "Oh."

Mackie smirked. "Yeah, *oh*. Welcome to the glamorous world of exotic dancing, sweetie."

* * * *

"Oh, honey, you are going to be the belle of the ball for sure tonight. The other boys and I are going to be fighting for pocket change once the patrons get a look at you."

Leaning forward, Quinn studied his kohl-rimmed eyes and glossy lips. He frowned and ran his fingertip across his glittery cheeks. "It doesn't make me too girly, does it?"

Mackie tossed the tube of mascara on the table and crossed his eyes at Quinn through the mirror. "No. It highlights the beautiful boy that you are, except, you know...*better*. Trust me. Your G-string is going to be bulging with money before your first shift is over."

"She's got that right," chimed in another boy, Shawn, who was putting on his own finishing touches a few seats away.

Mackie grunted. "I told you not to use female pronouns when referring to me."

Shawn huffed as he stood and perused himself by turning this way and that. "I would think an ass that takes Val's big dick every day wouldn't be so tight." Then he blew a kiss in their direction before adding, "Good luck, Quinn." He sauntered out, swinging his impressive bubble butt.

Mackie glared at the boy's back for a few seconds before turning his attention to Quinn. "Come on. It's showtime. Don't worry. The patrons are going to be so excited about seeing a new boy that they won't care how well you dance."

Standing, Quin inspected himself in the mirror. He hardly recognized the boy he'd been his whole life. The image he projected was of a male siren, a little slutty and way too young. Although his thong just covered his junk, his ass didn't project the kind of sexy invitation that Shawn's did — or Mackie's, for that matter. He wasn't even sure he wanted it to, except for it adding to his income. The plain truth was, his ass was cherry. Other than in the locker room at school or the doctor's office, no male had seen it bare since he'd hit puberty, let alone touched it. Would a mature male find it enticing?

Would Alex?

Shit, where did that stray thought come from? The last person he needed to attract was his boss. Lux might be a sex club, but it was still a business and dancing was his job. Sleeping with the owner could end in disaster. Quinn needed the work too much to risk losing it over something like a bad hook-up. Besides, the guy scared the crap out of him.

"Hey, is this the new boy?"

Quinn glanced at the doorway from where the question had come. A lanky boy with the same coloring as all the Stelalux men, plus an Asian appearance to his face, came sauntering in. He gave Quinn the once-over before heading to the make-up counter and picking a tube of lip gloss.

Mackie sighed. "Demi, you know you're not supposed to be here." When the boy just shrugged and proceeded to dye his lips, Mackie grunted. "Fine. Don't listen to me. Your fathers will find out, anyway. They always do. Don't come crying to me when they take away your electronics as punishment."

The boy, Demi, straightened and preened in front of the mirror. He was gorgeous and undoubtedly knew it. "Two more years and they won't be able to stop me." He patted his somewhat-flat ass. "By then, this will have filled out and the world can see how fabulous it — and I — am."

"Oh my God!" Grabbing Quinn's arm, Mackie fled the room. "That's Harry's son. He and his husband Lucien used a surrogate to make him, and I swear he's been giving them fits since he came out of the womb."

Because focusing on someone else helped ease his jittery stomach, Quinn gave that bit of news some thought. "Is Lucien Asian?"

"Yup. Thai, I think."

"They must have used an Asian surrogate and Harry's sperm, given how much that kid looks like a Stelalux."

Mackie shrugged. "I guess. Never really thought about it, to be honest. I just try to keep him out of the dressing room as much as possible. Harry and Lucien have big plans for that kid because he's off the chart intelligent and being a go-go boy is *not* on their agenda."

The reminder of their job brought Quinn back into his own current circumstances as they entered the main floor. It was a few minutes before nine, the time when the dancers started the first of their two-hour shifts. Shawn and another boy, Kenny, had already started gyrating to the song playing. There weren't more than a dozen patrons milling about, but Mackie had told him that things started to get swinging by eleven. That was when more boys would come in to mingle with the crowd and take over at the stages when the first shift ended.

Quinn would have two hours off to either mingle and give lap dances or join a patron in a private room. Otherwise, he'd take another turn on the stages at one. Being a private club, it could stay open as long as the owners wanted and was available twenty-four seven, but the boys only had to work until five a.m. Quinn hoped he'd be able to last that long. Despite having eaten a couple of times and even taken an afternoon nap in his very comfortable bed, he still felt a little weak and tired. Alex had given him a pass about working that night and he'd been tempted to take him up on the offer. Fear drove him, though. He needed to prove that he was capable of doing this job that he needed so desperately.

Mackie squeezed his arm and whispered into his ear, "Good luck and don't worry. You'll be fabulous. You'll see."

Mackie sauntered to one of the free stages, giving every man he saw a sexy smile. The boy reached for the pole and twirled himself around to stunning effect. Knowing he could never match that kind of skill, Quinn nevertheless squared his shoulders, put on what he hoped was a mirror image of Mackie's expression and propelled himself onto the one remaining stage.

* * * *

"The new boy seems to be settling in okay."

Alex didn't spare Val a glance. His attention was entirely focused on said new boy, as it had been since the moment he'd stepped into the main room. *Hell and damn*, as the humans would say. At this rate, he'd get nothing done all night.

He took a deliberate sip from his tumbler of Maker's Mark before answering. "I suppose, although his dancing technique is a bit pedestrian compared to the others."

Val snorted, one of the many human mannerisms they'd acquired over the centuries, whether they'd intended to or not. "Nobody seems to care about that. They've been three-deep around his stage since he started."

Indeed they had. The way they kept groping the boy in the guise of stuffing bills into what there was of his thong set Alex's teeth on edge. One man in particular, a member named Crowell whom Alex heartily disliked, kept circling like a carrion-eater eyeing roadkill. Alex's grip tightened around his glass.

"That's good. Poor boy needs the money." He took another sip of his drink and fought against his fangs' sudden desire to descend. Crowell had slid a finger down Quinn's crack at the same time that he tucked yet another bill inside. A human eye wouldn't have detected it. His did. A low growl rose. That was a sound they tried to suppress, not being one humans typically made.

Val chuckled and put his hand on Alex's shoulder. "You'd better hurry and fuck the guy before you give us all away."

Annoyed, Alex shrugged off the touch. "I don't dally with employees. Unlike you," he added in a biting tone. "And speaking of which, you'd better make a decision about your boy. Either commit to him or cut him loose.

He's the one most likely to discover who we are. Your dithering puts us all at risk."

As soon as the harsh words were out of his mouth, Alex regretted them. For the first time in the last hour, he peeled his gaze away from Quinn and focused on his comrade. "I'm sorry. I didn't mean to be so blunt. I understand why you hesitate, but it doesn't have to end badly this time. Mackie's a strong boy, fortified by modern medicine and nutrition. He's not like —"

"Don't say it." Val gave him a shuttered look. "Please don't say his name."

Alex struggled to think of a suitable reply, knowing that he'd left this old wound festering in his subordinate and friend too long, the same as he had his own, so perhaps he had nothing to offer the man after all. Before he could say anything, however, Val's expression changed. He morphed into head bouncer mode.

"The new boy has attracted too much attention."

Alex followed Val's gaze, and their conversation was instantly forgotten in the face of what he saw. Crowell had wormed his way in even closer to Quinn and now had a grip on the front of the boy's G-string. Alex zeroed his sight to the spot where the man's fingers held onto the thin fabric. He could see how tightly he kept the boy in place. For his part, Quinn was trying to pull away to free himself while still keeping a smile on his face.

With a heavy-lidded gaze, Alex watched the tug of war and filtered his hearing until he homed in on the boy's heartbeat. It was easy enough to do. He already knew what it sounded like and its rapid hammering told him all he needed to know.

Throwing his arm out to stop Val from advancing, he hissed — another sound that marked his species as different — yet his sudden fury left him heedless of the fact. "I've got this."

He'd never hated his need for secrecy so much as he did in the few seconds it took him to reach the stage. But for the humans, he could have arrived at his destination in a split second instead of the agonizingly slow pace he forced himself to take. By the time he got to them, Quinn had already pulled so hard to escape that he'd tumbled off the stage. Elbowing other men aside with no thought as to how hard he hit them, Alex raised his arms and caught the boy.

Quinn landed sprawled in his embrace with a whoosh of breath and a wide-eyed stare. The boy's slick skin dampened Alex's Ferragamo shirt. He didn't care. Human currency had proven to be easy to acquire and his closet was stuffed with clothing. Instead of standing the boy on his feet, Alex tightened his grip as he gazed at the startled face. His nostrils flared at the sweet scent of the human's blood. It rose past the more cloying fragrance of whatever body spray Quinn had splashed on before taking to the stage. Alex's cock stiffened, although, in truth, it had never truly subsided from earlier in the day.

He stared at the slender neck and the rapid pulse at its base. The temptation to dip his head and take a sip was so strong that he almost threw away a thousand years of secrecy to give in to it. His need to protect his men overrode his impulse, as did the reason why Quinn's heart was beating so fast. Setting the boy down with a sudden tilt of his arms, he gripped his shoulders instead until he was sure Quinn was steady.

Alex made himself let go and take a step back. He called forth his legendary strength of mind and patience so that he wouldn't pick the boy up and carry him off to his bed the way his hard dick urged him to.

"Go in back," he ordered.

Licking his lower lip, Quinn shot a look at the enormous steampunk-styled clock hanging over the bar. "I have ten minutes left on my first shift, sir." His voice was soft and wary.

The boy's very vulnerability egged Alex's fury. He leaned forward. "Your first shift ends now. In fact, all your shifts for the night are over." He pulled back to put more distance between them. "Go shower. Wash off that glitter and clean that paint off your face."

He didn't mean to sound so harsh and could see the sudden hurt and even fear that leaped into Quinn's eyes. There was nothing to be done about it, though. His ire was up and he barely held onto his control. There was only one person responsible for it, of course, but he couldn't address that man until he was sure Quinn was out of harm's way. Keeping his gaze fixed on the boy, he waited until Quinn had turned and fled toward the dressing room as ordered. His small, taut ass was on full display, except for the bills flapping against it. It seemed as if every male eye tracked those globes until they disappeared down the back hall.

Val entered his line of vision. "Let me take care of Crowell, boss."

Turning, Alex narrowed his eyes. "No fucking way." He shifted his stance to find where the asshole had scurried off to once Quinn had fallen. Finding the guy, he took a step in that direction, only to have Val plant himself in the way.

"Come on, Alex. Crowell is an entitled shithead who drinks too much. I'll get him out and give him a talking to."

By way of answer, Alex stood and let his man see his feelings inside his eyes. Unlike humans, their species easily read each other's emotions. It took only a heartbeat for Val to sigh and step aside.

"Just don't kill him," he pleaded in a low voice. "I hate cleaning up messes."

Alex ignored the plea, yet held himself under control enough to not race over and snap Crowell's neck. He did put on some speed, assuming that everyone had drunk a sufficient amount of alcohol not to notice the inhuman swiftness he used. Crowell stood talking to a few other patrons and didn't notice Alex until he'd grabbed him by the front of his shirt and hauled him onto his toes.

"Hey!" The human clawed at Alex's fist. "What gives, Stelalux? You're going to rip my shirt."

Alex bared his teeth, careful to keep his biting fangs retracted, much as he would have liked to rip the man's throat out. "I'm escorting you off my premises, Crowell."

He didn't wait for an acknowledgement or even a response before dragging the man toward the nearest door. It was one that led to the public alley, not the front. Alex didn't care one way or the other. He only wanted the human scum away from his Quinn.

No. That isn't right. Away from my club. That's it.

The scene he caused attracted quite a bit of attention. Most of the men they passed smirked or even gave the thumbs-up. Crowell wasn't well-liked. Young and handsome in an obvious way, he flaunted his inherited wealth and connections to the irritation of many of the other members. He was also younger than most of them, having paid Alex's high membership fees with a kind of ease reserved for men who'd worked hard for years.

"Jesus Christ, what are you doing?" Crowell sputtered and struggled to free himself from Alex's punishing grip.

"Kicking you out of my club." Now that he had matters well in hand, Alex's usual sangfroid had returned.

"What? Why?" Crowell continued to squirm and even dug his heels into the rug. His human muscles were no match for Alex's. "You can't be mad over that slut fighting me. Stupid newbie didn't understand that members have special privileges."

"My rules are very clear. My boys are not whores. You know better than to grope one like that without his permission, and you certainly didn't have it."

"That's not true. He said he'd go into one of the rooms with me then kicked up a fuss when I wouldn't pay him what he wanted."

Alex paused long enough to spit out, "Liar," before moving again. "Your membership is hereby revoked."

"You can't do that. I've paid my dues through the end of the year."

Pausing by the door, Alex hauled the man's face to his own. He could smell the fear and the human's pulse beat a rapid tattoo. This blood, though, held no interest for him. "I will gladly refund you the entire amount."

With that, he popped the bar to the door, threw it open and tossed Crowell out onto his ass. Crowell landed in an undignified heap. He sat, cursing and sputtering. "You son-of-a-bitch. You can't treat me this way."

Alex gave him a brittle smile. "And yet I have." He turned away.

"I know the mayor. I'll get this place closed."

Pausing, Alex looked over his shoulder. "Don't ever show your face around here again, Crowell or you'll regret it." His patience at an end, Alex let his eyes briefly turn the deep red they became before his kind went for blood.

The way the human's face turned white, Alex knew he'd seen the change. It was a calculated risk, one he'd taken before. Even if Crowell didn't put it down to a false memory fueled by booze and fear, who would ever believe him? With one last contemptuous glare, he shut the door behind him.

He cracked his neck and took deep breaths to calm himself as he made his way around the room. Time to reassure his other members that the scene they'd just witnessed wasn't of any concern to them. It took effort, but he forced a smile to his lips and glad handed everyone not dancing. This was his business. It mattered to him. Of all the things he'd done to make money and pass the time while on Earth, running a nightclub had turned out to be the one that suited him the best. It allowed him to operate at night without humans wondering why, saving his eyes and skin from the heat and light of the too-close sun. He loved the way music thrummed in his blood and how he and his men could be more themselves out in the open and not raise suspicion.

Here and now, in twenty-first century America, males could find pleasure in each other without fear. The desire for blood could be hidden behind a façade of kink-friendly patrons. He'd finally established a domain in which he could relax more than he'd ever been able to do before and not have to look over his shoulder so much. Those who'd deserted him and his command were a continent away, and so far, they had left him and those still loyal to him alone for more than half a century. If they were making mischief somewhere in the world, he was unaware.

He loved this city and this club and he'd do anything to keep it his for as long as possible. And, if that meant making stupid small-talk with humans, well, he could do that. It would not disturb his tranquility. But, something else did, and although he wanted to chase after it—him, Quinn—he didn't. He needed time to cool off, get his baser urges under control. What he'd do after that, who knew?

One thing was painfully clear, however. A sweet, vulnerable human had already turned his world upside-down.

* * * *

"Eat! You're too skinny, and I've never known a boy to turn away a hot fudge brownie sundae."

Quinn gave the chef, Emil, a wan smile and dug into his treat with more enthusiasm than he felt. The big man, who looked more like a pro-wrestler with his bulging muscles and man bun, had taken him under his food wing the moment Quinn had slinked into the kitchen after his first shift—his only shift. Embarrassed, demoralized and, to his mortification, a little teary-eyed, Quinn had only intended to grab a piece of fruit or something before heading to what would undoubtedly be his one night sleeping in that wonderful bedroom.

Emil had tsked at the notion, sat Quinn at a small table and had plied him with a turkey club sandwich, tall glasses of cool milk and now a treat the size of Quinn's head. He had a feeling the man wasn't going to let him leave until he'd swallowed every last bite. *What the hell?* It wasn't as if he had to worry about his waistline. Not anymore. Not after causing that scene with one of the members. *God, Alex was so angry.* The memory of those piercing violet eyes boring into him made the ice cream curdle in his stomach.

And speaking of which — the disturbingly appealing man sauntered in and homed in on him in an instant. At his approach, Quinn had trouble swallowing his mouthful, yet couldn't stop staring. There was something compelling about his soon-to-be-former boss. He didn't want to be attracted to the guy but couldn't help himself. Even when he was wary of him, he still felt that unsettling twinge way down low that stirred his mostly untrained cock. It twitched now as Alex's eyes pinned him to the spot. *Thank God, the table is hiding my reaction.*

Alex shot him what Quinn supposed was intended to be a charming smile. It was more predatory, and still, his dick only got stiffer. Maybe he had more in common with Mackie's love of being dominated than he thought. He swallowed hard, trying to return the expression.

Pulling out a chair opposite him, Alex slid his large body onto it with enviable grace. He frowned at Quinn's bowl before calling out over his shoulder. "How come I never get a brownie sundae, Emil?"

The big chef strolled over with another bowl and a spoon in one hand and a bottle of amber liquid in the other. He slapped both on the table in front of Alex.

"Because it's disgusting enough that you like vanilla ice cream and bourbon. I'm not adding chocolate into that mix." With a shake of his head, the guy walked away.

Alex chuckled, the sound winding its way around every one of Quinn's nerve endings. The boss man splashed a healthy swig of the liquor over his ice cream and, scooping a big mouthful, hummed in appreciation. "Don't let me interrupt," he said, waving his spoon at Quinn. "I expect you haven't had many treats lately."

Quinn shrugged and dug into his dessert once more. They ate in companionable silence, the only sound the clanking of metal against china. The kitchen workers' activity faded into the background until it seemed as if he and Alex were the only two people in the room — the club, the entire universe, for that matter. The only thing marring the experience was Quinn's nagging worry.

The horrible events of the night eventually closed in on him so that he blurted out, "I'm sorry." Dropping his spoon, he sat back and ran a hand down his face. He was afraid he might start crying.

Alex dragged his spoon past his lips and cocked his head. "Why are you apologizing?"

Seriously? This was like being sent to the vice-principal's office and being forced to confess one's misbehavior. He couldn't hold Alex's gaze, and he felt his cheeks heat. "For…um…upsetting one of the club's members." He took a shaky breath. "I'm sorry I fought him off, but he was so grabby that it startled me, and he wouldn't listen when I told him I didn't want to do anything more than dance, and…"

His voice failed him. He'd been babbling. It wasn't like that was going to help, anyway. At least he had an amazing six hundred and forty dollars' worth of tips tucked away in his pocket. That was more than he'd had when he'd come in earlier in the day, broke and desperate. It was something, he supposed.

He rubbed his thumb against a worn spot on his jeans. "Can I please sleep here tonight? I promise to leave first thing in the morning."

Alex sighed. "Quinn, look at me."

It was hard, but he raised his gaze to do as he'd been told.

Alex appeared sympathetic. "You have nothing to apologize for. I have strict rules about how the club members treat my employees, especially the go-go boys. That man was way out of line. I've banned him from the club."

Quinn widened his eyes. "Really?"

"Yes, really." Shaking his head, Alex started in on his dessert once more. "And you're not fired, if that's what you're thinking," he said around his mouthful of ice cream.

"I'm not?" Quinn straightened, half-expecting the man to scoff at his naiveté. "But you were so mad."

"At him, not you."

"You took me off the floor for the night," he added in a low voice, because really, *why am I arguing with the guy?*

Alex licked the back of his spoon before tossing it into his now-empty bowl. "Because I was worried from the start that dancing tonight would be too soon for you. Once I realized Crowell was not only crossing a line but had gone into sexual assault territory, I decided to pull the plug." The boss pushed back and stood. "You're not fired. Until Crowell's abhorrent behavior, you were doing great. The members obviously loved you. Now grab that bowl and come to bed." Alex froze and his expression turned almost sheepish. "I mean, I'll escort you to your room. You can finish your dessert there. And," he added with a crack of his neck, "there will be no more talk of being fired. You don't want to quit, do you?" Now he appeared alarmed.

Quinn's cheeks got even hotter as he stood. "No, sir. I like it here." He clutched at his food to give himself something to do and a place to concentrate on other than on Alex.

"Good. I'm sure you're going to be an asset to the club."

The man walked out without a backward glance, assuming Quinn would follow, which he did, sundae bowl in hand. They rode the elevator to the fourth floor in silence. When the doors slid open, Alex held them with his hand to allow Quinn to step out.

"Sleep well," Alex said, eyes averted. "And," he added with a heavy breath, "I promise that you are safe here. I'll make sure of it." He raised his gaze then, and the seriousness Quinn saw there was unnerving. "I won't let anyone hurt you—ever. Now, go."

"Yes, sir," he replied in a quiet voice. "Thank you," he added.

But the doors had already closed.

Chapter Three

"Jesus, just when you think you've seen it all."

Trey tore his gaze away from the bloody scene in front of him and shook his head at his partner. "Come on, Karl. You know saying something like that is like spitting into the wind. I don't want to tempt fate and have her throw something worse at us tomorrow."

He returned his attention to their vic and watched the coroner finish his preliminary examination of the corpse. There was no arguing with Karl's assessment of their newest case, however. The man lying in the far corner of a public alley looked as though his throat had been ripped out. Strike that. It *had* been ripped out, and pieces of flesh and trachea lay next to the head. The victim's face wore an expression of abject terror. The coffee Trey had gulped on his way over roiled in his stomach.

"Hey, Almadeo," he called over to the coroner. "Can we assume that was the cause of death?" He jutted his chin in the direction of the gaping neck.

Almadeo stood. He'd been at his job for many years before Trey had even left the academy. The man knew what he was doing and usually didn't offer speculation until he had his body on a slab.

The guy shook his head. "Hard to say."

"Really?" Karl interjected. "'Cause from where I'm standing, it doesn't seem like something you'd survive happening."

Almadeo raised his eyebrows. "Needless to say, I can tell you that if it wasn't the cause of death, it happened soon thereafter. There's virtually no blood left in the body." He studied the dirty ground around the corpse. "Obviously this wasn't the location of the murder."

Trey grimaced, but he'd come to the same conclusion himself. Not enough blood coated the pavement. "So, he must have been killed somewhere else and the body transported here after the fact. But, why?"

Karl grunted. "And why bring the neck bit with it? I mean, how freaky is the perp?"

Almadeo stepped around the victim and held out a clear evidence bag. "That I can't explain, although given the lack of blood left compared to the size of the wound, I'd say the killer made some effort to drain the body."

Trey took the offering and studied it. Inside was a wallet, keys, a tin of breath mints and a cloth handkerchief. "What? Like he hung it for a while or something?"

Almadeo gave him a shuttered look. "Perhaps. I'll know more after the post-mortem. That's all I found in his pockets," he added with a nod toward the bag.

"Thanks." With his gloved hand, Trey removed the wallet and studied the driver's license. "Richard

Crowell. And wouldn't you know that he has a Beacon Hill address."

Karl shot him a smile. "Awesome. I love it when the vic is high profile. It means the press and the pols will be breathing down our necks."

"Mmm." Trey couldn't argue with his partner's assessment. "What's he doing here? Not exactly where the tony night spots are."

A piece of black plastic caught his attention. He'd thought it was a credit card, but it turned out to be a membership one. "Lux," he read the bold silver lettering above the victim's name and picture. "Ah."

Turning on his heel, he headed back to the mouth of the alley then made a left. He pointed to the sign above the double doors for the building. "That's why he's here. It's a private club."

Karl stepped next to him and stared first at the card showing through the plastic bag Trey still held, then at the sign. "Sometimes you get lucky, huh? It would seem like the place to start our investigation. It's probably not open now, though. We may have to call the owner." Karl pulled out his phone and started searching the Internet.

Believing in trying the most direct approach first, Trey stuffed the evidence bag into his pocket and went over to the front door. The knob turned easily when he tried it so, opening it, he stood aside to wave Karl in. With a shake of his head, his partner obeyed the silent command. Trey followed him into the hushed, muted entryway.

It took a few seconds for his eyes to adjust to the dimness. Once they did, he passed Karl and led the way into a large room. The club was empty, which wasn't surprising, although jazz softly filled the space. The sound of glass clinking caught his attention. All the way in the back, someone was working behind a long, wooden bar.

The lush pile of the carpet muted their footsteps as he and Karl walked in that direction. Nevertheless, the bartender turned before they'd made it halfway. He could tell it was a very tall woman with a bald head. She was the kind of woman who could pull off the look, though. If he'd been into females, this one would have piqued his interest.

She gave them a blinding smile. "How can I help you, officers?"

The fact that she'd made them as cops right off told him she'd probably had a run-in or two with the law herself. He put that thought aside, however. Unless and until the investigation implicated the club, he'd assume everyone here was a potential witness, not a perp.

He flashed his badge, as did Karl. "I'm Detective Sergeant Trey Duncan. This is my partner, Detective Karl Anderson. We'd like to speak with you about a homicide."

The smile dimmed a bit. "Who's dead and where?"

"A man out in the public alley that abuts this building. I'm surprised you didn't see or hear the commotion when it was found."

The woman shrugged. "I've been in the club the whole night. We're open all the time to members, so I stay until noon when my second-string bar manager arrives. These walls are reinforced for maximum sound-proofing. It keeps noise in *and* out. Who's dead?" she asked, again in a calm voice.

"A member of yours, as it happens. Richard Crowell." He watched her to see how she reacted to the news. He was surprised when she didn't even try to hide it.

Her face scrunched in disgust. "Can't say I'm bothered hearing that." She tossed a towel onto the counter and turned. "You'll need to speak with the boss."

Trey took another look around the large room as he listened in on her deferential call to someone she called 'Alex'. Apparently the guy was in bed, and given the nature of his business, that wasn't surprising. The place was gorgeous and he imagined membership didn't come cheap.

"He'll be right down," she said once she'd hung up.

"Down?"

"His apartment is on the fifth floor."

Trey nodded. "Ah. Thanks, Ms.?"

"Houlihan," she replied with another flash of her teeth. "Katherine Houlihan. Everyone calls me Kitty."

He smiled back. "I would never have guessed that."

She laughed, a full-throated sound that reverberated around the empty space. "No one ever does."

Leaning against the bar, Karl wore a more charming smile than Trey could ever pull off. "So, Kitty, just what kind of club is this, anyway?" He nodded toward the very obvious small, round stages with poles embedded in them at the corners of a parquet floor. "A strip one, I presume?"

Kitty shrugged. "Of course, except not the sort you'd enjoy." She gave Trey a sly look. "Your partner, maybe, although the dues would be steep for a cop."

Damn, how did she peg me so quickly? Not that it mattered. He was out and proud, as the kids would say. Karl didn't care, nor did their lieutenant, but he didn't want to be known as a gay cop, just a good one.

Karl opened his mouth but didn't get a chance to pose his next question. A quiet ding to the right caught their attention. Elevator doors opened and out stepped one big mother-fucker sporting a Mohawk and wearing a pair of ripped jeans. He had more muscles on display than a MMA fighter and he didn't appear to be happy. Trey instinctively shifted his weight to the balls of his feet and noticed Karl straightening and doing the same, not that they expected to be attacked. The guy just put them on their guard.

This wasn't the boss, though. Another man strode out behind him — amazingly, even taller. The first guy had to be the muscle of the club, and given Trey's own six-two height, he judged Mohawk as being about six-five. The club owner had to be more like six-seven and their features were enough alike for them to be family members — *a family of giants, apparently.*

The boss overtook the muscle and approached Trey and Karl with a serious expression on his face. He wore black silk sleep pants and nothing else. He wasn't quite as jacked as the other guy, but he still wasn't someone Trey would want to tangle with. Because both of them were shirtless, a lot of pale and hairless skin was on display, not that he was into that type. He favored annoying twinks who took him for a ride before dumping him for some other daddy-type. But he could imagine these two guys never lacked for company. He also found it easy to imagine either of them ripping a man's throat out.

"Sorry to keep you waiting, gentleman. I'm Alexandru Stelalux, the owner of this club. This is my head of security and cousin, Valeriu Stelalux." The words were uttered in a clipped tone of English that made it obvious it wasn't the man's first language. There was only a hint of some underlying accent.

Trey held up his badge once more and reintroduced himself and Karl. "Sorry to have to wake you, sir."

The man ran the fingers of one hand through strands of ink-black hair that fell straight to a few inches below his shoulders. "Not at all. Kitty tells me there was some unpleasantness this morning."

The stilted coolness of the response put Trey on alert. "You could say that. The body of Richard Crowell was found this morning by city garbage collectors."

Stelalux's eyes narrowed. "Indeed. Shall we sit to discuss this?"

"Sure."

Trey slid into the booth indicated by the proprietor, making enough room for Karl to sit next to him. Stelalux sat on the other side. Mohawk man remained standing with his hands clasped in front of him. He went as still as a statue while his boss lounged with his arm slung along the back of the seat. Trey noticed the man had no hair under his arms, meaning he waxed, which Trey found incongruous with the guy's overt masculinity.

He took out his battered notebook and pen to get to more important things than the witness's personal grooming habits. "You knew Mr. Crowell, I presume, given that he was a member here?"

Stelalux gave him a hooded look. "Former member, and yes, I knew him."

Trey looked at him sharply. "Former? When did he quit the club?"

"He didn't." The man's eyes glowed with some unnamed hunger. "I kicked him out."

Trey exchanged a quick glance with Karl. *Okay, so this is going to be an interesting line of inquiry.* "Why was that?"

"He assaulted one of my boys. I don't tolerate that sort of behavior, so I showed him the door — quite literally."

"You tossed him out bodily?" Karl asked.

"With the greatest of pleasure. He was an entitled little shit whom I should never have admitted in the first place." He paused and shifted his gaze sideways. "In fact, I took him out the side door to expedite matters. It leads directly to the alley."

"Which is where his body was found." Trey tapped his pen against his notepad, weighing whether he should say anything more. Knowing that Crowell had been found right where he'd been shoved out made the idea that he'd been killed elsewhere more bizarre.

"His throat was ripped out."

Because he was watching the man closely, he had no trouble seeing the shift in Stelalux's expression. The calmness remained, but he tensed, became more serious. More tellingly, he glanced again at the bouncer guy, who in turn twitched a bit in reaction. The change was subtle and almost instantly gone.

"And, drained of blood," he added because he wanted to see how the two men took the news. Ignoring Karl's sharp intake of breath, he even pressed the matter. "Not a lot of blood was found around the body, either, which is strange, don't you think?"

The club owner and his bouncer each made the sign of the cross over their massive chests, although neither of them wore a crucifix or anything. The gesture struck Trey as being an automatic one, not particularly heartfelt.

"How disturbing," the club owner murmured. "I do hope you're not going to insinuate that, given our heritage, my cousin and I had anything to do with such a ghoulish situation."

Trey cocked his head. "I'm sorry I'm not following you, sir."

"We're Romanian."

It took Trey's brain about second too long to work out the implications. It was Karl that tripped to it first, barking out a laugh. "You mean like Count Dracula?"

Stelalux's expression turned icy. "Exactly. You can imagine how tedious it can be having to field comments and questions about vampire legends." He sighed. "Utter nonsense. I suppose the nature of this club gives you the wrong idea, as well — or will, once you learn of what goes on inside this private space."

Trey sat back against the luxurious leather cushion. "You might have to enlighten us there, sir. All we know is that this is a gay men's club."

"It is, but we also cater to clientele that practice the BDSM lifestyle." He flicked his gaze toward the ceiling. "We have playrooms on a higher level for the members and their guests to use. All perfectly consensual and, as I said, private. We conform to state law in that regard."

Trey felt an odd little goose to his dick at this new piece of information. That particular lifestyle had intrigued him for years, even though so far, he hadn't found the courage to explore it. Being a cop and in a state where it was, though not illegal, was frowned upon, had always stayed his hand. He found himself wondering if the investigation would afford him a chance to explore those rooms — in a professional capacity, of course.

Those were dangerous thoughts, however, so he turned his attention back to the interview. "Was Crowell into those kinds of games?"

"On occasion, I believe, except that he was a dilettante at best. And I did have to warn him when he overstepped the bounds of acceptable behavior. I'd actually given him a time out on the upstairs until he proved to be more trustworthy."

"So, his run-in with the stripper wasn't his first transgression?"

"Go-go boy, and yes, it was the last of his strikes."

"What's the difference between a stripper and a go-go boy?" Karl interjected.

The club owner gave Karl an indulgent smile. "Strippers take off their clothes as part of the performance. Go-go boys come out already wearing their G-strings and simply dance."

Not liking the image that popped into his head, Trey said, "I'm going to have to interview the boy. What's his name and address?" He poised his pen over the paper, ready to write the information.

"His name is Quinn Cooper, and as it happens, he's living here at the moment."

Trey frowned at the man's tone. There was an underlying menace and Stelalux's expression had turned fierce. He was almost baring his teeth.

"Is he your boyfriend?"

Something — heat, maybe — flared in the man's oddly-violet eyes before he banked it. "No, merely a down-on-his-luck employee that needs a place to stay until he's back on his feet."

"I see. Well, we need to interview him, so maybe you could call him."

Those teeth were showing again. "He had nothing to do with Crowell's death, I can assure you. Crowell had at least five inches on him and probably forty pounds.

Quinn couldn't even free himself from the man's grip, let alone kill him."

Trey shot him a bland look. "I appreciate your assessment of the situation, sir. We still need to interview him."

The club owner was clearly working to suppress his irritation. Finally, he said, "Very well. I'll fetch him for you."

Not much liking the idea of one witness having the chance to coach another, Trey tried to work it so the man didn't leave his sight. "Can't you simply call him?"

Stelalux slid out of his seat. "There's no extension in his room, and I don't know his mobile number, assuming he even has a phone at all. He's been on the streets since his family kicked him out because he's gay."

Trey didn't have anything to say to that. It was still an all-too-common story. Resigned, he settled back once more. "I see. Thanks for getting him."

"Not at all. I'm happy to help solve this unpleasantness to the extent I can. Would you care for some coffee while you wait? I bet you haven't even had breakfast," he added with his host expression on full display.

"We're fine, thanks."

"I could use a cup and maybe a doughnut if you've got one," Karl countered. He shot Trey a look when he kicked him under the table. "What? I didn't get a chance to eat."

Stelalux smiled. "I think we can do better than that, detective. Our kitchen is open twenty-four hours. Kitty, would you please see about coffee for the gentlemen, and how about an egg sandwich on an English muffin?"

Karl perked up like a dog scenting a bone. "With cheese and bacon?"

"Absolutely." The man appeared delighted to ply them with breakfast.

"Jesus Christ," Trey muttered, but he knew when he was out-gunned. Maybe if he appeared to let his guard down, his witnesses-potential suspects would, too.

"I'll be back as soon as I can. You know how teenage boys can be—hard to wake."

With that convenient warning, the club owner strode over to the elevator and disappeared inside.

Alex used the brief time riding to the fourth floor to calm his seething nerves. The humans had an expression that appeared like they were waiting for the other shoe to drop. Well, he'd been waiting more than half a century for his old friend and former first officer to rear his head again. The last time they'd clashed, Alex had come out on top at the cost of two men on the other side and one on his, not to mention millions of human lives lost. He was determined that this time he would suffer no loss and keep the collateral damage to a minimum. He hated killing the others, given how they'd once all been his men. But they'd fractured into two camps long ago, despite his efforts to hold them together.

Worse, the Stelanyx family couldn't seem to just live their lives quietly. If they weren't slaughtering humans, they harried Alex's family for sport. Even now, apparently Dracul hadn't learned his lesson. Alex recognized the killing on his doorstep as being the first volley in the next phase of their never-ending war on

Earth. That Quinn was going to be dragged into the mess made him even more furious and the fact that it *did* disturbed him. Since arriving, the young human had wormed his way into Alex's blood, quite literally. He couldn't allow that to continue. If Dracul learned of this new vulnerability, it would end as badly as it had the last time.

He pounded his fist on his thigh as the doors slid open and he left the elevator. *I will* not *let that happen.* One human lost because of Alex's devotion was more than enough for his conscience to bear.

He approached the boy's door with his usual quiet tread. Humans lacked grace, clomping their way through life like boar crashing through the undergrowth, while his species moved almost silently on this planet. In fact, they were superior to humans in almost every way. Conquering them would have been all too easy, especially in the beginning when human technology was non-existent. Sometimes, when he felt weary, he wondered whether he should have taken a different path than he had. Did being morally right after all this time and so far from his own people matter?

Alex chided himself. That was fatigue talking. He knew that all he and his men had left was integrity and the chance to forge a new life that didn't include casting aside all that they'd been taught. He stopped outside Quinn's door and listened. The sound of the boy's rhythmic breathing met his ears. The human was sleeping, and he hated to wake him. This was probably the first chance the boy had had in days—maybe weeks—to sleep soundly and safely.

But the cops downstairs weren't going to leave before interviewing Quinn, so with regret, Alex knocked a couple of times. When there was no response, he did it again and called, "Quinn? Can you wake, please?"

There was a break in the breathing, indicating that the boy had woken, a rustling of cloth that invoked a sudden image of Quinn turning in bed. *Is he naked under the sheets? Have my cool sheets wrapped around all the lustrous pink skin?* Oh, that was a bad train of thought. Hadn't he just reminded himself not to get attached?

"Quinn?" he called out again with less patience than he intended.

More cloth moved, feet hit the floor then padded over. A brief hesitation and the door opened. Lovely Quinn peeked out. "Alex? Is there something wrong?"

He tried not to be pleased at the sound of his name tripping past those luscious lips. He tried, as well, to ignore the rumpled hair and sleepy eyes that reminded him of bed and the fun that could be had there.

"Sorry to wake you." He made his voice brisk, business-like. "There's been some unpleasantness concerning that man who harassed you last night."

Quinn's eyes widened. "What's the matter? Did he return to the club?"

"Not exactly." Alex winced, hating to have to bring trouble to the boy's door. "I'm afraid the police have come because Crowell was murdered last night in the public alley next door."

"Oh, God!" Stumbling back, Quinn allowed the door to swing open, giving Alex a fetching view of the boy standing in his boxer-briefs. Somehow, it seemed even more provocative than seeing him the previous night in a thong.

It was the setting. Being in a bedroom made it that much more sexual. Alex's cock stiffened at the sight. He took a deliberate step back, even though he very much wanted to go forward. He could grab the boy, toss him on the bed, sink his teeth into all that lovely pale skin while he thrust inside what was undoubtedly a very tight channel.

Shit. Alex took another step backward. "Don't worry. The police only want to ask you a few questions."

Quinn's chest heaved. "They think I killed him."

"Nonsense. One look at you and they'll cross you off any list of possible killers they have. I'm the one they likely suspect."

The boy worried his lower lip with his front teeth. "But you didn't."

It came out as sounding like a statement, yet Alex chose to treat it like a question. "No, I didn't. I never deal with a problem using a sledge hammer when a tack one will do." He flashed a smile to ease the edginess in his voice. "Now, get dressed as quick as you can. I'll wait by the elevator."

"Yes, sir."

Alex didn't linger, resisting the desire to watch the boy turn in order to catch a glimpse of his enticing ass. Instead, he waited by the elevator, forcing control back into his mind and body. Quinn didn't make him wait long, either. Within a few minutes, he joined Alex, wearing a T-shirt, jeans and flip-flops. He looked as if he'd run his fingers through his hair, but he smelled sweetly of mint—toothpaste, no doubt, and likely deodorant, too. Humans had become obsessed in the last hundred years in eliminating body odor. He rather wished they hadn't. He'd found their earthier smells appealing.

"I stayed in my room the whole night after you escorted me from the kitchen," Quinn said as they entered the elevator.

"Of course you did." Alex made the mistake of placing his hand on the boy's shoulder in reassurance. The warmth of the human's body seeped into his palm, causing his heartbeat to accelerate. So did Quinn's. Alex could hear it, feel it and see it by the way the pulse at the base of the boy's throat thrummed faster.

Alex pulled his hand back as if scorched. "Don't worry," he said, staring straight ahead and laboring to keep himself under control. "Just tell them the truth and all will be well."

That was a lie. At the very least, Alex and Val would have to track whomever of their former shipmates had killed Crowell and deal with him themselves, not that the police stood a chance of finding him and bringing him to their form of justice. Even if they could, Alex knew that the killer was his responsibility. He was still the captain, even though his ship had been destroyed on his orders. If he didn't deal with this latest problem, he knew from experience that more humans would die. He couldn't let that happen.

The moment the doors opened on the ground floor, he smelled coffee, eggs and bacon. The two cops were still seated at the booth, except now they were eating a breakfast that Emil must have put together in record time. The man had gone from botanist to chef almost immediately and loved nothing more than creating in the kitchen. There was always food ready for consumption, no matter the time of day.

When Quinn hesitated to step out, Alex pressed his palm against the small of the boy's back. The touch was just as electrifying as it had been earlier but he ignored it. Soothing the human's nerves mattered more than anything at the moment.

"It will be fine," he reassured him. Using a small amount of pressure, he propelled the boy forward. "Here's Quinn, gentlemen."

The sandy-haired detective looked at him from over his fistful of egg sandwich, before taking another bite. The other one, the leader, put his meal down on the plate to focus on the boy approaching him. This was the man that Alex watched most keenly. The cop was an attractive man with light-brown skin and dark curly hair that hugged his head. He was big for a human, although nowhere near as tall as even the shortest of Alex's men, and keen intelligence showed through his brown eyes. That was all to the good. Alex expected him to quickly dismiss Quinn as a suspect.

Ushering Quinn over to the table, Alex made the introductions. Then he urged Quinn to sit in the space Alex had occupied earlier and he stood next to him. If he gave the appearance of a guard for the boy, then so be it. He wanted the cops to know that the boy wasn't without friends — strong friends.

Duncan pushed aside his mostly uneaten plate of food and gave Quinn a reassuring smile. "Thanks for coming, Mr. Cooper."

Quinn seemed startled by the formality. "Oh, um...sure." He glanced at Alex, as if for reassurance.

That gesture of trust pleased Alex and he gave a nod before turning to Val. He wanted Quinn to have something to eat, too. He didn't even have to ask. Emil was already out with a plate and a glass of orange juice. Alex intercepted him and grabbed it, placing it in front of the boy with a resounding *thunk*.

"Given that you're awake, you should eat." He flashed a warning look at Duncan when the man frowned. "You don't mind, do you, sergeant?

"No, of course not." He turned his attention to Quinn. "Now, Mr. Cooper — ah, can I call you Quinn?"

"Sure." Hunching his shoulders, the boy took a sip of juice.

Duncan gave him a reassuring smile, and that act of kindness caused him to rise in Alex's estimation. "So, I expect Mr. Stelalux has filled you in on why we're here." At Quinn's nod, the man continued. "Can you walk us through what happened last night?"

Fiddling still with his glass, Quinn began to tell his side of the story in a low and halting voice. His cheeks pinked when he described the way Crowell had laid his hands on him and tried to get him to go upstairs.

Duncan tapped his pen against his notebook. "I see," he said when Quinn fell silent. "Did Crowell threaten you or hurt you in any way?"

Quinn shrugged. "Not exactly. Except when I tugged to get free from him, I fell off the stage. I would have hit the floor if Alex hadn't caught me."

"Oh?" Duncan trained his gaze on Alex. "You were that close when it happened? I assume that means you heard any words exchanged by Quinn and Crowell?"

Shifting a bit to lean against the booth, Alex shook his head. "Not so close. The music is always loud for dancing. I saw the problem unfold and raced over. I got lucky enough to arrive just in time."

Duncan tapped his pen some more. "Hmm. So, Quinn, what happened after Mr. Stelalux caught you?"

The boy recited the rest of the evening, ending with Alex dropping him off at the door to his bedroom. It all sounded boring and plausible, even to Alex's jaded ears. He felt certain that the police would dismiss Quinn as a possible suspect.

Duncan leaned back. "I see." Putting his pen down, he grabbed his egg sandwich and took a big bite. After chewing and swallowing, he gestured to Quinn's plate. "This really is an excellent breakfast. You should have yours before it gets cold."

Quinn did as he'd been told, taking an almost dainty bite of his food. The boy was clearly used to doing what an authority figure said. The knowledge gave Alex all kinds of bad ideas. Dominating the human would be a delight that he needed to resist experiencing.

Duncan chewed some more. "Thank you for your time, Quinn—and yours, Mr. Stelalux. Now, if you'd be so kind as to give me the use of this booth for a while longer, I'm going to need to interview everyone else who was working last night." He looked at Val. "I assume that includes you, sir. And you, ma'am," he added, calling to Kitty.

Alex answered for them both. "Yes, they were both here last night, as they are virtually every night. As was Emil, the chef, and a few others that are currently working or otherwise in the building."

"Great. I'd like to speak with each of them, one at a time."

"Of course." Alex forced a smile to his lips. "We're only too happy to cooperate. The faster you can eliminate any of us as suspects in this sorry affair, the better."

And as soon as he got rid of these cops, he and Val could start the necessary process of finding the killer themselves. He turned to gather the rest of his people together but the cop stopped him.

"Before you go, I have one more question. Do you have security cameras in the alley, by any chance?"

Alex stared straight into the cop's eyes and lied. "No, I'm afraid not."

Duncan sighed. "Didn't think so. No reason to, really, but I thought I'd ask."

Alex nodded and strode away. There was no point in letting the cops see whatever security feed Val would pull from his system. Whoever had killed Crowell would have either interfered with the system or let it get a good look at the proceedings, depending on whatever game was starting. Either way, he couldn't let the humans have any more information than was absolutely necessary. This was family business—hive business—when all was said and done, and in the absence of a queen, the duty fell to him.

Chapter Four

Quinn grabbed the pole with both hands and swung his body around it before sticking the landing on one foot and striking a provocative pose.

Watching over by the railing, Mackie clapped a few times. "That was great, nearly perfect."

Quinn straightened and grinned back. "I'm not sure I'd go that far, but at least I didn't fall on my ass this time."

He caught the towel Mackie threw at him and wiped sweat off his face. They'd been practicing for hours. The club was quiet in the late afternoon, patrons rarely coming in at that time and the police having concluded their interviews hours ago. He sauntered over to Mackie and after grabbing a bottle of water, took a long pull.

"Thanks for working with me. I think I'm going to be more confident tonight." He grimaced. "I just need to put this murder stuff out of my mind."

Mackie mimicked his expression. "I know it's so creepy to think of that guy getting his throat ripped out right outside. I'm mean, that's grisly, even for an asshole like him." The boy shuddered. "Nothing we can do about it, anyway. The 'family'," he added in air quotes, "is on top of it, so…" He shrugged.

"What exactly does that mean? What 'family'?"

Mackie rolled his eyes. "You know, Alex, Val and the others. They've been holed up in Alex's suite since the cops left. Val didn't say much when he brought me to talk to Detective Hottie. I assume he and Alex are going to increase security or something. This won't play well for the club. Members getting their necks chewed off sends the wrong kind of message."

Quinn got that. From what Mackie had told him, those members who practiced the BDSM lifestyle put a high value on safe, sane and consensual activity. Crowell's murder fell under none of those standards. If the killer turned out to be another member or, God forbid, one of the employees, it could prove disastrous for the club's reputation and membership.

He took another swig of water. "Which one was the hottie, in your estimation?" *And if you have a guy like Val for yourself, why would you even look at another man?* If he had someone like, say…Alex in his life, other guys would probably cease to exist for him. Not that he had any chance of catching his boss' eye, of course. It was a foolish thought.

"Well, they were both attractive, but I was referring in particular to the one who could be the love-child of Denzel Washington and Vin Diesel."

Quinn chuckled. "Yeah, I guess he was pretty hot. He was also gentle in his questioning. It wasn't anything like you see on TV."

"Oh, honey! As if he seriously thought you were a suspect. No way. He's focusing on the giant Stelalux boys. Now, they could yank out a man's larynx without breaking a sweat."

The very notion had beads of moisture forming on his own skin. Alex had been furious with Crowell. *Could he have really done such a thing?* Quinn hadn't seen him for more than an hour after he'd sent him scurrying away from the stage. He could have done it, he supposed.

"You don't think one of them is the killer, do you?" he asked.

At the question, Mackie blinked with exaggeration. "And be stupid enough to leave the body at their own back door? No fucking way! If you think their bodies are big, you should see their minds at work. They are *massively* smart, even Val—not that I care two shits about the size of his brain. That is definitely not the organ that catches my attention." He broke into a fit of giggles.

"What's so funny?" Demi called out as he raced by them, leaped onto the closest stage and twirled around the pole with more speed and grace than Quinn would ever master. The boy made three rotations before stopping then wrapping one foot around the pole and flipping backward. He hung there with his long hair almost brushing the floor.

Mackie stopped laughing. "Nothing you need to know about, show-off. And you shouldn't be eavesdropping on our conversation or playing go-go boy. Don't you have school work or something? He's home-schooled year-round," he added for Quinn's benefit.

Demi righted himself and struck the same pose Quinn had moments earlier. This boy was sexier than

Quinn had imagined he was. The dark, exotic allure of the kid was going to get him into a boatload of trouble if his fathers didn't keep close tabs on him.

"The 'rents have been behind closed doors with Cousin Alex and Val for hours, and calculus bores the shit out of me." He climbed the pole using the strength of his arms only, wrapped his thighs around it and hung upside down with his arms folded over his chest.

Mackie made a noise of disgust. "You look like a bat!" Dropping his voice for Quinn only, he said, "Sometimes I really hate that kid. All that beauty and strength plus an intelligence that would make Einstein weep. He doesn't get how lucky he is to have so much going for him, especially having two parents that love and support him."

"How about we trade places?" Demi called out.

"Ugh, he has hearing like a bat, too."

To prove Mackie's last point, the boy flipped himself right-side up and landed on his feet a second before Val came striding over from the elevator. Quinn hadn't heard the doors open, yet there was Val, Emil peeling off to the kitchen and Alex. The sight of the boss made Quinn's heart beat a little faster and it caught his entire attention. The man's presence filled the big room the moment he entered. Quinn had the sudden and fleeting thought that whoever the killer was, he would do well to worry about Alex coming after him, compared to the police.

Val stopped by the railing. "Mackie, come on. I need a break." Not waiting for an answer, the man turned and headed for the staircase in the far corner.

With a huff, Mackie cocked his hip and folded his arms in front of his chest. "I'm sorry. I didn't hear a *please* in that invitation."

Without a hitch to his stride, the bouncer reversed direction and was on Mackie with dizzying speed. Before Quinn could even register what had happened, Val had grabbed Mackie by the waist and tossed him over his shoulder. The boy squealed in alarm, but when Val turned to walk away, Mackie winked at Quinn before struggling to free himself. With a loud smack to the boy's ass, the bouncer stayed on course and took the stairs two at a time.

A warm presence along with an earthy scent caught Quinn's attention. Alex had taken Mackie's place next to him. The large body made him feel crowded, yet instead of wanting to inch away, he felt the urge to get closer. He didn't. Any fantasy he might be spinning about him and this man needed to stay inside his head.

"Demetrius," Alex said in that mild tone he used that nevertheless came out with command, "your fathers are undoubtedly searching for you. I suggest you return upstairs."

"Yes, sir." The teenager's normally snarky expression had disappeared and he trotted off.

A few seconds later, Alex focused his attention on Quinn. He felt the heat of it even before he saw it. "Please don't let me interfere with your practicing."

Quinn's usual flush burned his cheeks. "Oh, um…yeah." *Awesome. So articulate.* Any idea that a man as obviously cultured and educated as Alex would find an awkward high school dropout like him interesting was plain stupid.

Feeling ill at ease, he returned to the stage and re-started the routine he and Mackie had worked out for him. The low-level music held the right tempo for what he wanted to do. It was that intense gaze that made him clumsy again. He'd rather face a crowd of drooling men than this one. Wiping his palms on his thighs, he jumped to grab the pole and lost his grip. He slid right onto his ass with a jarring *thud* that stung his tail bone and rattled his teeth.

Perfect.

In what seemed like a split second, Alex was there, kneeling beside him. "Are you all right?" His concerned face loomed in close to Quinn's.

From across the mere inches between them, he could see the man's violet irises. They seemed to change right in front of him to a shade of purple that was almost black. Alex's nostrils flared with a sharp intake of breath before he grabbed Quinn's right hand. Without breaking their locked gazes, Alex did the strangest thing. He placed Quinn's palm against his lips.

It wasn't a kiss. Alex lapped what Quinn now felt was stinging skin. As he did so, those mesmerizing eyes staring over the edge of his hand got even darker. Their intensity pulled Quinn in. He felt trapped, helpless to look away. He became aware of the heavy beat of his heart. His palm seemed to pulse with the same rhythm while Alex's tongue bathed it. All other sound became muted and his vision tunneled so that all he saw were those amazing eyes.

His breathing slowed, too—a steady, yet harsh, in and out that burned his lungs. Blood rushed to his cock, making it hard with painful intensity. Even his hole clenched as if demanding to be filled—by Alex, with whatever Alex had hiding within his perfectly tailored slacks. The thought alone made Quinn moan with a wanton need that echoed inside his head.

And just like that, the spell broke. Alex dropped Quinn's hand and pulled back. The man shook his head as if he, too, had been caught in some trance. He stood and hopped off the stage, putting a few feet between them. There was no hiding the bulge behind his fly. The guy wanted him, that much was obvious. He also appeared as flustered as Quinn felt.

Alex flashed a smile. "Sorry. I thought you'd hurt yourself."

With slow movements, Quinn studied the palm of his right hand. The skin was slightly abraded. "I guess I did," he replied with a frown. "I must have given myself a rope burn of sorts." Even as he said the words, though, he saw no evidence of blood, only red skin. "No real harm."

Quinn started to stand. Alex was on him in another flash, helping him, then with an arm circling his waist, pulling him off the stage. Their bodies collided with Quinn's feet dangling a few inches above the floor and his crotch mashed against Alex's. Their hard dicks made contact, eliciting a gasp out of Quinn — *and a growl from Alex?* Yes, low and feral. It gave Quinn goosebumps.

Alex stared at him, warm, spicy breath bathing his face. "I'm sorry," the man said in a husky voice. "I seem to lose all sense of propriety around you. I could blame it on the heightened emotions of the day, but that would be a lie."

Reaching around Quinn with his other arm, Alex cupped Quinn's ass and tugged him in even closer. "I find you absolutely irresistible, despite my better nature telling me I shouldn't. I don't want you to be afraid of me," he added with a heavy-lidded gaze that made Quinn's hole clench once more.

"I'm not." Quinn's reassurance came out in a whisper. With his hands pressed against Alex's chest, he felt as if he were touching marble. He couldn't resist caressing what he could reach.

Alex growled some more and squeezed Quinn's ass. "Careful, boy. My control is not as tight as I'd like."

"What if I don't want it to be?" he dared to say back before licking his lips.

Alex's gaze tracked the movement, and for a second he thought the man might kiss him. Quinn even tipped his head back to give him better access. But instead, Alex lowered his face to place his lips at the base of Quinn's throat. He didn't even touch him, merely hovered a fraction of an inch above Quinn's skin for a few seconds and inhaled deeply. Then, he pulled back and dropped Quinn onto his feet.

"What?" Quinn blinked at him while he steadied himself. When he rocked back, Alex grabbed his shoulders only long enough to make sure he didn't fall before letting go again.

"I think that's sufficient practice for today. You're going to have a long night, and given that I woke you early for the police, you should go and take a nap before dinner."

Quinn frowned. "A nap? I don't need —"

Alex's expression hardened. "Go upstairs and rest for a few hours, Quinn." The man's voice had taken on a hard edge.

Quinn blinked some more and frowned harder, except that he couldn't muster the energy to argue. "Yes, sir," he replied in a voice that sounded petulant to his own ears.

"Take the elevator."

With a nod, Quinn turned. His ass and his palm still both stung from his fall, and a big yawn escaped his mouth before he could stop it. Sleep did seem like a good idea, after all. "I'll see you tonight, sir."

"Fuck me, not if I can help it." The response was uttered in such a low tone, Quinn wasn't even sure he'd heard it.

He turned to look over his shoulder and found an empty room.

* * * *

"So, what can you tell me?" Trey stared at the body laid out on the cold, metal table. He'd been a cop long enough to view the remains for what they were — evidence. The man who had once lived, breathed and suffered inside it was long gone. The best he could do for him was find the killer. Weeping over the corpse served no purpose.

Almadeo pulled off his shield and ran his fingers through his damp hair. "TOD was sometime between ten and midnight. I can't pin it any more accurately than that."

"You don't have to. We know from what the club's owner told us that he booted the vic out shortly before eleven. That narrows it down."

"If we can believe the guy," Karl added.

"Everybody's story confirms that fact, and before you say it," he added, raising his palm, "I get that Stelalux runs a tight ship. If he said the sky was green, I'm betting his people would back him on that. We'll see what other patrons have to say about it once we track and interview them."

Karl just grunted. "It's a weird group working there. They give off an us-vs-them kind of vibe, almost like it's a cult, especially the family members." He gave an exaggerated shiver. "Biggest fuckers I've ever seen, and what kind of name is Stelalux, anyway?"

Almadeo pursed his lips before saying, "Starlight, roughly translated from Latin."

"Oh, yeah? The owner said they were from Romania, not Italy."

Trey resisted rolling his eyes. Karl was a great cop but not a scholarly guy. "It's a Romance language, so Latin is embedded in it. Anyway, their first names ring true, and I put in a request to ICE for confirmation of their immigration status. According to their statements, they came over about fifteen years ago and were eventually naturalized. I don't think their ethnicity is going to turn out to be relevant."

The coroner smirked. "You might change your mind about that once you hear the rest of my report."

Trey raised his eyebrows, not liking that prediction at all. "Oh?"

"Yeah." Almadeo lost his smile. "Take a look at the edges of the wound." They all peered at the gaping hole that used to be the victim's throat. "The cause of death was exsanguination, no doubt. This is the only exit site on the body."

"So, having his throat ripped open is what caused him to bleed out." Tray stated it as a fact, not a question, because even a two-year old could see where this was going.

"Correct." Almadeo hovered his finger over the jagged edge of flesh. "The tear marks on the skin suggest that the weapon used was teeth."

Karl swore. "Shit. I hate the freaky ones."

Trey had to agree with his partner, although he wasn't yet buying the coroner's findings. "You're telling me that a human being managed to do this kind of damage using only their teeth?"

Almadeo nodded. "They started here" — he pointed to the base of the neck — "at the jugular, then ripped up and at an angle, stopping right beneath the chin."

A cold streak gripped Trey's spine. "That would have taken a great deal of strength."

Almadeo gave him a hard look. "Determination, I'd say, more than anything else — and perhaps fury."

Memories of the corpse as he'd seen it in the alley rose in Trey's mind. "There wasn't any blood on the victim's face and hardly any on his clothes. Ripping open the jugular would have caused a massive spray." The coroner's expression caused even more cold to seep into Trey. He ignored it.

"Yes. I'd say that almost all the blood had left the body before this wound was created."

The man's words hung in the air. Karl swore again and paced away. More irritated now than freaked out, Trey studied the body again. From what he could see, there was no bruising marring the skin except near the shoulders. He focused on that.

"Is this the only evidence of a struggle?" he asked, pointing to the mottled spots.

"Yes. The killer grabbed the victim by both shoulders and pinned him. Other than a little scraping along the palms, I see no sign of the poor man reacting. He rubbed them along the pavement, hard enough that pebbles imbedded into his skin. I'd say he lost consciousness very quickly."

Karl rejoined them. "Are you saying that the blood got sucked out of him?"

Almadeo gave a frosty smile. "Of course not. It would be impossible for a human being to ingest another's entire body of blood — in one sitting, at least." He shook his head. "No, you'd have to drain it by some artificial means, even if your kink runs to vampirism."

Trey's stomach roiled. "Is that really a thing?"

"Everything is a *thing* when it comes to humans. There are people who get off from drinking other's blood. But, as I said, it would be impossible for someone to simply drain a body completely by sucking on their jugular." He shook his head. "No, your killer used something to accomplish it after he incapacitated the victim then ripped the throat open. It's the only explanation. I'm running a tox screen to see if the victim was knocked out by a drug. Although if he was, I haven't found a puncture wound."

Shoving his hands in his pockets, Trey rocked back on his heels. Various scenarios for what had happened swirled in his head. "All of that would have taken some time. If it had been done right where we found the body, it would have been a big risk. Someone could have seen it happening simply by walking past one of the ends of the alley. The area isn't that remote. If it happened somewhere else, the killer would have had to transport the body back, and that could have been seen, too."

He paced away. "And why bother?" He turned back to Karl. "Why kill someone in a place where people are still out partying? Or why dump the body by the club? The Starlight clan strikes me as being too savvy to shit in their own bed without sanitizing the mess right away, even if I buy into the idea that Crowell pissed the head guy off that much."

"It's the boy," Karl interjected. "Cooper. Alex likes him. You can see it in the way he hovered when he brought the boy to be interviewed. It's in his eyes every time he looks at him. Crowell put his hands on what's Alex's, so he lost his temper."

"Maybe. It still doesn't explain why we found the body in the alley." He started pacing around the small, cool room. "Let's play it out. Fresh-faced Quinn Cooper comes in for a job as a go-go dancer. Part of the job description is getting pawed by patrons, I'm assuming, at a minimum, if not more. Stelalux interviews him, and maybe part of getting the job is you let the boss paw you first."

Karl flanked him. "Sure, why not? What's the point of having pretty boys working for you if you don't get to sample the goods now and again?"

Trey shook his head. "Yeah, but if that's the way the game is played, how does that square with the guy getting into such a fit of jealousy within hours that he kills a man? See, even if we treat the guy like your average pimp — and the private rooms the club offers its members kind of suggests that — you make your money off your stable. You can't afford to be stingy, even with your favorite. The most that makes sense is that Crowell crossed a line in public and the boss man had to make an example of him, again publicly. But, this bloodletting and neck chewing?"

"Crazy people don't have to make sense. You know that," Karl reminded him.

"Yeah, yeah." Trey ran a hand over the top of his head. "It doesn't mean stupid, though. Even if he's a psychopathic killer with a blood fetish, Alexandru Stelalux is *not* stupid. Leaving the body near the club is massively so. Why would the perp bother to kill close to an open business or haul it back there? Unless it was meant to be a message?" The obvious conclusion hit him square between the eyes.

Karl grimaced. "You think there is some kind of vendetta going on here? Mob related maybe? Romania is near Russia, right?"

"Sort of, except a bullet to the back of the head gives the same kind of warning. Why this elaborate method of killing?"

"Because," Almadeo interjected, "the killer liked it. This kind of thing?" he added with a nod to the body splayed out beside him. "It's a fetish, a compulsion. And I can almost guarantee you that it won't stop with just this one."

Trey's heart thudded with the news that he'd already known on some level. "In other words, regardless of whatever else we're dealing with, we've got a serial killer on our hands." He sighed. "Awesome."

* * * *

Boston nights in the early summer could be perfect as far as Alex was concerned. The oppressive heat that humans often loved, but made his species miserable, hadn't yet settled in. The air ruffling his hair as he stood on the roof of his building was cool and delicious. It helped his warm body calm, although his dick refused to settle into anything more than semi-hardness. It had been plaguing him all day, ever since he'd given in to his baser urges and had practically attacked his new employee.

Christ, the humans would say. He'd really lost his well-honed control. Bad enough to lick the few beads of blood welling on Quinn's palms, but to practically fuck the boy through their respective pants was beyond the pale. Hadn't he resolved only a few hours prior to ignore his interest in the human? That way led to possible disaster for both of them. He had to do better or risk the boy being swept into his private war.

And, speaking of which…

Alex inhaled, taking in the scents of the public alley below him. The police had finished their scouring of the place where Crowell had met his fate. He was aware Duncan believed that the man had been killed somewhere else and dumped here after the fact. Alex knew better.

"It was Adrian," he said to the man who came to join him on the roof.

Val sauntered to his side and sniffed. "Yeah, no big surprise there. He's always been Dracul's lap dog. I checked the security footage and the fucker blacked out the cameras. I got a nice picture of a hand before it all went dark. Stupid, really, considering he knew we'd identify him by scent."

"It's a game, as always — a deadly one."

"Yeah, he must have crawled down from the roof to take out the cameras. My system only alerts me if it's been breached, not vandalized superficially. I'm going to have to adjust that now."

"Do whatever you feel best, although I don't expect there will be a repeat performance out here."

"Yeah, he must have waited a while for a victim to show."

"And I hand-delivered one to him. He must have been delighted."

"You can't blame yourself, boss."

"Of course I can. I was in charge. It's my fault ultimately that we are stranded here and I couldn't keep the surviving crew together." Closing his eyes a moment as if to shut out the truth, Alex added, "I keep hoping he'll stop. After all this time, why does he continue to seek power and wreak havoc on this planet? He knows I'll never let him achieve dominion."

Val grunted. "At least he laid low longer this time."

Alex huffed. "Well, after nearly causing the world to implode more than seventy years ago, you'd expect he needed at least a bit of rest."

"I bet his whelps have finished growing, too, giving him new soldiers to utilize — and loyal ones at that," Val said.

"Yesss," Alex hissed out. Dracul had been the first to discover a successful way to procreate with humans. Of course he had, not giving a damn how many of them died before his experiments had worked. That gave Alex one more reason to resist the temptation that Quinn presented. Capitalizing on his nemesis' experiments rubbed him the wrong way. Harry had been successful, of course, as had others of their coterie, demonstrating that breeding with a human could be done in a loving relationship. Still, Val's foray had ended in disaster, and that was confirmation enough that he shouldn't try it himself.

"If this is the opening salvo," Val observed, "it's his most subtle to date. I'll give him that."

"It reflects how this world is rapidly changing, I think. A lurid murder at our doorstep can become fodder for the world through the Internet within hours. These days, you don't have to instigate a multi-country war to sow the kind of fear he likes to feed on. He can sit in that castle of his and watch the humans lose their collective minds over the possibility of a superhuman killer."

"You think there will be more?"

"Oh, yes. I expect Adrian's orders are to litter the streets of Boston with bloodless corpses. Talk of vampires will feed the humans' natural inclination to see the supernatural. Space travel and pocket-sized computers notwithstanding, as a species, they are still ruled by their baser emotions. What they don't understand, they fear. And they are prone to concoct the most outlandish stories as to the 'how' and 'why' of things rather than to seek knowledge and truth. They remain easy to spook and lie to. That hasn't changed since we first arrived."

Val stepped closer to the edge and peered over. "Just because they dumped this at our door doesn't mean we have to react."

Alex scoffed softly. He'd had the same fleeting thought earlier in the day when he'd held Quinn's delectable body in his arms. Abandoning the fight and letting Dracul do what he wanted in this world was tempting. They'd been fighting so long that he was tired. If this was to remain his home for the rest of his long life, he'd prefer to live it in peace.

"We have no choice," he replied, letting his weariness seep through. "Earth has always been a volatile, violent place. The humans don't need us to accomplish that. But they have been getting better, slowly, yet relentlessly more caring of each other and peaceful. Dracul would end that trend, turn this planet into his personal playground, and humans would become his unfortunate toys."

"We could carve out a quiet piece for ourselves," Val reminded him.

"We could, ignoring our sworn duties to protect those in need and preserve the hive."

"An oath we took for our people, not humans. They don't even have a collective hive."

Alex shook his head. "We never qualified it in that manner." This was an old debate.

Val sighed. "We had no way of knowing at the time we kneeled before the queen and spoke those words that we'd ever have to apply them to a species not our own." He looked at Alex over his shoulder and gave him a tired smile. "Would anyone really blame of us if we left the humans to their own defense? They're hardly helpless now."

"I don't know." He dropped his gaze and studied his own feet. "But if nothing else, I'm still the captain of our group. No event has relieved me of my charge and Dracul's mutiny cannot go unaddressed."

Alex took a step forward and looked at the alley. From this height, he could jump without causing himself any harm. Their strength and agility were two of the reasons humans viewed them as supernatural beings. "This is only the beginning. There will be another victim soon if we don't find and stop Adrian."

Val arched his eyebrows. "There is only one way to stop him."

"Yes, and as much as it might pain me, we need to take that path."

"I'm sorry to say, boss, but it will cause me no pain at all. Dracul must know how we'll react. I'm surprised he'd be willing to sacrifice one of his men."

"He's never cared for them much more than he has the humans. Besides, I'm certain it was Adrian who screwed the pooch last time, giving us the edge in the conflict. You know Dracul was merely biding his time before meting out the proper punishment."

Turning, Alex added, "Come. The club is full tonight, the story of the murder perhaps titillating our members enough that they want to come see for themselves.

Later, you can slip out and track Adrian's movements." He shot his friend a sly smile. "I trust you've blooded-up sufficiently this afternoon."

Val grinned. "Oh, yes. Mackie was quite generous in that regard. He always is."

"Watch him closely," Alex warned, all trace of humor gone. "He's at risk, even though you haven't committed to him."

"I know." Val growled. "I will rip Adrian into small pieces and feed him to the sharks if he so much as looks at that boy."

Alex said nothing more, but he understood the sentiment. He'd do the same if Quinn entered the crosshairs. He might not want to become involved with the boy, but his resolve in the matter was weakening. He was no longer sure he could remain strong.

Chapter Five

Wales

"Stop whining!" Dracul slapped the already-red ass of his pathetic not-quite-human mate. Of course, that bite of pain only made the creature mewl even more.

In truth, he liked the sound and only pretended to be angry — most of the time. As he slammed his cock into the channel that was still tight even after a few centuries, he groaned and dug his nails into quivering flanks.

Dafydd had yet to grow out of his delicate youth, the effect of a steady diet of Dracul's blood. He wondered idly — as he often did — how many centuries he would be able draw out the boy's lifespan. And would the beauty remain or would it wither, as was the norm for humans? He didn't know, but he wouldn't keep him if his desirability ever faded. For now, Dafydd's curtain of long black hair covered his pale face that was mashed into the bedding. Dracul liked fucking him this way — on all fours, taut ass sticking up where he could grab the hips for maximum control. He pulled back and rammed balls deep once more before drilling Dafydd at a brutal pace.

He'd had many humans in the long, boring centuries on this miserable planet. The pretty Welsh boy he'd plucked from the fields one day still gave him the most pleasure. Perhaps because, despite his slender form and innocent manner, he'd managed to survive. His human nature had weathered being bred by his master, as well, when others of his species had perished from it. There was a hidden strength in his mate that Dracul tried to break, almost on a daily basis. As entertainments went, it had a lingering appeal.

Digging his nails into the soft flesh, he yanked the ass in flush with his pelvis before draping his larger frame over his mate's bony back. The thrum of the human's heartbeat still called to him. He focused on the tiny pulse at the bottom of the pale throat a second before he sank his fangs into it.

Dafydd's scream, a sound that still made Dracul smile, echoed in the large, stone chamber they called their bedroom. Sweet blood filled his mouth. He still marveled at how he'd lived without it for nearly two centuries on this miserable planet before defying the weak-willed captain. He tugged at the vein, drawing the blood down his throat and quenching a thirst that seemed to only get stronger with the passing years.

The taste of it, hot and salty on his tongue, sent a signal to his cock. Embedded deep within his mate's ass, the throbbing length twitched and pulsed. He jerked and thrust as much as his position would allow, setting a rhythm between his swallows and the flicking of his hips. The pathetic human collapsed onto the bed, his legs splayed out and tears running over his chin. He knew how much Dracul hated that moisture getting in the way of his feast. He'd have to punish the boy later for that unacceptable weakness.

Just the thought of turning that satiny skin into rivers of blood that he could lap as a special snack sent him over the edge. He sank in his teeth in even harder as cum erupted from his dick to coat the human's channel. Maybe this time, Dracul's seed would find another egg to fertilize. This human had borne him two sons already, but that wasn't enough. He needed more warriors.

As if thinking of his sons could conjure them, a firm knock sounded against the chamber's thick wooden door. He knew by scent and sound alone who was there. Retracting his fangs, Dracul let his mate go and raised his head.

"Enter."

Bran and Cadoc entered, the sight of them giving him a sense of pride, as always. They were so clearly his, little trace of the inferior human blood visible in the tall, strong males they'd become. They wore their long hair as he did — shaved on the sides while hanging in a long queue down their backs. They always wore black leather, though, lacking his sense of style. But that was okay. They were young and full of themselves. He could indulge them.

He sat on his heels, wiping the trace of blood from his lips with the back of his hand. His spent cock ripped out of Dafydd's tight hole, causing the boy to whimper. Neither Dracul nor his sons paid any attention to the pathetic being. Bran and Cadoc had learned early and well how contemptible the being who'd given birth to them was.

"What is it?" He knew the boys wouldn't interrupt his fun without good reason.

Older by a few minutes, Bran took the lead. "We have been monitoring the news out of Boston, sir, and the media is already speaking about a ghoulish murder."

Dracul smiled. "What a wonderful boon this Internet is. It took these pitiful creatures long enough to develop fast-paced communication. I only wish I could see the look on Alex's face." He tsked. "He won't be able to resist getting involved."

"Sir?" This from Cadoc. "With respect, would you please reconsider sending us there to help Adrian? He is outnumbered."

Dracul's lips curled. The question irked him. He needed his sons to be able to think ahead. "No. You are not for the frontlines in this war with Stelalux."

"But, sir," the boy persisted, "Adrian will be killed if he doesn't receive support."

"That's the whole point," Bran scoffed, and his understanding caused Dracul's smile to return. "Isn't that right, sir?" He appealed to Dracul for confirmation, his eyes gleaming with excitement.

"Exactly. Adrian is there to test their appetite for engagement and their numbers. They have become more scattered in the last half-century. You'd do well to learn from your brother, Cadoc. Bran is proving to be the better strategist."

Cadoc glared at his brother. *Good.* He'd always fostered a certain rivalry between them. One would have to emerge to take the soon-to-be vacant leadership spot at Dracul's left side. Petru had always occupied the spot on his right and he had no intention of casting his most loyal and capable male aside to make room for a less-deserving son. When Adrian failed, though, there would be a vacancy to be filled.

"Adrian is loyal to you, sir. May I ask why you are sacrificing him?" As much as he didn't like Cadoc questioning him, the query did show some amount of thought and courage, so he answered the boy.

"Adrian has served me well, but he got clumsy in our last endeavor. At the time, I forgave him, but that was always a temporary reprieve. He can demonstrate his devotion one last way in flushing Stelalux out to start the new chapter in our conflict."

Cadoc nodded. "I understand now, sir. Please forgive my impertinence."

Dracul flicked a wrist at the pair of them. "Go and paste your eyes to those screens of yours and keep me apprised."

They were both smart enough to recognize the dismissal. They bowed, turned and strode out of the chamber.

"One day, you'll sacrifice them, too, won't you? Your own sons don't matter as much as your thirst for power."

Dracul turned his gaze to his mate. The human had risen and sat staring at him with surprising contempt—surprising because the boy wasn't usually so bold.

With a speed he knew Dafydd could barely see, let alone avoid, Dracul backhanded that pretty face. Dafydd's head snapped to one side before he returned to stare at him. Blood trickled from his split lip, the sweet sight causing Dracul's hunger to rise once more. And while fear showed through the human's dewy brown eyes, so still did defiance. Yes, he was an entertaining little pet. Feasting could wait.

"I was going to fuck you again, but I think punishment for all those tiresome tears is in order." Placing his hands on his hips, he glanced around the stone chamber. "Now, where did I put my whip?"

* * * *

Boston

Alex loved Boston when it was quiet and dark. In the few hours between night revelers dragging themselves back to their homes — or someone else's — and the morning light brought by the too-hot sun was the time when his people thrived the best. He could make his way through the city in relative secrecy, not having to hide his true nature.

To be safe, even at this late hour, he started on the roof of his own building. He kept his clothing black, a color that reminded him of his rank and duty as a warrior. It also helped to hide him from whatever prying eyes might be about. His pants were made of supple leather that wore well, no matter what he scraped against, and his cotton crew-neck was long-sleeved to hide as much of his pale skin as possible. Sturdy boots helped to cushion hard landings.

Val had called with his location and, knowing the route well enough, Alex figured he could at least start his journey above ground. Standing on the brick edge, he eyed the next building over for a brief moment before leaping across the very alley where Crowell had met his fate. The scent of the killer was still detectable, although barely. He was glad he'd dismissed Val early from the club to start the tracking. If they'd waited one more day, the trail would have gone too cold.

He landed on the roof next door with a quiet thump and sprinted across it. It took nothing for his long, strong legs to send him running and jumping from rooftop to rooftop. Even a human could have managed it if they'd tried hard and were lucky enough to judge the distances correctly. For him, it was like a stroll in the elevated world of the small city. He loved the freedom of giving his muscles a worthy work-out. Most of the time, he had to rein himself in, pretend he was slower and clumsier than he truly was. The reason for his journey might be troubling in the extreme, but he would enjoy the outing, regardless.

All too soon he reached a point where he had to return to the ground. He picked the back of the last building to make his descent. His heavy boots and muscular legs absorbed the impact of his jump. As he straightened, he concentrated his hearing on the sounds around him. With his hair pulled back into a braid, there was nothing to muffle any noise to be heard. Other than distant and sporadic traffic sounds, he detected no one nearby.

He raced to the end of the alley then stopped to case the street for anyone before crossing over to the other side. Although there was always the risk of being seen, he decided urgency trumped caution. If there had been someone watching, they would have seen a dark blur and would hopefully put it down to a trick of the eye or too much drink, perhaps. Humans were always using substances to alter their perceptions to degrees that didn't happen with his species, forever miserable with their lives and searching for something better. It was no wonder they'd been easily led by Dracul whenever that traitorous male had gotten the urge to meddle.

He made his way past buildings and over streets and bridges until he reached an area of the city that still contained warehouses. He wasn't surprised Val had tracked Adrian to this section. Although it was being revived and developed, it was still a place where one could hide away without anyone noticing.

The scent trail was stronger here, yet still fainter than he wanted. It was easier to catch Val's and find him, instead. When Alex reached a five-story building, he made a standing jump to grasp the ledge of a smashed window and climbed. Human architecture, with its bits and pieces always sticking out, made it easy. Throwing his leg over the edge to the roof, he vaulted onto it and stood.

He took a second to brush the dust from his pants before searching for Val. The loyal male stood in the shadow of the HVAC system. The most visible part of him was the glowing red ember at the end of the cigarette he brought to his lips.

Alex sauntered over. "I thought you'd stopped that filthy habit."

Val shrugged and blew out a puff of smoke. "I promised I wouldn't smoke at home." He scanned the rooftop. "This is definitely not home. Besides, it's not like it can kill me."

"Harry isn't completely sure on that point. It might just take a lot longer than it does the humans."

With another shrug, Val took a long drag. Then he dropped it and stamped it out. "Who the hell cares?"

The cynical response took Alex aback for a second. "I do, for one. And I expect Mackie would be most aggrieved if you died from lung cancer."

Val blew the smoke out. "Yeah, there is the boy. You're right about him. I need to make a decision. It's not fair of me to string him along." Taking a step, he scanned the area some more. "I ordered him to stay in, just to be safe. Sometimes this Dom persona I've adopted comes in handy. No telling how long Adrian has been scoping us out, and he might have seen me with Mackie."

"Excellent point." His mind flashed on Quinn and his gut clenched with the sudden notion that he should have done the same with him, except that was ridiculous. He was in no position to order the boy to do any such thing, and besides, there was no reason for Adrian to tie the human to Alex because there was *nothing* between Quinn and Alex. *Nothing at all.*

Irritated by his own musings, Alex turned his attention back to Val. "Why are you lingering here? Has the trail truly gone cold?"

"Take a whiff for yourself."

He did, turning in the direction where he caught a lingering sent. "This way."

Val shook his head. "Try some more."

Again, Alex tested the air, and this time, he detected something in another direction. Frowning, he glanced at Val. "He went in two different directions?"

"Three." Val pointed left of where Alex stood.

"Clever."

"Yeah, he must have doubled back and laid three different trails, knowing we couldn't follow all of them at once. We may find he repeated the process along one or more ways still, to really fuck with us."

With a sigh, Alex put his hands on his hips and surveyed the area. Val was right. Adrian wasn't the brightest of their lot, but he was a warrior, well-trained and formidable. "It would take three of us to even make a start of it, and given the hour, I doubt Emil would be able to get here in time for us to do it properly."

Val made a pained face. "Leave the guy to his pots and pans. We might want to consider bringing some of the others back in."

Now, it was Alex's turn to grimace. "I don't want to do that unless it's absolutely necessary. You know I want everyone to carve out what life they can on this planet. I hate for Dracul to shatter peace for all of us." He shook his head. "No. We'll handle this ourselves, even if it means forcing Emil and Harry to trade their domestic skills for their warrior ones."

He took one futile step in a direction his nose told him to go, then he stopped and forced himself to accept temporary defeat. "There's nothing more we can do tonight. We have to accept that, for now, it's a waiting game. Once Adrian makes his next move, we'll be ready to react quickly so he can't trip us up again."

"Fuck! You're right but it sucks. I hate being lured away from the club, too. I know security is tight because I installed it myself, and I know Harry and Emil are capable of mounting a good defense. Still..."

"Yes." Quinn's face swam in front of his mind's eye and a sudden sense of urgency overtook him. "We go back. Now."

With that pronouncement and an irrational need to return to defend his home and the people in it, he ran to the edge of the roof and leaped into the darkness below.

* * * *

"How'd you do tonight?" Mackie asked as he shuffled his tips into an orderly pile.

Quinn had just finished counting his own and still hadn't managed to stop gawking. "Better."

He stared at a little over a thousand dollars, and coupled with the money he'd earned the previous day, he now held more money than he'd typically earned in a month at the hardware store — and that didn't even factor in the wages Alex paid him. He'd yet to see a single paycheck.

"Is it always this good?" he asked the other boy.

Mackie shrugged and tucked the single wad into the thong he still wore. "Weekends tend to be, and we had a larger crowd than usual. I think the murder helped business, to be frank. Plus, you're new, so you're going to get a lot of attention for some time. Be smart and save while you can. Don't go off on a bender or anything. Lots of boys do, then lose their jobs because of booze or drugs."

"That's good advice. I don't do either of those things and I don't intend to start. I'm grateful that Alex took a chance on me and I'm not going to blow it."

Cocking his head, Mackie smiled. "I have a feeling you're going to be fine. You seem to have a good head on your shoulders. Must be all that clean living in Montana."

"Michigan," he reminded Mackie with a roll of his eyes.

Shawn wandered in from the shower area, dressed in street clothes. "Hey, a bunch of us are going to the Tea Cup for breakfast. Are you coming?" He directed the question to both of them. They were the last ones in the dressing room.

Mackie sighed. "Thanks, but I'm on lockdown for the night. Val ordered me not to go out. He expects me to be in his room when he returns from wherever he went."

Quinn frowned and he couldn't help shifting his gaze to the boy's groin. Bite marks were visible on his inner left thigh. "Is that okay with you?" He knew the question might be crossing a line, given their short acquaintance. But Mackie had been kind to him and given good advice, so where was the difference? He worried about how Val treated the guy.

Mackie fluttered his lashes. "Of course. He's my Master."

Shawn made a gacking noise. "Don't even try to figure out what makes this one tick. Are you coming?" He directed the question to Quinn.

"Oh." A big yawn tore out of him before he could say more. He smiled. "Sorry, no. I'm exhausted."

Shawn gave a little wave. "Suit yourselves. See you later."

"Don't worry. Going to that diner is pretty common among the boys. It's the only one open all night in this area. You'll get on the right schedule pretty quick, then eating after your shift ends will seem normal."

Mackie headed out, apparently not concerned about parading his naked ass around the club after hours. Quinn followed, having thrown on a pair of jeans. Even so, he felt exposed in a way that he didn't while dancing. Something about flashing so much skin while going about his ordinary life seemed embarrassing, except that he and Mackie were only going to their rooms — or Val's, in the other boy's case. There probably wasn't going to be anyone seeing them, anyway.

Because he was walking behind Mackie, he got a good look at his new friend's exposed ass. It was covered in welts that had been an angry red when the evening began and now were more mottled. He winced at the view.

"Doesn't that hurt like hell?" he asked without thinking as they entered the elevator.

Mackie pushed the fourth-floor button before turning guileless eyes on Quinn. "What? My ass-paddling? Of course. That's the whole point." A look that was pure sex crossed his friend's face and his eyelids drooped.

Embarrassed, yet unable to let it go, Quinn flicked his hand in the direction of Mackie's groin. "How about that?"

Now the boy's eyes closed for a moment before he shot Quinn a mischievous smile. "Only a little and just at first. After that, it sends me flying to this floaty plane that is the best high ever."

The elevator dinged and they got off on the fourth floor. "He doesn't really drink your blood, though, does he?" The very idea was repellent.

Now Mackie popped his eyes out. "Sure, he does. That's the whole point. It's part of his kink, and it's not like he drains me of it. He's not a vampire or anything," he added with a little chuckle.

They'd reached the door to Val's room. Mackie leaned on the jamb. "It's part of our negotiation. You know..." he continued when Quinn raised his eyebrows in confusion. "Those of us in the lifestyle discuss in advance how we play. We set respective limits, soft and hard.

"I like a man to take charge, put me in chastity from time to time and wallop my ass. I wear these welts with pride, not shame, and it doesn't hurt that the members tend to tip me more when they can see how much punishment I took from Val."

Quinn wrinkled his nose. "Isn't that kind of sick of them?"

"Nah. That's their kink and I don't mind. Val would totally respect my limits if I asked him not to mark me on nights when I dance. I don't, so if he tells me he needs to spend time with me before I work, then I give him what he wants." Mackie looked at the floor and chewed at his lips. "I was a real mess when I came here. I'd been living on the streets for a while, turning tricks when things were really bad. I needed a firm hand to get my life back on track and Val gave that to me. If he wants to suck my blood, that's fine with me."

Quinn glanced at the bite marks while he digested Mackie's explanation. "How do they close so quickly? They seem like they were done a lot earlier than this afternoon."

Mackie shrugged. "Val has some kind of ointment he uses. I don't really pay any attention. I'm so deep into subspace that you could land a plane in the room and I'd never notice." He held up his hand. "I know your next question is, what is subspace?"

Quinn grinned. "Ah, yeah?"

"I'll give you the BDSM primer tomorrow. Right now, I'm going to lock my horny self into a cock cage — I'll explain that tomorrow, too — and watch TV until Val gets back. I count on him to set limits for me, and he insisted I not go out tonight. I don't expect him to explain why because that leads me to question his judgment, which also leads me to fighting him and getting into trouble. The whole point of having a Master is to simply obey. It's liberating in its own way." The boy pushed the door open. "I'll see you tomorrow, sweetie. Get some sleep. You were positively fierce tonight." Blowing a kiss, he shut the door.

Quinn continued to his own room, which was a concept he still couldn't quite wrap his mind around. Once inside, he stashed his tips in the drawer of the nightstand where he kept his other money. Eying the tidy sum, he came to an obvious decision. He grabbed two hundred dollars and threw on a T-shirt and flip-flops, because slinking around in only jeans seemed too skanky. Then he took the back stairs to Alex's floor. He hesitated only a moment before pushing the door open.

He walked right into the man himself.

Alex grabbed his new go-go boy by the shoulders before he toppled over. Maybe the humans were right after all about the existence of some cosmic manipulator. It seemed as if he was destined to cross paths with this boy in a way that constantly tempted him.

"I beg your pardon." He forced normality in his voice even though he felt his world go off kilter as much as the boy's body was. A sudden thirst rose in his throat and it took tremendous effort to swallow it back.

Quinn looked at him with wide blue eyes. "I'm sorry, sir. I didn't mean to barge in on you." He blinked a few times.

"No apologies necessary," he replied with another hard swallow. He forced his hands to release the boy, although he hovered a moment to make sure he was stable. "My door, as it were, is always open."

Alex took a step back for good measure. "I was actually just returning from an errand." Which, considering the hour, must have sounded farfetched, yet given that they'd run into each other — literally — in his vestibule, what else could he say? "Is there something you require?"

Quinn stood staring for a few more seconds before breaking his gaze away from Alex's face. "Oh, um…no. Not exactly." He held out his hand and opened his fingers. "I wanted to give this back to you."

Alex stared dumbly at the bills in the boy's palm. "Money?" he finally said with furrowed brows.

The human licked his lower lip, likely an unintentionally provocative gesture that nonetheless caught Alex's attention as much as a sledgehammer to his head would. "I wanted to repay you the advance you gave me." Another swipe followed by a brief bite of the pink flesh sent Alex's blood pulsing. "I've made so much in tips alone that I don't need it."

Alex's thoughts had already scattered. "Need what?"

Quinn blinked again. "The money?" He raised his hand another inch, putting the wrist that much closer to Alex's saliva-flooded mouth.

It would take almost no effort to clasp that hand and bring all those luscious veins within biting distance. He would be so gentle, sinking his teeth into the flesh covering the wrist with as much care as something inherently violent could be done. He'd found drinking from the wrist to be the most civilized way to partake of a human's blood. No tempting cock brushing against one's cheek. No need to mash and grind bodies in a way that would encourage another basic claiming by way of a dick sliding into a tight hole.

The errant thoughts caused him to shudder and he must have uttered some primitive noise, because Quinn's eyes went wide while he took a half-step back. He continued to offer the repayment, however, and that simple show of faith undid Alex even more. This boy was guileless and trusting, even after the way his family had betrayed him. He needed protecting. *From me most of all.*

He forced his baser instincts down and brought a smile to his lips that he hoped looked reassuring and friendly and not desperate and predatory. "That's terribly kind of you, Quinn, but I assure you I have no need of repayment. Besides, it was an advancement of your pay, not a loan. Repayment was never required."

"Oh." The human still stared at him, still blinked a number of times. One could almost see the gears churning inside his pretty head. He lowered his hand and fisted the bills by his side. "I guess I forgot that. Sorry."

"Sorry for what?" He was losing the thread of the conversation again. It kept disappearing into the bright blue pools of Quinn's eyes.

"Disturbing you?"

Now it was his turn to blink as he struggled to formulate a suitable reply. It didn't help. Instead, he heard himself saying, "My dear boy, you disturb me simply by existing."

Seeing the sudden confusion morphing into hurt in the human's expression, he was forced to clarify what he'd meant. He had only himself to blame. The humans would say he'd let the cat out of the bag, and while he'd witnessed the true meaning of that expression, it didn't change how apt it was under these circumstances. He was lashing himself with each unguarded word.

He took a step closer to Quinn, pleased when the boy stood where he was instead of instinctively trying to distance them again. "What I meant was that I find you compelling, against my better judgment." He took another step closer. "I really shouldn't. It's entirely inappropriate, and yet..."

Quinn took a shallow, shuddery breath. "You mean because I work for you?"

Alex nodded. "Because of that and for other reasons."

Once again, the boy licked that bottom lip before truly testing Alex's resolve by taking a half step *closer*. "What other reasons? Like because you're a little older than I am?"

Alex chuckled at the innocent observation. "Dearest boy, you have no idea just how much older than you I truly am."

Quinn roamed his gaze down Alex. It was like a visual caress that made Alex hard even while his blood pounded in his head, not his groin.

Quinn refocused his attention on Alex's eyes. "It doesn't matter. You're gorgeous for any age." His breath hitched. "I'm sorry. I shouldn't have said that."

Whatever resolve Alex had held on to with a death grip nevertheless slipped from his grasp. Leaning toward him, he cupped Quinn's jaw and raised the boy's face while he lowered his own. He hovered his lips over the pulse at the base of the boy's throat. "Apology not accepted. Do you mean you want me?"

Alex froze, waiting for the answer, telling himself that he was stupider than any human he'd ever cursed for being so. He was also more of a predator than he'd accused Dracul of being. The right thing to do would be to let go of this boy, rebuke him for his insolence and banish him from the fifth floor, if not the entire club. Staying here, becoming involved with him, put Quinn at risk in all kinds of ways... Adrian targeting him was only one of them.

"I..." A flutter of warm breath caressed his cheek. "Please."

The ambiguity of the response should have been enough for him to pull back and let go. Instead, he closed the bare inch between them and pressed his lips against the gently pulsing skin. He felt the warmth of the human body, so unlike his species' core temperature, and the slow beat of the smaller heart.

Quinn shuddered at the contact. If the boy had made the slightest effort to evade the kiss, or had tried to repel Alex in any way, he would have stopped. He would have released his hold, stepped back and apologized for his unforgiveable lapse and he would have corralled his interest in the boy. Instead, the human leaned in, grasped hold of Alex's arms and all but melted into his touch. That was what caused him to lose what little restraint he'd held on to.

Pressing his mouth more firmly into Quinn's neck, he pulled him in closer. He dropped his hand from the boy's chin to wrap it around his shoulders, giving him greater leverage. He pressed opened-mouthed kisses all the way up the slender column of Quinn's neck, making his journey slow. He was in no hurry and wanted to taste every sweet inch of flesh he could.

Far from remaining passive, the human angled his head to expose himself more to Alex's touch. The grip of his fingers on Alex's arms tightened in testimony to how affected he was by such a small amount of attention. A sigh escaped those pretty lips, then a soft moan. The sound was so intoxicating that Alex was inspired to heighten his efforts. He worked along the jaw line before taking the boy's mouth.

He had intended to keep the kiss light and closed-mouthed. It was Quinn who demanded more. On another sigh, the boy parted his lips in invitation — or maybe he only did it on instinct. Regardless, Alex lacked the strength to ignore the opportunity. He slipped his tongue inside the welcoming warmth and began a gentle assault. Quinn's tongue met his and joined in the dance.

I am the first.

It seemed both impossible, yet just as obvious, that no one had ever even kissed this beautiful boy. How sad and how irresistible that realization made him. Alex wanted to go where no man had been allowed before. Knowing that he might very well set the tone for the rest of the boy's sex life, he tried to go slow to make the exploration of Quinn's mouth a leisurely journey with no expectation of anything more.

Quinn was having none of that, either. With a loud groan that echoed down Alex's throat, he pressed closer. Being weaker than he'd like, Alex responded by grasping the boy's hip and pulling him against as much of his larger body as he could. A hard ridge pressed into his thigh, testament to how much effect he'd had on the human. Quinn wanted him. There was no denying that. The question was what to do about it. *How far should I take this?*

Not far. Kiss him then send him off to bed. His own *bed, you weak-willed lunatic.*

He intended to act on his inner command, pulling away as a prelude to ending the kiss, except the second he tried to throttle back, Quinn whimpered and clutched at him with greater strength.

So instead of doing the right thing, he did what they both wanted and swept the boy into his arms. Quinn stiffened only for a second before relaxing into the embrace. He swirled his tongue around Alex's with obvious, if clumsy, enthusiasm. In the face of it, Alex abandoned any pretense of restraint. Keeping their lips fused, he marched the boy over to the apartment door.

Val had installed a security pad that worked on both a code and a thumb-print. And because Quinn weighed next to nothing, it was easy for Alex to hold the boy with one arm while reaching to press their way into his apartment. He didn't stop to consider how he'd never brought anyone else into his current home — not for this. Not for sex. He'd always sought out basic gratification elsewhere, either with strangers or occasionally club members in the lower rooms designed for those kinds of assignations.

This floor was his domain and his only. Here, he could be himself without worry of being discovered as 'alien' by the humans. Bringing Quinn here made no sense. He should turn around and take the boy back to his own room. *It would be safer that way. Wiser.* Nevertheless, he made no effort to abandon his course. The only question left in his mind was, where should he put the boy down so that he could access the rest of his lovely body?

He chose the quickest solution and, taking the short flight of steps in one bound, strode over to the very place where he'd placed Quinn a mere two days ago. Perforce, he had to release those welcoming lips in order to lay the human on the sofa without crushing him. The small, distressed mewl at their parting was most gratifying.

"Greedy boy," he chided with a grin. "I'm not going far."

Quinn gazed at him, his mouth all puffy and pouty from their long kiss. "I don't know what to do. I don't even know what I want."

"Not to worry. I do." Kneeling by the side of the couch like the supplicant he was, he brushed a few strands of hair from Quinn's forehead. "You must tell me if I do anything you don't like. And, if you tell me to stop, I will. Immediately. You have my word. Understand?"

Quinn gave a quick nod before reaching for Alex's cheek. "Will you kiss me again?"

"My dear, nothing would please me more."

He pressed his lips to the boy's palm before reclaiming his mouth. This time, he started slow and stayed that way. Despite Quinn's entreaties, he didn't invade with his tongue. Instead, he pressed wet kisses along the lips and at each side of them. Then he trailed his tongue along the edge of the jaw and down the throat, repeating his journey from the earlier one in the vestibule, except in reverse.

When the collar of Quinn's T-shirt impeded his progress, he took a moment to strip it off the boy and toss it aside. He'd seen this naked chest before. Of course, he had. This time, though, he touched it, running first his palm then his lips along all that satiny smoothness. He allowed only a brief detour to the small, pink nipples. When he swirled his tongue around each hard nub, Quinn gasped and bucked.

"So responsive," he murmured against the skin. "I could spend all night on these delectable pecs."

Quinn's chest rose in an undulating wave at the remark, testament to how reactive he was to everything. There suddenly felt like not enough time in the waning night to do all the things Alex thought the boy would enjoy before exhaustion overtook him. So, he went with simplicity and the one thing guaranteed to please any boy, virgin or not.

Alex licked a path past Quinn's navel. He swirled around the indentation, registering each hitch of the boy's breath and every twitch of his body. The low-riding jeans were an impediment. He solved that problem with a flick of the snap and a strong pull of the waistband. He groaned in appreciation when he saw that the boy had gone commando. The slender cock sprang unimpeded. It already glistened with pre-cum.

He blew on the tip and watched the rod jerk in response. "I must have a taste of this irresistible treat. If you want me to stop, now would be the best time to voice your concerns."

"Please." Again, the ambiguous reply was punctuated with body language that made Quinn's meaning clear. He flexed his narrow hips, brushing the cockhead against Alex's mouth.

He didn't need anything more. The cock fit perfectly into his mouth and he took it to the root with one long swallow. Quinn's shout and shudder reassured him. He grinned around the hot, hard rod. Unlike a human, Alex had no gag reflex and he could hold his breath much longer, too. It took no effort to suck and lave Quinn's dick while it remained lodged inside his throat.

With his eyes still open, he had no trouble seeing the effect he was having on the boy. Quinn scratched at the sofa and his head was thrown back. He trembled and cried, tossing as much as Alex's hold would allow. He wouldn't last long, but then why should he? Alex would bet anything that this was the first time the teenage boy was getting blown.

Because he wanted it to be extra good and because he wanted more for himself, he stuck one middle finger inside his mouth alongside the shaft. He kept it there only long enough to coat it with spit. Pulling it out, he then cupped Quinn's ass and slid the moistened finger along the puckered ring of Quinn's hole. Other than a moment of automatic resistance, the boy's hole opened for him beautifully when he pressed the finger inside.

Alex drew his head back, dragging his tongue along the underside of the rod. He slipped the tip into the salty slit of the glans. Quinn stuttered out an oath before bucking his hips. Understanding the boy's need, Alex took a deep breath and plunged his lips back to the base of Quinn's dick. At the same time, he pushed his finger in as far as it would go. The bundle of nerves he sought was right where his fingertip stopped. He pressed against it while he swallowed in a strong wave all the way down the shaft.

That was all it took. But for Alex's hold on him, Quinn would have likely have launched himself off the couch. The boy gave a strangled cry as cum shot into Alex's mouth. He pulled back a little so that he could taste the exotic flavor of human seed. All the while, he continued his throat massage and matched the rhythm with his finger circling the boy's prostate.

Toward the very end, Alex's self-control snapped. His fangs descended a little bit and he scraped the taut skin of the still-hard dick. Sweet blood trickled over his tongue and he closed his eyes as he savored the taste. Quinn's cock jerked once more in response to the pain and a small amount of additional cum pulsed out.

Alex breathed noisily while he got himself back under control. He pulled his finger from Quinn's ass and his mouth off the boy's cock. His heart raced and his lungs burned as if he'd run at top speed. His blood sang through his body, beating his own cock into a painfully erect state. He'd only thought he'd been aroused during this interlude with the human. Now, his dick strained within his pants as if it were trapped in some kind of eternal misery, desperate to come out. He'd never been so hard, not even when fully feeding from a willing partner. It *hurt*.

But he couldn't allow himself any indulgence. Not coming would be his penance. He had to focus on covering his tracks by licking the tiny scrapes closed on Quinn's dick. The last thing he wanted was for his lapse to mar the boy's first sexual experience. The moment he opened his eyes to view what he'd done, he saw that there was almost no trace of the abrasions, his saliva having done a proper job. Relief morphed into pride when he realized that he needn't have worried in any event.

Quinn had fallen fast asleep.

Chapter Six

Quinn woke with the kind of disorientation that reminded him of the one time he and a friend had stolen his father's beer and gotten drunk off their asses. His head felt fuzzy and his gaze was unfocused. The cotton mouth that came from being dehydrated was there, too, making him swallow and lick his lips. His heart skipped a beat when, for a second, he didn't recognize where he was. He relaxed the moment he realized he was lying on Alex's couch.

Again.

This time naked.

Because after his boss had given him a blowjob — that he remembered with heated cheeks — he'd fallen asleep. Passed out, really. *Oh, wow*. He'd had sex for the first time. Not fucking, but something just as intimate, maybe even more so. The memory of it made his cock start to rise. He slapped it with his hand over the soft blanket covering him. Alex must have done that, a kindness to a kid too dopey to know that he shouldn't stay over unless asked.

God. He was mortified. A quick glance around told him that he was alone. With the heavy drapes closed, he couldn't tell what time it was. He'd left his phone back in his room and he'd pawned the watch that his grandfather had given him days ago. He needed to leave, that was for sure. If Alex had wanted him to stay, he'd have carried him into the bedroom, surely. The blowjob didn't mean anything, just a one-night thing. Maybe even done out of pity, although Alex had seemed into their kissing, at least — except that Quinn had fallen asleep before reciprocating, so Alex could hardly be happy with him.

Throwing back the blanket, he forced his sluggish body to move. His first thing was to pull on his jeans, which lay on a hassock, then his T-shirt and flip-flops. He had a vague memory of Alex stripping the shirt off but neither of the other things. He inwardly shrugged. No good would come from dwelling on those kinds of details. The important thing was to get out and back to his room. After that, he could relive the better moments of his experience and figure out how he was going to be cool with his boss the next time they met.

His bladder would not wait, however. He dashed to the nearby half-bath. After that, he debated with himself about whether he should maybe leave a note to his host — and, say what? *Thanks for the blowjob, sir. It was awesome!* That seemed like a bush-league move. Just leaving also seemed wrong. As he pondered the pros and cons, he realized he was too thirsty to think straight. He eyed the gleaming stainless-steel fridge in the open kitchen and figured Alex wouldn't mind if he looked for a bottle of cold water.

He padded over to the steps that led to the kitchen. Reaching for the handle to the fridge, he'd barely pulled before a larger hand slammed the door shut again. Quinn yelped in surprise and jumped back.

Alex grinned at him. The man really was ridiculously tall. "Sorry, dear boy. I didn't mean to startle you."

Quinn stared at him wide-eyed. *Where the hell did you come from?* He ran a shaky hand through his disheveled hair. "Oh, I didn't see you."

Alex's grin widened. "I'm a bit like a cat in that way — light on my feet and quick. I just didn't want you to have to go foraging for yourself." He pressed his shoulder against the fridge and pointed to his right. "I brought breakfast from Emil's kitchen. His ice box and larder are much better stocked."

"Oh?" Turning, Quinn saw a tray sitting on the dining counter that separated the kitchen from the living room. It was overflowing with covered dishes, carafes of water, juice and coffee, as well as napkins and utensils. The thing must have weighed a ton. Of course, Alex was strong. Quinn could testify to that himself based on how effortlessly the man had scooped him up.

That additional memory, plus the overabundance of breakfast, made him feel shy. He hunched his shoulders. "That's very kind of you, and really, there's no need. I understand I overstayed my welcome. I was actually only hoping for some cold water." He couldn't even look Alex in the eye as he said it.

Wrapping an arm around those very shoulders, Alex steered him over to the counter. "Not at all. I was delighted to have you spend the night. I hope the couch was comfortable. I didn't dare move you to the bedroom for fear of waking you."

Quinn allowed the man to maneuver him onto one of the high chairs. He was hit with amazing smells that made his stomach growl. He knew he should say something about falling asleep and apologize, but his thoughts scattered in the wake of all the different foods Alex was revealing as he lifted each metal plate cover.

"I didn't know what you might like, so I brought a little of everything. Technically, as it's going on eleven, this is brunch, so indulging is warranted."

"Thank you so much. I eat just about anything, but I can't eat all this." He looked at Alex, feeling even shyer. "Are you joining me?" He held his breath. The answer would tell him whether he was a nuisance that a well-bred man was trying to usher out of his home or a welcome guest.

Alex's ready smile, laden with a certain predatory gleam, reassured him even before the man spoke. "I would like nothing better. However, as I grazed a bit while I was waiting for Emil to finish, the edge is off my hunger. You must take what you want and I'll pick at the rest."

"Okay, thanks."

The need to eat overrode anything else, so he helped himself to eggs, bacon and a pancake to start with. There was butter and real maple syrup, as well as the other usual condiments. Alex had left nothing out. Soon Quinn's plate was heaped with so much that he couldn't wait another second to tuck in to it.

Alex handed him a glass of ice water. "Here you go."

"Thanks," Quinn mumbled around his full mouth. He could feel Alex's gaze on him.

The man reached out and tucked a stray lock of hair behind Quinn's ear. That briefest touch sent a shiver down his spine. "Would you like some coffee?"

Swallowing, he answered more politely this time. "Yes, please, but I can get it."

"Nonsense." Alex batted his hand away and filled the two mugs he'd brought on the tray. "How do you take it?"

"Just a little cream, please."

Out of the corner of his eye, he watched Alex doctor the coffee. The man was so graceful in everything he did and his fingers were elegant — unusually long and slender. The casual domesticity of sitting for a meal and being catered to kind of freaked him out. He didn't know what to say or where to look, so he concentrated on his food and stuffing it into his mouth.

"Here you are. You must tell me if this meets your specifications so I can adjust it next time."

Next time? The first gulp of coffee scalded Quinn's mouth. He couldn't hold back the wince.

Alex peered at him from over the rim of his own mug, which apparently he drank black. "Careful. You don't want to damage that lovely tongue of yours."

The implication of that statement wasn't lost on Quinn. Washing away his bite of food with a more careful sip of his coffee, he turned toward his boss. He needed to learn to be braver, bolder, and that lesson started now.

"Does the state of my tongue really matter to you?" He licked his lips, and the way Alex's gaze tracked the movement, he knew the man was still interested in him. "I guess what I mean is, was last night a one-time thing?"

Putting his mug down, Alex lounged against the counter and stared at Quinn. The man really was graceful, especially given his size. Cat-like, as he'd said himself. "You're the only one who can answer that question, actually. And," he added with narrowed eyes, "you must give me an honest answer. I promise you that your job is not depending on my liking it."

Quinn furrowed his forehead and bit off a piece of bacon as he pondered that statement. "I don't think I expected that it was." He shrugged. "I've only been worried that I might have pissed you off."

Now it was Alex's turn to look perplexed. "In what way could you have possibly done that?"

"Well, besides staying overnight without an invitation, which I get you just said was fine," he hurried to add, "I, um..." Once again, he felt embarrassed. "I didn't exactly reciprocate after you gave me my first blowjob." Unable to hold Alex's gaze, he started in on his pancakes, stuffing a big, syrupy piece into his mouth.

Beside him, Alex took in a deep, noisy breath and let it out hard enough for the air to hit Quinn's cheek. It felt surprisingly cool, although it made no impact on his blushing. "Did you want to?" The question was asked in a soft, rumbly voice laced with heat.

Quinn's dick responded to the tone. *Thank God, I have my jeans on.* He put his fork on the plate and stared out into the living room. "Yes?"

Alex chuckled. "I'm afraid I'm going to need more of a commitment than that, dearest boy. I don't want you to feel pressure because I'm your boss. Would you look at me, please, when you answer?"

Quinn forced himself to turn his head and gaze straight into Alex's eyes. "Yes."

* * * *

"I'm not sure what the point is in coming here again."

Trey spared his partner a glance before continuing his scan of the alley. "Where else are we going to go? We've got nothing so far that indicates Crowell was specifically targeted by someone. There's no money issue that we can see. The one ex-boyfriend we found insists they parted amicably and hasn't seen him in over a year. There was nothing in his home to indicate he'd been into anything illegal. So, we're left with the serial killer angle.

"I'm hoping that there's something we missed." Even as he said the words, he spied a lump behind the dumpster that hadn't been there before. He approached it cautiously, giving it a wide berth before he confirmed that it was a street person, complete with an overflowing shopping cart.

"Excuse me, sir?"

The shaggy-haired form covered in khaki jerked before sitting up. A dirty and heartbreakingly young face scowled back at him. "I'm a woman!"

"I beg your pardon, ma'am." He held out his badge. "May I ask you some questions?"

"You can't arrest me." The woman pointed to the farthest back door of the club. "That guy in there, the one who looks like he's an MMA fighter? He gives me food when I knock. Not scraps, neither. Real nice stuff. I just had my lunch and I'm taking a little nap. They don't mind, so why should you?"

Squatting, Trey tucked his badge back in his pocket and gave Karl a subtle sign to stay away. "I'm not here to hassle you, ma'am. I was hoping to ask you some questions. That's all."

The woman ran the back of her hand across the end of her nose. "About what? I haven't done anything wrong."

"I'm sure you haven't. My questions concern something you might have seen the night before last."

The woman stilled and she stared back at him with narrowed eyes. "Was there something to see?"

Trey strived for patience. If this homeless person was a regular in this alley, she might have witnessed something. "That's what I need you to tell me. Do you come here at night or only during the day?"

She shifted, scooting to lean against the wall. "I come and I go. Those guys in there are open all the time and willing to help out a vet when she needs a bit of food."

Trey tried smiling, although he figured it might appear more like a grimace. "You're a veteran?"

"Yeah," the woman sneered. "Women serve, too, you know — and in combat."

He nodded. "I know that. I have a cousin who flies Apaches for the army."

The woman's spine straightened. "I was a marine. They called us 'lionesses'." She sniffed. "Now they just call me 'crazy'. I'm not!"

"Of course not." He kept his voice low and smooth, figuring this might prove to be the break they'd been searching for.

"Serving can change you, you know?" She looked off. "I saw things and did things. It's hard coming back to civilian life." She sniffed again. "I need my meds and sometimes I can't get them."

This was a story he was too familiar with. The VA was overloaded with veterans needing care, underfunded and with too few locations. He did grimace this time. "I'm sorry. I know it can be tough but I do need your help. There was a murder here two nights ago and I'm hoping maybe you saw something."

That suspicious expression crossed her face again. "I'm supposed to have seen something because there was something to see?"

Trey tried to parse what exactly he was being asked. The woman's phrasing was odd. "I don't want to put words in your mouth, ma'am. Whatever you can tell me would be really helpful, no matter how unusual you might think it is."

"I'm *not* crazy."

"No, ma'am."

"Sometimes, when I'm off my meds, I think I see things, then find out I didn't really." She tapped her head. "It's in here, and I get confused about that."

She shifted some more. "I come here when I come here. There's always food, even if it's really late." Her gaze moved back to him. "I might have been here two nights ago." She licked her lips and once more her gaze skittered away. "I might have seen something—something weird."

"Anything you can tell me would be helpful."

"I'm *not* crazy," she said again.

"No, ma'am." He had a feeling she'd heard the opposite too often in her life.

Twisting her body, she pointed toward the roof. "He went that way."

He tried to rein in his excitement. There was no sense getting ahead of himself, despite the fact that the woman's story already sounded far-fetched, and by her own admission, she sometimes hallucinated. "Who did, ma'am?"

"Some guy in black. Big motherfucker, like a lot of the guys in there." She jutted her chin toward the club wall.

Trey glanced at Karl, who stood out of view but was taking notes. He looked as interested as Trey felt. "Was it one of them?"

"Nah, just had the size and coloring." She rubbed at her cheek. "I could see the other one lying on the ground. Could smell the blood." A visible shudder went through her. "I know that well enough."

"I'm sure you do." He shifted slightly on the balls of his feet. His calves were starting to feel the strain, yet he was afraid to move for fear of spooking his witness. "How exactly did this guy leave? You pointed to the roof?"

Now, the woman's lips thinned. "Maybe I didn't see anything."

"Please."

"I told you that sometimes I imagine things, see things that aren't there. Flashbacks, a doctor once called them." She spat off to one side—in commentary, perhaps. "I'm *not* crazy."

"Please tell me what you saw. I promise I don't think you're crazy or seeing things that aren't there."

Bending one knee, she laid her hand on top of it. "He jumped, then he crawled."

Trey blinked a few times. "Crawled?"

"All the way to the top of the building." She made a motion with her hand from the ground to the roof, five stories high.

* * * *

"I need your help moving my blood supply to Emil's secure storage off the kitchen."

From his seat across Alex's desk, Val pursed his lips. "Keeping a supply of blood in the refrigerator then microwaving it is a dumb way to feed."

"I do not have the time or energy to negotiate my way into a fresh source on a routine basis. Buying it on the black market has gotten easier, thanks to the Internet, and having it in the ice box in my own kitchen has always been handy."

"Refrigerator."

"Hmm?"

"You have trouble keeping abreast of the changes in human vocabulary. Stop talking like you're from the early twentieth century."

Alex huffed. "This constant evolution of language is tedious. Humans are so restless in everything, even speech. Before long, we'll be holding entire conversations using emojis."

"I think the young ones already are, if Mackie is anything to go by. Anyway, I'll handle moving your supply. No worries. I take it your fridge isn't safe anymore? I wonder why?" He shot Alex a feral grin. "You're finally allowing a human into your personal space, I gather. Blood bags aside, is that wise?"

"You think I'm making a mistake." He stated it as fact and spoke again before his friend and confidant could reply. "I'm afraid I am, too." He sat back and stared at the ceiling. "You know it's been a very long time since I dared become close to a human, and I've never become involved with a subordinate before."

"Employee. We're not military anymore, not on this planet or our own."

"Same concept." He shook his head and choked out a laugh. "There's something about him that I can't resist. I mean, not even for two days."

"Well, he is pretty irresistible." The growl passed Alex's lips before he could hold it back. With a chuckle, Val held his hands out in surrender. "I'm just making an observation. You know I don't stray from Mackie."

Alex got himself under control. "Yes, of course. Do forgive me. As I was saying and you've just experienced, I don't seem to show my usual restraint where this boy is concerned."

"How far have you gone?"

Alex sighed and tipped back his head. "Too far and yet not far enough. I haven't fucked him, but that's only a matter of time. Perhaps a matter of hours, the way things are progressing. I haven't bitten him, but I have tasted his blood." He closed his eyes briefly at the memories. "Once was when he skinned his palm. One second I was helping him, and the next, I was lapping that delicious sweetness." The mere retelling of it had his cock hardening. "Thank God, he hadn't seen that he was bleeding before I sealed the skin."

When he paused, Val jumped in with the obvious. "Once implies there was at least one other time."

"Hmm, yes, one other. Last night." He straightened and gripped the arms of his chair. "I sucked him off and, at the point of climax, I couldn't resist the urge to mix the fluids, shall was say."

Val grinned. "Dick blood? Very nice."

"It was incandescent. No one has ever tasted better nor given me such a feeling of joy and power, even." He gave his friend a hard look. "If that's how I react to a drop or two, what would drinking a more substantial amount do to me?"

"I have no idea, boss, but I know you're going to find out—and soon. If you've already progressed to the cocksucking stage, then bloodsucking can't be that far away."

Alex sighed. "I'm afraid you're correct about that. It would be hard enough to accept falling for another human, but with Adrian prowling around, it's that much more...terrifying, I must confess."

Before Val could even make an attempt at reassurance, Alex's phone rang. He answered with impatience then modified his emotions when he saw that Kitty was calling from the bar. She wouldn't disturb him if it weren't important.

"Yes?"

"The police have returned and they want to talk to you and Val again."

Shit, just what I need. "Tell them we'll be right out."

Ending the call, he narrowed his gaze. "The homicide investigators request the pleasure of our company."

"Christ." Val stood with a huff of frustration.

Alex joined him, echoing the sentiment. "Amen."

They had long ago adopted human expressions and mannerisms to blend in better, but he had to admit that their colorful swear words added a certain satisfying punctuation to his feelings. There was something soothing, as well, in the religious rituals they'd been forced to participate in for assimilation purposes.

They found the cops at the bar drinking mugs of coffee. Hospitality, both offering and accepting it, was both a human custom and one from their own culture. As much as the presence of the two men grated, he was glad that Kitty had stepped in and represented the family properly.

"Gentlemen," he said in way of greeting, trying to keep his irritation out of his tone. Ingrained politeness and a need to stay off their radar as possible perpetrators drove his effort.

The senior man, Duncan, sat closest to them. He swiveled in his seat and finished his sip of coffee before putting his mug down. He slid off the stool. "Mr. Stelalux, thanks for taking the time. I'm sorry to barge in on you unannounced."

"I appreciate the apology, but I'm not convinced it's heartfelt, sergeant."

Duncan grinned. "You may be right about that, sir. Then again, investigating a brutal murder makes me a little rude."

"I can well imagine." He stopped a couple of feet away, gratified that even this tall human had to tilt his head back a little to keep their gazes locked. "Any luck?"

"Maybe. We talked to a witness who might have seen the killer."

"Indeed?" Alex worked hard to keep his expression mild and his sudden tenseness invisible to the humans. Beside him, Val stiffened a small amount. If what Duncan said was true, it presented an unwanted complication. "Can you say who?"

Duncan gave him a fake pained look. "No, sorry. But I can say that the description was surprising."

"In what way?" Apparently, the cop wanted to play a boring and irritating game where Alex was forced to drag information out of him.

"The description given sounded a lot like you, your uncle and your cousins." The cop glanced at Val. "Very unique."

Alex stiffened in an obvious way. "I trust you are not suggesting that any of us are the killers. I believe we've been more than cooperative in answering all your questions."

Duncan scratched at his chin. "Yes, sir, you have, and we appreciate it. The witness was actually quite clear that it *wasn't* any of you, because this witness is familiar with the club and its inhabitants."

"Then what is it you hope to gain from coming here?" Unable to keep his blasé demeanor, he stepped aside and leaned against the bar. "Would you be so kind as to pour me a cup of coffee, Kitty?"

She gave him a knowing smile. "Sure thing, Boss."

He turned his attention back to Duncan, giving him a deliberately patient look.

"I'm hoping, sir, that with this new information, you might be able to add to what you've already told us. We might be searching for a man who is very tall with pale skin and long, black hair."

"Thanks," Alex shot at Kitty before taking the mug she offered. He deliberately took a long swallow while staring at the cop from over the rim. The scalding temperature didn't bother him in the least.

Lowering the mug, he said, "Are you suggesting that anyone who shares my appearance is someone I know? As if we must be from the same ethnic group and therefore familiar with each other? Isn't that rather racist? That's like my asking you if you knew Paul Robeson simply because you're both African-American."

"I identify as mixed-race, actually, sir, and Robeson died quite a few years before I was born. I'm a bit surprised you're familiar with him, given that you aren't much older than I am."

Oh, if you only knew how long I've actually been alive. "His magnificent bass voice transcends time and generations."

Duncan offered him a tight smile. "I guess my tastes run more to grunge bands. But, I take you point, sir. My apologies if I've offended you."

Taking another gulp of his coffee, he put the mug on the bar counter and sighed. "You haven't, not really. I simply find this vicious murder right outside my door quite disturbing. Nothing would please me more than to help you find the perpetrator." The lie tripped off his tongue. "I wish I could help. Other than my family members here, I don't know anyone in the Boston area that is related to us or even has similar coloring and features." He shrugged and picked up the mug again, if only to give his restless hands something to do. "Our ancestry is a bit murky, and we really don't fit in with modern-day Romanians in any event. We were as much an oddity there as we are here." He took another long swallow of his coffee. "Standing out in a crowd gets wearing after a while."

"I think I can relate," the cop replied, and that simple show of some wit did make him more endearing. Absent the murder, Duncan was someone Alex would have liked socializing with. "In any event, it was worth a try."

The cop glanced at his partner over his shoulder. "Let's go, Karl." Nodding at Kitty, he added, "Thanks for the coffee, ma'am." Then he trained his intelligent eyes on Alex once more. "To be frank, sir, the witness was a bit unreliable. They actually said the possible killer climbed the side of the building, like a big bug or a bat, maybe. Or, you know, a vampire," he added with a chuckle. "Ridiculous, right? It really puts into question the entire story."

Alex kept a pleasant expression plastered on his face. "Yes, that does sound ludicrous."

"Anyway, thanks again for your time." With a nod at Val as he passed, the cop left with a confident stride, his partner at his heels.

When the sound of the front door closing reached their ears, Val let his breath out with a whoosh and a curse. "This is starting to heat up fast. Who was the witness, do you suppose?"

"You've fixed the security cameras outside, I gather?"

"Yes, sir."

"Let's go take a look at it then and see if we can spot this mysterious witness the cops talked to."

Val fell into step when Alex headed for the control room where Val kept all his electronics. "We don't know that they interviewed the witness here."

"No, but it's the only place we have to start."

He texted Harry to join them. The older man often had a keen eye and a cooler head. Certainly, when it came to humans, he understood the species better than any of them. Not only was the man a doctor, he had a long-time mate with whom he'd fathered a mixed-race child, as Duncan would likely refer to Demi.

Harry met with them outside the control room door. He stood beside Alex while Val took a seat in front of the massive computer console and started clicking at the keys. An image materialized on the main screen showing the alley where Adrian had done his dirty work. A familiar lump lay by the dumpster. Duncan and his partner wandered farther and stopped in front of it.

"It was Logan," Val observed, as the lump stirred and came to life. "No real surprise there."

Alex folded his arms in front of his chest and watched the conversation play out. "Of course. Emil feeds her, doesn't he? That would be reason enough for her to come to the alley at all hours."

Val huffed. "She was a warrior for her people, yet they do nothing to care for her."

Alex grimaced at the sight of the disheveled female. "It's abhorrent that she was put into war at all."

Harry shook his head. "Really, Alex, such outmoded thinking. Have you never heard of gender equality?"

Not liking that his subordinates thought he didn't move with the times as easily as they did, he stiffened. "It's absurd that humans have ever thought females inferior to males. Our species never did, but we also didn't put females into harm's way. They are far too precious."

Harry sighed with his version of being extra patient. "Only to us because of our hive-based society. Humans reproduce in an equal balance of genders. You know that. They can lose a lot of females without triggering the need for gender transformation, although I, for one, am certainly grateful the process has proven successful with humans."

Yes, Alex did know all this. Harry was very happy with his small and unusual family. There were times when Alex envied his friend's good fortune. To find someone to love in this alien world and to produce an offspring with him, no less, was an astounding blessing. It remained a bright point in the midst of their never-ending quest for survival.

That thought led his mind to visions of Quinn. The boy had proven so beautifully responsive to his attention. His pretty face had taken on a look of exquisite ecstasy in the moment of his release. What would it be like to retire at the end of each night with such a creature in his bed? He could easily picture spending the rest of his life with such perfection, except that wouldn't happen. Humans were not only fragile but short-lived. Even with their modern medicine, Quinn would never live as long as he would, not unless he changed him. Although they'd yet to learn how long they could extend a human life, they knew so far from those that had been turned that it lasted at least several centuries.

Would Quinn even want such a thing? Learning Alex's secret might send him screaming. It had happened before. In the modern era, when humans were willing to accept the concept of alien life-forms, it was riskier now than ever before to reveal the truth. One had to be certain that the human being let in on the secret could be trusted to keep it. As much as he wanted Quinn, he knew next to nothing about the boy. He might be the kind to go right to some tabloid and sell the story. Even as the thought occurred to him, his heart dismissed the notion. Quinn was a good kid, not a user.

"There." Val's voice broke Alex out of his reverie. He froze the image on the screen. "See where Logan is pointing? That's the way Adrian made his escape." He craned his neck to look at Alex. "She did see him."

"Hmm, I don't think I was ever really in doubt about that. The only thing we have going in our favor is the fantastic nature of the account itself and, regrettably, the poor woman's history of mental health issues."

"That's a horrible thing for us to be pleased about," Harry remarked.

Alex sighed and dropped his arms. "Agreed, but I must put the interests and security of our people first. I'd hate to exploit her weakness, except I don't think it matters. Duncan is taking her account seriously, at least to a certain extent."

Val turned around to face him. "You don't think the cop believes we're vampires?"

"Probably not. He's no fool, though. That much is clear. He knows something strange is happening and he's not going to stop digging until he solves the murder."

"Which only means we need to find Adrian first and make sure no one else can ever find him again."

Alex tamped down his growing frustration. "Yes, leaving where we've been all day—spinning our wheels and waiting for him to make his next move so we can hopefully track him better."

Harry shook his head. "I have to say this. I find myself hoping he'll strike again soon. I want this finished quickly, except that means some poor soul has to die."

"Unfortunately, yes. It will be tonight, I'm guessing. Dracul is not a patient man. Now that he's rekindled the war, he's going to escalate quickly. We just have to be ready for it."

Chapter Seven

"They're too big and hang off your ass."

Quinn twisted to get a look at his butt in the long mirror. Plucking at the modicum of fabric hanging there, he said, "I don't think so." He stared at Mackie's reflection behind him. "Unlike you, I don't want to *paint* my jeans on. Besides, I'm going to gain back the weight I lost recently, so I need my pants to have some give."

Mackie lounged against the entryway to the dressing room area, phone in hand. He tossed his head. "You're never going to attract Alex's attention with that attitude."

"That's fine, because I don't intend to try." It was a lie, of course, but while Alex hadn't forbidden him to discuss what had occurred between them, he still felt as if he shouldn't speak of it—not yet, maybe not ever. It could still end up being a one-night event, even though he and Alex had already agreed to meet again after his shift.

Quinn stood in front of the mirror and gave himself a critical review. Going shopping had been Mackie's idea. Although it was hard to spend even one dollar of his new income, he had to admit that he needed to stop dressing like a street kid. The artfully distressed jeans and simple green button-down shirt were attractive without putting too much of a dent in his wallet.

He tried to see himself through Alex's eyes and still couldn't believe that such a gorgeous and sexy man could possibly have an interest in the skinny hot mess he was — and, a virgin to boot. Quinn had only the Internet to give him any kind of guide as to how to please another man. Well, that and the fantastic lesson Alex himself had given him the previous night — blowjob one-o-one.

That experience might not be enough of a tutorial and there were other things for them to do, complicated ways for two men to find pleasure that alternately made him tingle with anticipation and want to vomit from nerves. What if he ended up being so bad at sex that Alex decided he wasn't worth the effort? Their budding relationship — or whatever this thing between them was — would die on the vine.

He believed Alex when he said Quinn's job wasn't on the line, no matter what. But the need for employment was only part of his worry. Now that he'd had a taste of what it would be like to be involved with Alex, he wasn't sure he could stand being around him as just an employee.

"You worry too much." Mackie didn't even look up from his phone as he spoke. "You're adorbs." He flicked that shock of hair hanging over one side of his face. "Not that you're my type, natch. For an alpha guy like Alex, I'm betting you make his dick hard enough to poke a hole in his thousand-dollar Gucci pants."

Quinn ran his hands nervously on the front of his thighs. "What makes you think I care?"

Mackie tossed his head again. "I'm sorry. Are we really playing that game?" He eyed him through the mirror. "Do you think there's *anyone* at the club who doesn't know you spent the night in Alex's loft?"

"Really?"

"Ah, *ya*. It's big news." He went back to playing with his phone. "No one's ever done that before, like *ever*. Alex is a really private kind of guy. If you think he fucks every boy he hires, think again. You are *numero uno*, sweetheart. Congrats, by the way."

As stupid as it was, his heart did a little dance at the information. Part of him had wondered if bagging the new boy was Alex's norm. It made him happy to learn that he was the first. *If* Mackie could be trusted to tell the truth, and from everything he'd seen of the boy so far, he was inclined to believe him. *Why would he bother to lie, anyway?*

He worried his lower lip. Alex was way out of his league on so many levels. "Does he really spend that much on clothing?"

"*That's* your question?" Mackie gave a high-pitched chuckle. "Have you not tripped to the fact that the Stelalux family has major bank? I think it's old money, too — not just from the club." He flicked his gaze. "And they are really generous. Val pays for everything. Other than for Starbucks, maybe, I rarely spend my own money."

"Doesn't that bother you? Being, you know…kept."

"Nope." Mackie went back to fiddling with his phone.

Quinn stared at himself some more, trying to work up the nerve to buy the clothing and knowing he was fooling himself. He wanted to look good for Alex when they met later. Wearing his G-string was not going to cut it. And it didn't matter if these clothes were just stripped off quickly. At least he'd be going in appearing like his own man and not a go-go boy being paid for sex.

A face loomed in the reflection. For a second, Quinn's breath caught. He thought it was Alex peering into the street-side window, except no. It was a pale-faced man with long, black hair, but it wasn't Alex. Quinn whipped his head around to get a better look. *Nothing.* Staring across the showroom, he saw only a few pedestrians walking along the sidewalk outside the store.

Mackie straightened. "What is it?"

Grimacing, Quinn shook his head. "Nothing. I just thought...nothing." He took a deep breath and let it out again slowly. "I'm going to buy this shirt and these jeans."

Mackie grinned. "Now you're talking." He yawned. "I need a nap before our shift starts. And," he added with a smirk, "if I'm lucky, Val will plow my ass before I have to go on."

Quinn shook his head again and headed back into the dressing room. He wondered if he'd ever be as open about sex as Mackie. Probably not, and he hoped that would be okay with Alex, because the more he thought about it, the more he couldn't wait to get back into the man's arms.

* * * *

It hadn't taken long — only a few days, really — for Quinn's body to adjust to his odd working hours. As he shimmied against his pole during the second half of his shift, he felt surprisingly comfortable. His routine was shaping up, enough so that he didn't have to concentrate as hard. And he hadn't fallen or skidded or made any other embarrassing missteps the whole night. It helped that the club was quieter this night, with fewer patrons milling about and everyone a little more subdued.

He smiled at the man who sauntered over and stuffed a twenty into the side of his thong. "Thanks." Leaning down, he gave the man an air kiss. "My time on the stage is almost over. Want a lap dance?" It hadn't taken long for him to become bolder, either.

The man opened his mouth but never got a chance to respond. A large figure covered in black hip-checked him out of the way. "I beg your pardon, Frank. Quinn's dance card is filled for the rest of the night, I'm afraid."

The member frowned at Alex before stalking off. Alex gave Quinn the kind of smile a cat might give a mouse. "I hope you don't mind."

Before Quinn could formulate a reply, Alex held up a hundred-dollar bill, licked it lengthwise and slapped it against Quinn's left pec, where it stuck like wallpaper. The move was so wanton that it sent a shiver down his sweaty body.

Alex leaned in to speak directly into his ear. "I've been patient all night, but I've reached my limit." His breath tickled Quinn's skin, making him shiver again. "Come and dance for me, Quinn — only me."

The man didn't wait for a reply. Instead, he straightened and held out his hand. Quinn licked his lips and stared at the offering. He let go of the pole, peeled the bill off his chest and crushed it in one hand while he took Alex's with his other. It felt as if all eyes were on them as he allowed Alex to lead him up the stairs to the more private space.

Only a few couples occupied the wide, velvet seats intended to make lap dances easy to give. One included Mackie, straddling the thighs of a member and gyrating in a lascivious way that was nevertheless emotionally detached. He winked at Quinn when he passed, before moaning and reassuring the client that he was so very sexy.

Alex led Quinn to the far end of the wall for maximum privacy. With a fluid grace that Quinn had become used to seeing, he settled into the seat and pulled Quinn in between the V of his thick thighs. Quinn had to brace one hand against the wall to avoid tumbling into him.

The man let go of Quinn's hand and grabbed his waist to steady him. "I've been waiting all night to do this," he confessed.

Up here, the music was a little more muted, making it easier to talk, if that was what someone wanted. Placing his hands on Alex's shoulders, Quinn smiled at him.

"What do you want? Shall I stay here or straddle your lap?"

"I want whatever you're willing to give me. So long as I get to touch you, I'm content." Alex slid his hands down to cup Quinn's naked ass.

The bills tucked into the thong rustled, reminding him that he was still holding Alex's tip. It was mashed against the man's black shirt. Opening his hand, he showed it. "You don't have to pay me. I want to be here." He dropped his gaze, because it was all too intense for him to keep eye contact.

Alex let go with one hand to pluck the bill from him. Then he slid it under the string of the thong to join the others before clasping Quinn's ass cheek once more.

"That is for the lap-dance, not anything that might come after." He nuzzled Quinn's neck, pressing a kiss at its base. The man seemed to like that boring part of his body.

Quinn stuttered out a breath, surprised that boring or not, his neck was becoming an erogenous zone. "Lap dances are twenty bucks, not a hundred."

"Mmm." The sound vibrated through his chest. "I guess I want five of them." Alex kissed the spot he'd been brushing with his lips, then sucked gently at the skin.

Quinn's mind went blank and his head dropped back. He gasped when Alex grabbed the back of his thighs and hoisted him up. *Well, that settles the question of how I should position my body.* Now he was right where he needed to be to start moving his hips against the man's crotch. If only he had the energy to do so. He felt both aroused and languid.

The conflicted reaction was brought home in the next instant as Alex tugged him even closer. Quinn's growing erection bumped against a bigger, harder bulge standing from Alex's lap. The lips at his throat increased their pressure. Every nerve ending came alive and it seemed as if his blood rushed to both that spot and his dick in equal measure.

Alex dug his fingers into the fleshy underside of Quinn's ass and mashed their groins together. He easily heard their moans above the music. Quinn clutched the fabric of Alex's shirt and tried not to give in to the urge to hump in rhythm to the pounding beat of the song. The situation had morphed at a dizzying pace from a teasing lap dance to serious arousal. He leaned in to Alex, pressing his forehead against his shoulder.

"Please," he pleaded softly, not sure if he could be heard, yet unable to draw in enough breath to raise his voice. "I don't want to do this here."

Alex relaxed his hold and raised his head. "I'm sorry. I forgot myself. Do you want to go upstairs?"

Yes. Oh God, yes! Except... "My shift—"

"Has just ended."

That was all Alex said before he stood with Quinn still plastered to him. Quinn instinctively wrapped his legs around the man's waist and held on like a monkey. The situation had shifted once more. Alex was taking him upstairs—to fuck him, he hoped. He was so consumed with the enormity of his situation that he didn't even feel embarrassed to be carried away.

Eschewing the elevator, Alex trotted the two flights of stairs to his fifth-floor loft with Quinn in his arms. The guy wasn't even breathing heavily by the time he let himself and Quinn in and shut out the world. He bypassed the couch, striding to the far end of the room and up a curving set of stairs.

Quinn barely had time to register that he was in the open loft bedroom before Alex placed him onto an enormous king-sized bed draped in a black sheet. He lay against a mound of equally black pillows as Alex followed him and knelt between his legs. Those violet eyes had darkened once more. They peered deep into Quinn's own with such intensity that it felt like being mesmerized. He was unable to look away.

Alex's nostrils quivered. "It's important for you to remember that you are in control here. We'll only go as far as you want."

Quinn's brain registered the words and they did bring him extra comfort, but he had no intention of crying uncle. He'd waited too long for this experience, and although part of him was terrified, the other part was grateful that this monumental event in his life was happening with this man. He trusted Alex. Even though they'd known each other for a short period of time, there was something profoundly comforting in being cared for by Alex. The man had almost an ancient quality about him that made Quinn feel safe.

Quinn widened his eyes, trying to convey his sincerity. "Please believe me when I say I want it all. I'm *ready* for it."

Alex smiled. "I'm going to assume you know your own mind. Still, I also assume you're a virgin, yes?" When Quinn nodded, Alex continued. "We're going to take this very slowly. I expect you're eager, but something so momentous mustn't be rushed."

Quinn gave a smile of encouragement. "I know you'll do it right." He turned, though, on a thought. "Only…"

"What? Ask me anything you want. Please."

Quinn broke his gaze away for a second. "Those things that others do. You know, downstairs. Like Val and Mackie?"

"Yes, what about them?"

"Are you, um…into that stuff, too?"

"Oh, my dear boy" — leaning down, Alex brushed his lips against Quinn's forehead — "don't worry about that. Other than a little bondage now and again, I'm not into that scene in particular. I have no interest is paddling your pretty rump, or any other part of you, in order to be stimulated. The very sight of you arouses me more than enough."

"Oh." A little of Quinn's tension drained away, except… "What about the other thing?"

"Other thing?" Alex seemed genuinely perplexed.

Quinn licked his lips, unsure of whether he should shut his mouth and just let Alex have his way with him. But he couldn't quite let the issue go. "The, ah…blood thing. Like what Val does to Mackie. Are you into that, too?"

"Ah." Alex sat back on his heels, sliding his hands along Quinn's arms until he held onto only his wrists. He put his thumbs on top of each of Quinn's pulse points. "As it happens, I am." He stared at Quinn's throat for a second before returning his gaze to his eyes. "Does that frighten you?"

Quinn swallowed hard. He couldn't help it. "It does. A-a little," he confessed. Because the idea of Alex sinking his teeth into his flesh to suck blood *did* scare him. Of course, it did.

That was assuming he would bite him instead of starting the blood flow in some other fashion. Regardless of the method, it was mostly a terrifying notion. A more primitive part of him quivered at the idea. His already hard cock twitched in response.

Alex didn't react to the confession right away. Instead, he focused his gaze on one of Quinn's wrists before moving his thumb to place a kiss against the pulse. Alex shuddered and straightened again.

"I would never hurt you, Quinn. Giving me permission to taste your blood has to be something you want, not something I demand. It is a gift that you bestow or not, at your discretion. It's not necessary in order for me to find pleasure in your body. Kissing your lovely lips, licking every inch of your delicious skin, sucking your succulent cock and sinking into what I know will be your welcoming heat will make me the happiest and most grateful of men."

A nervous giggle escaped Quinn. "You make me sound so appealing. I'm afraid I will disappoint you."

"Never. Let me prove just how desirable you are, dear boy. May I?"

"Yes, please." Quinn recognized the sudden pleading in his voice yet couldn't regret it. He wanted to give himself to this man. Letting Alex take control was both a relief and exciting.

"Thank you," Alex replied, as if Quinn had just granted him a great boon. "First, we need to divest you of this."

The meaning of the man's words became clear when he tugged the bills still jammed into Quinn's thong and piled them on his night stand. Then off came the thong itself, but not by Alex sliding it down Quinn's bent legs. No, this giant of a man with his incredibly long fingers just ripped the fabric at both sides and tossed it away. It was an impressive display of strength and desire that made Quinn's breath catch.

His dick lay happily stiff against his groin. Already a pearly drop of pre-cum hung off the tip. He watched as Alex stared at it. There was no surprise when the man bent and ran his tongue up the shaft from root to tip. Quinn groaned and bucked his hips in invitation. Another blowjob would be just the thing to take the edge off. Alex, damn him, had other ideas. Grasping Quinn's wrists again, he pushed them to frame Quinn's head and held them there while he leaned in to claim his mouth once more.

Quinn moaned and opened to let Alex explore. He loved kissing with this man. It wasn't the sloppy, clumsy effort he'd experienced with other boys on a few occasions. Alex was a master at employing the right amount of pressure, the perfect amount of spit and a hint of teeth to make things spicier. He leaned into Quinn as he deepened the kiss, pressing their bodies together. Quinn gasped into his mouth and wiggled in an effort to give friction to his dick. He only worried vaguely that he'd be getting cum on his boss's very expensive slacks.

Too soon, Alex broke the kiss. Quinn gave a distressed mew of disappointment that morphed into another moan as Alex gave him open-mouthed kisses all along his jaw and down his throat. The man stopped at the pulse point at the base, confirming his interest in Quinn's blood. But he didn't linger too long and he didn't break the skin in any way. He was keeping his promise and that show of restraint caused Quinn to let go of any lingering doubt.

Those kisses turned into licks and nips. Alex peppered Quinn's chest and pecs with attention before settling in to suck at his nipples. The pleasure of having those nubs sucked and laved came out in breathless moans and fast, little jerks of his body. It was a direct pipeline to his cock, as well. It pulsed and dribbled more pre-cum. His balls tightened against his body. He might come from the nipple play alone, except once again, Alex just teased. He didn't linger.

Down the man went to draw on the taut skin of Quinn's flat abdomen. There would be hickeys visible in the morning and likely the next time he danced. The idea that other men would see how Alex had marked him was thrilling. He understood now what Mackie had meant. It didn't even matter if this was a one-time experience with this particular man. After this night, he'd be forever changed and no other man would be able to claim his body the same way.

With a small amount of incoherent pleading on Quinn's part, Alex landed his mouth on Quinn's dick. He licked around the flared head and slid his tongue inside the weeping slit. Quinn bucked in invitation but was disappointed. Alex did everything except take Quinn's cock into his mouth. By the time Alex had finished teasing his dick with his tongue, Quinn had turned into a writhing mass. With his wrists still locked in Alex's grip, there was almost no give in his movements.

Alex scraped his teeth up the shaft and pulled back. "Poor boy. Do you want me to suck your cock?"

Quinn gazed at him with heavy-lidded eyes. "Yes, please."

Alex's eyes gleamed back at him. "Very well." The next moment, however, he released Quinn entirely. When he started to protest, Alex shushed him. "None of that, now. Be a good boy and lie still. Otherwise, I won't take this any further."

Oh, damn. It was hard—and not—to do as the man commanded. *Is this what Mackie feels?* It was almost liberating and very arousing to be under a strong man's control. He watched with labored breaths and an itchy desire to move while Alex sprang off the bed and practically ripped his own clothing off. He stood like a god with pale, almost hairless, skin stretched over sleek, yet powerful, muscles. The man's cock was large, almost alarmingly so. Because there was only a small, short thatch of hair around it, the hard shaft appeared even bigger, like a club. *How is that thing going to fit inside my ass?* His hole clenched involuntarily at the idea, clearly eager to find out.

Reaching inside his nightstand drawer, Alex pulled out a bottle of lube and a condom. "We'll need this in a bit." Excitement flared inside Quinn. Alex kneeled back between his legs. Quinn still had them bent, his hole exposed and vulnerable. Alex palmed the back of Quinn's thighs and pushed them forward.

"First," Alex said. "I want a taste."

The meaning of his words eluded Quinn for about two seconds before Alex bent forward and licked along the seams where his leg met his pelvis. Quinn jerked at the sensation but had little time to process how erogenous that part of his body was before Alex proceeded to lap the entire area. He took Quinn's balls in his mouth and sucked them briefly. Then he licked his way around Quinn's puckered hole.

"Oh, God!" he gasped and even tried to break free. "That's…" He wasn't sure how he intended to finish that statement. *Unnecessary. Amazing.* He was on sensory overload, not sure how he should respond to something that he hadn't even dreamed of.

Then he came. It took him by surprise, his cock jerking and spitting out ropes of cum onto his abdomen. He wanted to grab it and tug it to completion, but Alex's admonishment to stay still somehow held him in thrall. He was helpless to do anything other than cry out and shudder with his release.

His hole clenched and loosened repeatedly. Alex took advantage by slipping his tongue inside, which sent another wave of climax coursing through him. Quinn fisted his hands and tossed his head back and forth. He almost didn't notice when Alex replaced his tongue with a lubed finger.

"Oh!" Quinn's eyes flew open and he stared at the plain white ceiling as he accustomed himself to the strange feeling of being invaded.

"That's it, darling boy. Relax." Alex's voice was pitched low and soothing. He fucked Quinn slowly with that finger.

In and out, it dragged against his swollen tissues. The invasion wasn't at all painful. The rhythm lulled him into closing his eyes again. He relaxed his fingers and melted into the soft bedding. He could have fallen asleep, except that Alex crooked his finger to scrape against a spot that sent a jolt through Quinn. He gasped and rolled his hips to try to hold Alex's finger in place.

The man chuckled and pressed his free palm against Quinn's abdomen to keep him still. "Like that, do you?" Quinn could only grunt in reply.

A second digit joined the first, stretching Quinn's hole a little bit more. It burned for a few seconds before he relaxed his muscles and fell back into the soothing rhythm of being finger fucked. Then Alex goosed his prostate again, and this time he kept at it. With each pass of his fingers in and out, Alex rubbed the sensitive bundle of nerves.

It drove Quinn mad. His arousal built once more, sending blood surging into his cock. It rose just as hard and Quinn's balls ached just as much as if he hadn't come mere minutes ago. The fact that he could barely move under Alex's physical and mental control only served to heighten the experience. Soon he shut his eyes again and squirmed.

Alex grasped Quinn's dick and tugged. He flicked his thumb across the leaking slit, making Quinn whimper.

It was all too much. His senses were being assaulted on multiple fronts and overloaded by the attention. He became desperate to come again and would have if Alex hadn't gripped the base of his cock to hold the climax back.

"No. Please." He begged shamelessly for release. He was so wrapped up in his need that he almost missed how his hole had been abandoned, only to be filled once more with something bigger, wider and harder.

His eyes flew open as his slickened ring of muscle was stretched far more than it had been before. Alex still knelt between his legs, still held his rod in one hand. Now, though, his thick thighs pressed against Quinn's ass. The man's large, wide cock invaded Quinn's tight hole. It was looser than it had been, those fingers having done their job, but still not enough to keep the pain from coming. Quinn whimpered and Alex stilled.

"Easy now," Alex crooned. "I'll go slowly."

He began jerking Quinn's dick again with sure strokes that went all the way to the top of the bulbous head then down to the root. He rubbed his thumb against the sensitive spot right below the cockhead. It made Quinn shudder and squirm. The second he moved his ass, Alex pushed forward. The man's dick slid in a little bit more before he froze again.

"That's it, darling boy. You're doing wonderfully. We just need to give your precious channel a chance to adjust."

The words of praise and encouragement warmed Quinn. He kept his gaze on Alex's eyes. They'd gone almost completely black, yet he saw safety in those endless depths. Something inside him snapped like a band pulled too tightly. His body relaxed. So, too, did

Alex apparently, because he took advantage of the change by sliding his dick balls-deep inside Quinn's ass.

They both sighed at the same time, and Alex grinned. "There now. It's all done. You're no longer a virgin." His eyelids fluttered closed for a second, his pleasure obvious. "And, yet so delightfully tight that I find it hard to stay still."

The man's breathless voice and the way in which his massive chest seemed to labor gave Quinn a new thrill. He'd done this to him. It was a kind of power, even though he was the one on his back with his ass filled with dick. Emotion welled up, strong and invigorating. He wanted to please Alex, make him come.

He licked his lips and grinned. "Then don't—stay still, that is. Go ahead and fuck me. Please," he added and squeezed around the invading shaft.

Alex grunted and grimaced. "Oh, Christ! What you do to me."

Then he did as Quinn requested and began to thrust slowly. At the same time, he resumed jerking Quinn's dick. Arousal built once more with increasing speed. Alex pushed the back of Quinn's thigh with his free hand to angle his ass higher. He increased his speed at the same time, and now he nailed Quinn's prostate with each stroke of his cock.

Quinn lost it. He couldn't keep his eyes open and tossed his head back and forth. He made fists once more and pounded the mattress. He bucked his hips as best he could within the stranglehold of Alex's grasp, urging the man to go faster and harder.

"Please. Please." He didn't even know what he was pleading for, except he knew something had to give. *He* had to give—and soon.

Alex forced his eyes to stay open. He didn't want to miss a moment of the beautiful sight laid out before him. He was fucking Quinn with fast, sure strokes now, giving him all his passion. Control was slipping away as the tight, slick channel he drove himself into clasped and dragged his dick to orgasm. Had he ever been imbedded in such a welcoming heat? If so, the memory of it had been wiped away by the perfect pleasure of fucking this boy. Not even the unnecessary use of a condom marred the experience.

Quinn's virgin body blossomed in response to his relentless assault. With each pass, Alex's dick was sucked in deeper. The hot human cock in his grasp throbbed and leaked so much cum that his grip slid along the satiny, taut skin. He could feel the orgasm climbing the shaft, ready to erupt.

He redoubled his efforts, drilling Quinn in an increasingly frantic race to empty himself. The boy came first, sticky, warm cum pumping out to coat Alex's fingers. With the first spurt, the human's hole clenched around Alex's shaft. That was all it took to send him over the edge. With a howl, he threw his head back and pounded out his release.

The maelstrom swirled through him, making him wild. He felt the pounding of Quinn's heart through the pulsing artery at his groin. Pressing his thumb against the spot, Alex bit his own lip to taste the salty blood he imagined coursed through Quinn's veins. The urge to drop his head and tear at the boy's artery almost undid him. Instead, he roared out his frustration and, grabbing Quinn's hips with both hands, yanked the boy's pliant body flush against his pelvis. He ground out the last of his orgasm.

When it was over and sanity returned, Alex forced his eyes open. Quinn lay limp against the sheets with his eyes closed. Carefully, so as not to hurt him any more than he might have already, Alex eased his softening dick out of the quivering hole. A quick glance told him all was well. He released the boy's legs and climbed over to lie beside him. He tugged off the hated condom with a tissue and tossed it aside.

He gathered Quinn into his arms and kissed the top of his sweaty head. "Are you all right, dearest boy?"

Quinn mumbled something quite incoherent before turning in to Alex's embrace. A few seconds later, he realized the boy had fallen asleep. He smiled and hugged Quinn a bit tighter. He didn't even question the wisdom of letting the human sleep in his bed. This was where he wanted the boy — nowhere else. And that was a terrifying realization.

* * * *

Alex popped awake at the sound of his phone going off. Quinn still lay curled within his arms, which pleased him. The incessant ringing couldn't be ignored, however, and he knew that it must be important for someone to rouse him from his sleep. Releasing the boy, he leaned over the side of the bed and snatched his pants. He pulled the phone out of his pocket and saw that it was Val calling.

"What's wrong?"

"Turn on the local news."

Alex didn't waste time asking why. He grabbed his remote and clicked on the flat screen mounted on the wall opposite his bed. What he saw dismayed and angered him, but it wasn't a surprise.

A shot from a helicopter zoomed in on the pale white body of a naked man hanging from the Longfellow Bridge over the Charles River. A plethora of emergency personnel swarmed the area, working, no doubt, to free the corpse while preserving the crime scene. Even via television, one could see that the victim's throat had been ripped open and his body drained of blood.

"Fuck me. Adrian's been busy." Alex said the words without thinking.

"Who's Adrian?"

Shit.

"The boy's with you?" Val's tone dripped with surprise.

Alex ignored the question. "Get the car. I'll join you out front in ten minutes." Disconnecting the call, he turned off the TV then tossed both the remote and his phone onto the nightstand.

He turned to Quinn, and the adorably rumpled appearance of the boy made him smile, despite the horror of Adrian's latest kill. He pressed a soft kiss on those swollen pink lips. "Good morning. Sorry to wake you."

Quinn blushed and dropped his gaze for a second. "Good morning."

"How are you feeling?"

The human wiggled a bit. "A little sore, but in a good way, you know?" His blush deepened, which only served to make him even more irresistible.

Alex kissed him again and indulged himself enough to deepen it to the point that they both ended up breathless. He pulled away reluctantly. "I'm sorry. I have to go, but you should go back to sleep. It's early yet."

"Oh, is that okay?" He peeked at Alex from under his lashes. On a more experienced boy, he would have thought it a calculated coquettish move. Knowing Quinn as he already did, it was pure shyness.

He tucked a stray lock behind the boy's ear. "Of course. I rather like the idea of you tucked in my bed while I'm out." He stood, and grabbing the sheet at the foot of the bed, spread it over the human.

"That should keep you warm until I return."

Quinn smiled and snuggled under the sheet. "Thanks. Do you really have to go?"

"Yes. There's been another murder, and given the proximity of the first one to the club, I want to keep abreast of what's going on."

"Oh, yeah, I got that from the TV." He gnawed at his lower lip. "Who's Adrian?"

Of course, the boy wasn't so distracted by Alex's charm that he'd forgotten what he'd heard. "That's simply the nickname that Val and I gave the killer. Adrian is someone we knew back in the old country who was a bit of a bully." He gave an artless shrugged. "Juvenile, I'll admit, but there you are."

"Oh." Quinn smiled again. "I guess that's better than calling him the vampire killer, like some of the boys are doing."

Alex kept a fake smile in place. "Yes, indeed." Leaning over, he gave Quinn one more kiss because…just because, before heading to the bathroom.

Ten minutes later, he climbed into the black Escalade Val had arrived in. They didn't need the vehicle much, but when moving quickly in human fashion, the thing did come in handy. They'd both dressed as they did when forced to go out in the summer sun—long-sleeved tees, jeans and boots, although Val's style tended toward Alexander McQueen or some other trendy designer, whereas Alex stuck to the old standbys like Armani.

They hid their sensitive eyes behind glasses designed to filter out the worst of the sun's rays. There again, his companion liked the flashy aviator style, and Alex just wanted something functional and more conservative. Val also shielded his head with a Red Sox ball cap. It was a sensible choice, but Alex didn't like hats and had chosen to put his hair in a messy man-bun. He felt like an idiot every time he did it. Still, the clump of hair helped keep his head from baking.

He had developed a surprising level of vanity while living on this planet. On their home world, clothing was functional, not decorative. Males and females dressed alike. He'd first scoffed at the human need to pretty themselves with ever-changing fashion trends. Yet over the centuries, that which he'd done merely to blend in had become more important to him. Add to that a ridiculous amount of wealth, and he could indulge himself—and Quinn, too. That thought popped into his head. He pictured dressing the boy in clothes worthy of his beauty. The idea made him smile.

"Not for nothing, boss, but I think you should wipe that well-fucked look off your face. We're headed to the site of a murder, after all."

Alex scowled at Val's insubordination. Even after a thousand Earth years, their command structure held, although it was fraying a bit, despite his best efforts. "I do not have a 'well-fucked look' on my face. And, technically, we aren't heading to the site of a murder so much as the place the body was dumped."

"Hung, sir. *Technically* speaking." Val shot him a wry grin.

"Whatever," he muttered back and slumped in his seat. "Damn Dracul to hell. He would have Adrian make a spectacle of the whole thing."

"Not his usual style. I mean, the low body count part, not the spectacle. He's always gone in before for the massive casualties and destruction of nations kind of trouble-making. Two dead people in a few days' time seems penny-ante for him."

"Hmm. I expect he's simply changed with the world. He recognizes that he has to tread lightly now that humans have developed the means to destroy everything, including us. It's one thing to goad and help the power-mad and insane to slaughter thousands, then millions, using conventional means. Splitting atoms to obliterate your enemies is an entirely different matter. Impossible to contain."

Val sighed as he weaved his way through the clog of traffic that was getting thicker the closer they got to the crime scene. "I was really hoping he'd stopped."

Alex shook his head. "Never. I don't think he's constitutionally capable of that now. It's a compulsion to manipulate humans for sport and to harass us."

He heaved a bigger sigh than Val had and lifted his glasses to pinch the bridge of his nose. "I'm tired of reacting to his every move. And I'm not leaving. Not again. I like Boston. I like the club."

I like the boy.

He stomped on that thought as soon as it formed. That was taking things too far too fast. One night didn't mean anything, nor did taking the boy's virginity. If he cared even a little bit for the vulnerable human, he'd pack him up and send him back to Michigan where he'd be safe—as safe as any human could be, at any rate. He knew the moment his brain formulated that plan, though, that he couldn't go through with it. The very thought of Quinn being out of his sight, out of his protection, made his hot blood run icy cold.

"If Dracul wants to play a new game, then so be it. We're taking a stand. This is our city and we're going to defend it for however long it takes."

Chapter Eight

"Jesus fucking Christ, this a nightmare."

Trey took his eyes off the coroner's tentative review of the still-hanging body and trained his attention instead on his partner. "Which part? The one where we have to figure out how in the hell the killer managed to string the victim over the side of a bridge without being seen? Or the part where we have to accept that we have a quickly-escalating serial killer, which means the feds are on their way to shove us aside?"

Grabbing the railing in front of him, he leaned over and studied the teeming crowd of looky-loos below. "Or the part where we're trying to do what's left of our jobs in front of the entire fucking city?"

The beautiful summer morning encouraged people to practically treat the horror show unfolding on one of the city's landmarks like a fun outing. Street vendors had followed the flow of people and even now hocked treats and drinks in an obscene display that put him in mind of old-fashioned executions. Worse, people were buying the stuff and sitting on the grass or strolling around, watching as the pathetic and bloodless remains of an as-yet unknown victim were poked and prodded.

"Hey, Doc, can you please move this along?"

Almadeo shot him an irritated glance from where he was bent almost in half, trying to examine the body. "Nearly done, Duncan."

Trey grimaced and busied himself studying the site, even though he'd already been doing so for the last couple of hours. The perp had managed to string the vic into an almost cross-like position, which would assuredly drive the media wild with its illusions to — as Karl had said — "*Jesus Fucking Christ*", even though his partner hadn't meant it quite like that. Even now, helicopters circled the Charles, getting close-up shots that were certainly being streamed live over television and the Internet, although the picture would be blurred, no doubt, given the victim's nudity. That was some small blessing, he supposed, to help preserve the poor man's dignity in death.

"Ah, shit." He swore without any real heat at the sight of two familiar men cutting an easy swath through the crowd to get close to the bridge.

The arrival of the Lux boys didn't surprise him — not really. They were either in this butchery up to their eyeballs or they'd seen the news and come out of the same curiosity as the others.

"Hey, Karl? Have a uniform call down for the Ghoul Quarterly models to be brought here. I want to see if they know this latest victim."

With a snort, Karl called out to a cop and relayed the order. Trey braced himself once more on the bridge railing and watched as a uniformed officer at the cordon received the command, sought out the Stelalux men and ushered them over. As the two approached, Trey could only mentally shake his head at the way their 'casual' clothing looked like it cost more than his monthly take-home pay. It struck him as odd, too, that they were covered so much, given the warmth of the day. There was something odd about these men.

Vampires.

He scoffed at his own flight of fancy. They were just privileged foreigners with a kinky lifestyle. He, of all people, should know better than to judge them for being different. Still, he wanted to sneer at the big boss's man bun. He didn't. The arresting masculine beauty got to him. It grated that the guy was probably the only man on the planet who could pull off that particular hairstyle.

A thump behind him had him turning in time to see the morgue attendants wrestle the victim into the waiting body bag. When they went to zipper it, he stopped them with a quick, barking 'wait' because he wanted the club owner and bouncer to have a chance to view the remains. Without a single shred of identification available, it might take days—or even never—to identify the guy. Trey half-hoped it was another club member. That at least would give them a firmer trail to follow, not that the feds would allow them to continue now.

Shit.

The Stelalux cousins approached him with sure steps. If the sight of the body bothered them, they didn't show it, not in the normal way. As they'd done at the club with the news of the first murder, they crossed themselves. Well, that made a mockery of any ridiculous notion that they were vampires. Maybe they were so tired of people cracking that particular joke their way that they'd adopted the gesture in defense.

He planted himself in their path. "Gentlemen, thanks for coming."

Alex Stelalux stared at him through his undoubtedly very expensive sunglasses, his eyes too hidden by the tinted lens to be readable. "Of course, sergeant. We came as soon as we saw it on the news. I assume you want us to view the victim to see if we know him." It was a statement, not a question, and the man's reading of the situation irked him for some reason.

He stepped to one side. "Yes, if you don't mind. It might be another of your members."

"Crowell was a former member, but I get your meaning." He didn't hesitate to approach the body.

Neither did his cousin, who gave Trey a carnivorous kind of smile as he passed. His spooky eyes were totally obscured in his aviator glasses. *Too sexy for his clothes* went through Trey's mind. There was no denying these guys had balls.

"Give them room," he called out.

Everyone gave the enormous men a wide berth, and he couldn't blame them. No matter what they wore, their power was on full display. Standing side-by-side, they stared at the sad remains of the victim. It occurred to Trey that someone of great strength and arm-reach would have had to have hung the body. If it wasn't one of these men, it had to be someone of similar height and build.

He sauntered up to them. This close, it was even more obvious that the victim bore the same marks of violence as Crowell, although his throat was more intact.

"Do you recognize him?"

"No." That was Alex speaking for the two of them. There was something about this man's authority over the other that spoke of more than mere boss and employee. Given their bearing and demeanor, he had a feeling they might have even served in the military together. *Does Romania even have one? They must. Virtually every country does.*

Alex turned to Trey, taking his glasses off. Trey had a good view of the man's unusual violet eyes. "I'm sorry, no. He wasn't a member and we don't know him otherwise."

Trey shifted his attention to the other man. "And you, Mr. Stelalux?" He knew the answer, yet wanted to hear it from the guy, anyway, if for no other reason than it was still his goddamn job to find the killer until the feds shoved him aside.

The bouncer, Val, joined his boss's side. He didn't take off his glasses as he answered, "No, sir."

Trey banked his disappointment. "I see. I'm also going to have ask you where you were last night." Logan's assertion notwithstanding, he couldn't dismiss the possibility that the killer was one of these men — or even both of them.

Alex raised his eyebrows. "Oh, are we still suspects, sergeant?"

"I have to pursue all avenues, sir."

"Of course. I was at the club most of the night then home in bed. And, before you ask if anyone can verify any of that, there were lots of members milling about. I really wish you'd be discreet about interviewing them, should you feel the need to." He paused. "Quinn was with me until Val called about this unfortunate discovery being on the news. That means the boy and I both have the necessary alibis."

"Yeah, sure." Trey wasn't surprised, and while it was possible the boy would lie for his lover and vice versa, he also knew that Stelalux still didn't play well with him as the killer. He turned to the bouncer. "I assume you have a similar answer?"

"Yup."

"Well, thank you for coming, anyway, gentlemen. We seem to have a serial killer on our hands. That's my problem, though, not yours."

Alex flicked his glasses back on and murmured something else. Something that sounded like, "I wish that were true."

"I'm sorry?"

Alex smiled. "We'll leave you to it, then." With that, they sauntered away as if they didn't have a care in the world.

Trey wasn't fooled, not in the least. Rational or not, he couldn't shake the idea that those men had more to do with this nightmare than they let on.

* * * *

Alex found his boy exactly where he'd left him. And Quinn *was* his boy. To say otherwise — to even think otherwise — would be a pointless exercise in fooling himself. With Adrian's murder spree breathing down their necks, he didn't want to play that kind of game. Despite his confidence in his ability to defeat Dracul yet again, he also feared the fall-out this time more than any other. Millions of humans had become collateral damage in the thousand-year war their two factions had waged.

One loss more than the others had cut Alex to the quick. He'd vowed to ensure that never happened again. Yet here he was, exposing himself to the possibility of that agonizing hurt. He just couldn't help it. From the moment that shy, vulnerable Quinn had entered his loft to beg for a job, Alex had been helpless to avoid his destiny. And now, he'd reached a crossroads. He either pushed the boy away or pulled him in close.

As he'd returned to his loft toting a breakfast tray for the second day in a row, he'd achieved a surprising measure of peace with his decision.

He walked up the bedroom steps in his usual silent way, not wanting to wake Quinn if he still slept. The sight of the small lump curled under the sheet made him smile. After placing the tray on the nightstand, he allowed himself the pleasure of simply watching. Quinn's lips twitched and he let out a puffy breath. Then he sighed and rolled over onto his back, one arm flung over his head. His pretty blond hair stuck out in adorable spikes.

Quinn's eyelashes fluttered open. A look of confusion crossed his sweet face before a smile broke out. "Hi."

Alex returned the greeting. "Hi." He sat beside Quinn and reached over to tuck a bit of hair behind the boy's ear. "I'm glad you were able to go back to sleep."

He immediately regretted saying anything. Quinn's expression changed as he remembered how they'd been woken earlier.

The boy pushed to a sitting position and frowned. "There was another murder."

Alex grimaced. "Yes."

"Anyone you knew?"

The strand of hair fell forward again. Alex tucked it back and took the opportunity to stroke Quinn's cheek.

"No. The poor man wasn't a member or anyone that I could recall ever meeting."

Leaning into Alex's touch, the boy closed his eyes briefly then he became more alert. "You were able to see him? The body, I mean."

Alex dropped his hand. "Yes. Duncan was there, of course, and he had us brought in close to see if we knew the victim."

Quinn chewed at his lower lip. "Was he like Crowell? You know?" He brought his hand to his throat.

Alex clasped it and brought it back again. "Don't think about it. You're perfectly safe here, you know."

Quinn huffed out a breath and his cheeks turned a soft pink. "Yeah, I do." He peeked at him from under his lashes. "You're like the biggest, baddest guy I've ever met."

"You know I'd never use that strength to hurt you?"

"Of course." He gave Alex an impish grin and slid his gaze sideways. "Is that breakfast?"

"It is." Alex picked up a tall, cold glass with a straw sticking out. "I brought iced coffee. Emil keeps cold brew in the kitchen." He handed it over.

Quinn took it and sipped eagerly. "Oh, man," he said, stopping for air, "that's awesome." He wiggled to lean against the headboard. "What's there to eat?"

"Egg sandwich." Alex grabbed the plate and held it out for Quinn to take the food in his other hand. He watched the boy alternate between big bites of food and long sips.

"Aren't you eating?" he asked Alex around his mouthful.

"I did already."

"Hmm." Quinn kept busy with his breakfast for a few more minutes. His gaze skidded to the side. "I'm not sure what to do."

Alex was perplexed by the confession. "About what?" He put his hand on the boy's covered knee and resisted the urge to slide it farther.

Quinn swallowed. "About this." He gestured around the room. "Am I supposed to thank you for taking my cherry and feeding me breakfast then pretend this never happened? Was it the last time we're going to be together?"

"Oh, dearest boy." Leaning over, Alex plucked the almost-empty glass from Quinn's fingers.

He kept going until he'd captured the human's lips in a bruising kiss. He dropped the glass on the tray and crawled onto the bed all the way so that he could wrap Quinn up and drag him close. His dick hardened as much as his jeans would allow. A similar hardness pressed against his thigh through the blanket that separated their bodies.

Alex slid his palm down Quinn's naked back and cupped his ass. He ground the boy against him, soaking each little moan into his own mouth. With his grip, he made Quinn hump his thigh. When he tucked one finger into the puckered ring of Quinn's hole, the boy jerked, then thrashed. He gave one long groan before shaking in Alex's embrace.

Alex held the kiss until the boy fell limp. "Does that reassure you on that point?"

Quinn dropped his head on Alex's chest and panted through the aftershocks of his climax. "Uh-huh," he managed.

Pulling his finger free, he slapped the still-quivering ass. "Then let's get you in the shower."

* * * *

Quinn didn't think he'd ever be able to shower again without thinking of blowjobs. Apparently, when two guys were in a relationship and they bathed together, one of them would land on his knees. At least, he thought that was the case. As he'd knelt on the tile to suck Quinn's insatiable cock, Alex had just laughed at the idea that doing it was somehow contrary to the original purpose of showering. Given that he'd only stayed upright because Alex had held him, Quinn hadn't been in any position to argue the point.

He'd never felt looser in his life. At the same time, his body ached in a few places in a way he'd never known before. His ass felt as if Alex's big cock was still inside, while at the same time, it also felt empty. His inner thighs were also sore, the result of having been stretched as much as his hole to accommodate the general hugeness that was Alex. He even had some finger-print-sized bruises on his hips and arms where his lover had held on to him with a punishing grip that also let Quinn know he was safe.

His lover.

That sounded weird. So did the notion that he was in a relationship, but Alex had made that clear, as well. They hadn't had a one-night stand, which would have been miraculous enough. No, Alex had looked at him with a proprietary gleam in his eyes and had asked him to join him in the loft later in the day for dinner — just the two of them.

Now that he had plans for sex instead of falling into the moment, he'd started to be even more nervous. Alex was a magnificent man. *What does he see in a scrawny twink like me?* Well, some guys liked that, of course. Val did, except Mackie was totally cool and sexy in a way that Quinn never would be. At the very least, though, he could do something to tone and build muscle.

With that plan in place, he'd come to the in-house gym as soon as his legs had been steady again. He'd never been one to work out. He'd been too afraid of the jocks in high school to enter their domain and too afraid that his attraction to them would be obvious. His gayness had been clear to many in school, no matter what he'd done. The bullying had been sporadic, yet routine. He hadn't wanted to invite even more abuse.

He found he liked using the fancy machines. The rhythm of pulling this and pressing that with the just the right amount of weight made exercise almost easy. It allowed him to relive his time with Alex without risking dropping something heavy on his foot.

"Someone's got that well-fucked look."

"Jesus!" The metal bar slipped out of Quinn's hand, dropping the weight with a loud clang. He glared at the grinning face on the other side of the machine. "Don't sneak up on me, Mackie."

The boy flipped his hair. "Why not? It's fun. Besides," he added, reaching out to grab Quinn's left bicep. "You don't want to overdo it. If you get too jacked, Alex might not want you anymore."

"Huh!" Grabbing the towel he'd brought in with him, he swiped at the meager perspiration on his face. "As if I could ever approach anything remotely like jacked." He gnawed at his lower lip. "Do you think Alex likes twinks?"

Mackie cocked his hip and flipped a hand in Quinn's direction. "Ladies and gentlemen of the jury, I present Exhibit A."

Quinn hunched in on himself. "Shut up," he said, without meaning it.

Mackie wound one arm around the machine and leaned in. "So, on a scale of one to ten, how was it? And, don't say an eleven."

His cheeks just got hotter and he gazed at the ground. "Even if it was?"

Mackie let out a whoop and came around to give him a bear hug. "Congratulations, sweetie! That's awesome."

Embarrassed and delighted in equal measure, Quinn returned the embrace. "I know. I can't believe it finally happened."

Pulling back, Mackie smirked. "So dish. I want all the details."

Quinn raised his eyebrows. "No. I can't do that."

"Can't do what?" An impish face popped into his peripheral vision.

"Jesus!" Quinn said for the second time in less than five minutes. "Demi, where did you come from?"

The exotic boy just shrugged then added more weight to the machine Quinn had been using. "I'm allowed to leave my room every once in a while, you know." He sauntered over and hip-checked Quinn and Mackie out of the way before pulling on the bar.

Quinn raised his eyebrows at Mackie. Despite his slight build, Demi showed some impressive strength. Mackie rolled his eyes and mouthed the word 'freaky' before moving away.

"So, what were we talking about?" The boy didn't even sound winded.

"*We* weren't talking about anything," Mackie sniffed. "Nothing for your little boy ears, anyway."

Demi made a face. "That means sex, which I already guessed. Hard to miss that Cousin Alex is fucking the new boy."

The blatant statement, especially coming from such a young guy, made Quinn gasp.

"What? I'm not a little kid. I know what fucking is. It would be nice for once to hear about it in real terms. My parents have only given me the clinical basics."

Quinn wiped at his forehead again, the conversation making him sweat far more than the workout had. "Are you gay?"

Demi let the bar go and shrugged. "More poly, I guess. I mean I'm attracted to all types. And, I'd like to know what to expect when I finally meet someone."

"You're too young, regardless. Tell him, Mackie," Quinn added when Demi made a face.

Mackie was no help, though. He went wide-eyed at the plea. "Why would I do that? He's not that young. I was thirteen my first time."

Shocked at the news, even though he thought himself worldlier than that, Quinn sputtered. "But thirteen is way too young for sex."

Mackie averted his eyes. "That's not what the man who popped my cherry thought." When no one said anything for a few seconds, he huffed. "Fine. Demi, you need to wait until you're married to that one special man — or woman — who will love you forever and ever. Satisfied?" he asked Quinn.

"Don't be such a dick." He redirected his focus on Demi. "Okay. I don't want to go into details with anyone. What Alex and I do is private. But you really are too young right now. Don't be in such a hurry."

He paced away, his emotions suddenly coming to the surface. "When I was your age, I thought life was passing me by, that everyone was having sex except me. I blamed it on being gay. If only I could come out, I'd meet some great boy and we'd lose our virginity together. Everything would be wonderful."

He turned and gave Demi a hard look. "I was too scared to come out then, and thank God I was. My parents kicked me to the curb the moment I told them. My whole family turned their backs on me because I refused to 'accept' that I had a problem that needed fixing. Can you imagine what would have happened if I'd still been a minor and totally dependent on them? As it was, I told them a few months too soon. I would have been forced to leave home even before I finished high school."

He pressed his hand against his stomach. The memories of having been tossed away by the people he'd loved his whole life were still fresh and the wound still raw. He shuddered to get himself under control. Mackie, bless him, came over and hugged him from behind.

"It's okay, sweetie. You're better off without those assholes. You have a home here with us, now."

Quinn took a deep breath and whooshed it out. "Yeah, I am lucky. I know you don't have to worry about any of that, Demi, but my advice still holds. Give yourself time to find the right guy. I think that sex with the wrong person is way worse than no sex at all. Alex has been amazingly kind and gentle with me. I know that's not true with all men."

Resting his chin on Quinn's shoulder, Mackie said, "That's true. There are some real shitheads out there. And even though your family would rip a guy that hurt you limb-from-limb, you can never get your first time back."

Because he could hear the hint of sorrow in Mackie's voice, Quinn shifted to give him a hug. The boy allowed it for only a second before wriggling free and dancing away. Apparently, Mackie was better at handing out sympathy than receiving it. Quinn didn't push the issue.

"Why don't we all forget about sex for a while and work out?" Quinn suggested. "That's why I'm here, anyway."

Demi sighed. "Fine. It's better than doing my school work, and the 'rents will let me take an hour break if it's for exercise."

"I suppose I should put some time in, too," Mackie said, heading for the elliptical machine. "After this, though, we should go out, Quinn. I'll show you the city."

"Thanks, but I'm not sure I'll have enough energy for that and work tonight."

Mackie giggled. "It's Monday, sweetie. No work tonight. The club is still open, but all the boys have off."

"Oh. It's hard to keep track of the days. Everything is still upside-down."

"You'll get used to it." After hopping on the machine, Mackie programmed in his work-out. "And Val's got me on a curfew, so we'll be back before sundown."

"Oh, good." Quinn decided to try leg exercises next. That meant he'd be back in plenty of time for his dinner with Alex, too. He stopped, frowned. "Why the curfew?"

Mackie glanced over his shoulder while he kept his arms and legs pumping. "The killer, remember? He seems to hunt at night and Val's being overly cautious. It's not like the ghoul is focused on the club or anything, not given that the latest victim was some stranger to us."

"Right. We'll be okay." Even as he said it, though, a shiver ran down his spine.

* * * *

Quinn peered into the world behind the circular glass tank with unbridled awe. "This is amazing." He glanced at Mackie's reflection. "Thanks so much for suggesting we come here."

"It's mostly for little kids." Mackie shrugged as if it were no big deal, but Quinn could read the boy easily at this point. He knew Mackie was pleased by his enjoyment of the outing.

The day was a beautiful one and they had spent a couple of hours wandering around Boston Common before coming into the cool dimness of the aquarium. Quinn didn't mind spending the last of his free time inside, though—not when there were penguins and sharks to see. A hammerhead loomed by the side of the glass, causing Quinn to take an involuntary step backward.

Mackie laughed. "It's almost like you're right in there with them."

"Yeah. I've never seen anything like this tank."

The entire internal structure of the building was a ramp that wound its way around the outside of the tank. With each step they took, there was more and more to see. Quinn figured he could spend hours in this place. The little kids pushing past him didn't bother him in the least. He envied their carefree experience, and for a few hours, he could join them in their innocence. He'd already spent time in the touching-pool area, allowing starfish to crawl on his hand and picking up horseshoe crabs.

He felt odd, teetering between the childhood he'd been forced to abandon and the obvious adulthood of having taken a lover. Did spending time in Alex's bed, as well as dancing around a pole, mean that he shouldn't hang out anymore in spaces designed to enthrall children? He didn't know, hadn't even considered it. Yet the aches in his body reminded him that he had crossed a significant line.

Mackie nudge him with his shoulder. "Get a load of that turtle. I bet they don't have anything like that in Missouri."

"*Michigan* does have an aquarium. I just never had a chance to visit it."

"Even though I'm from the Boston area, Val was still the first person to bring me here."

"Really?" He tried picturing the almost feral-looking bouncer bringing his boyfriend on a date to this kid-oriented place. It seemed incongruous.

"Yeah, he loves the sharks."

Okay, that makes sense. Quinn returned his attention to colorful fish swimming close to the walls. A movement caught his attention. A pale face framed by long, dark hair appeared across the crowded tank and through the glass at an angle just higher than he and Mackie stood. His heartbeat quickened because, for a second, he thought Alex had arrived. But between one blink and another, the face disappeared, the same way it had when he'd been shopping the previous day. With a jerk, Quinn stepped back and promptly bumped into a woman walking on the ramp behind him.

"Excuse me, ma'am."

He didn't wait for an acknowledgment. Instead, he scampered past people ahead of her to catch a glimpse at the man. There was no one anywhere farther along that reminded him of Alex or the other Stelalux men. He pressed himself against the railing, letting others pass while he taxed his brain to remember just what he'd seen.

"Hey, what's going on?" Mackie slid into a spot between Quinn and a little boy.

Quinn shook his head. "Nothing."

"You bolted like a spooked steer or something. I mean, if that's a thing in Mississippi."

"Michigan," he corrected absently. He studied the tank all the way up, seeking any hint of the man he'd seen on any level of the tank. "I thought I saw Alex here," he finally confessed, "or someone who looks like him."

"Nah. Alex would never come here. Demi is at that awkward age when anything that smacks of little kids' stuff is automatically off-limits, so he wouldn't be here with his dads. And besides, anyone from the family would come and say hi at a minimum. It was a trick of the tank lighting or something."

"I guess." His head told him Mackie had to be right, yet unease continued to prick at him. Maybe some long-lost relative of Alex's was wandering around Boston. He'd raise it with the man at dinner, maybe.

"It doesn't matter." He shot Mackie a smile, determined not to let anything mar the rest of their beautiful day. "Let's go find the giant lobster."

"I know right where it is. Come on." Mackie grabbed Quinn by the sleeve and tugged him along.

Chapter Nine

"Thank you, Emil. The table setting is lovely and the food smells delicious. You've outdone yourself."

The engineer-turned-chef folded his thick arms and nodded once. "First time you want a romantic dinner in your private quarters? Damn straight I pull out all the stops." He slanted his gaze at Alex. "I like that boy, you know?"

Alex raised his eyebrows and a spurt of anger had his fangs descending. "*Like?*"

The man held up his hand. "Put your biters back, boss. I meant that I think he's a sweet kid who deserves to be treated nicely. Since his family isn't here to say it, I'm taking it on myself to warn you to be careful with him."

"Oh." Alex pulled back his teeth and his anger. "You've always been very protective of the humans, more so than even I am."

"Yeah, well, they need it, don't they? They're so hard on each other, and with Dracul and his traitorous bunch always stirring the pot, someone has to play nursemaid."

Alex clapped his friend in the shoulder. "Your loyalty is appreciated. I couldn't fight against his horrific behavior without you. And your worry for Quinn does you great honor. Rest assured that my intentions are honorable."

"Fuck honor. *Sir,* you're always honorable, but you need to be careful, too, with this kid. He's vulnerable. I bet he's halfway in love with you already."

"Oh." Alex stepped back and frowned. "Surely not. I'm his first lover, yes, but that's physical with some mutual appreciation. Love, though? That's a different matter. And even if you're right, I doubt he'd want me if he understood what I am. My supposed blood fetish turns him off. I'm sure of it."

Shit, who am I trying to convince?

His rather alarming introspection was interrupted by Val storming in. "It's almost sunset." He stopped at the sight of the table set for two, complete with snowy white table cloth, fresh-cut flowers as a centerpiece and candles waiting to be lit. "Jesus, Alex. When did you turn into a girl?"

"I beg your pardon?" His tone had turned to ice, even as he worried that Val was right. The effort he was making for this dinner with Quinn was more than any he'd ever gone to.

Val worried his mobile phone in one hand, distracted. "It's like you're expecting the queen or something."

"The Queen of England?" he asked with a frown.

"No. *Our* queen."

"Oh." *Damn, we've been on this planet too long.* He'd almost forgotten his true monarch, a woman who had ascended to the throne shortly before their mission had started. And she wouldn't have given someone like him a second thought. He was a military man, a drone within their hive and not worthy of her notice, no matter how good at his job he'd been.

He shook off Val's easy mocking and focused on the man's obvious tension. "What's eating at you?"

"I told you. It's almost sundown."

"Indeed." The reminder of the hour caused him to go to the long curtains covering his windows. With a push of a button, the heavy material slid aside to reveal the darkening sky. He had a decent enough view — not very romantic yet more pleasant than a dimly-lit room. With the sun almost set, he could eat with the curtains open.

"The boys aren't back," Val bit out.

"Oh!" Alarm spiked within him. "I'm not expecting Quinn for another fifteen minutes, so I hadn't realized. Have you texted Mackie?"

Val's lips thinned. "About a million times. The little bastard hasn't responded. I am going to beat his ass so badly..."

Alex worried the back of his neck with his hand. "It should be fine. Adrian has done his killing at night so far."

"So far," Val agreed in a grim tone. "That can change, and now that he's leaving his kills in such public places, tracking him is near to impossible. Too many human scents are trampling it."

"His very thought, I'm sure. He's proving cleverer than I expected."

Val's phone chimed. "Finally."

The man stormed out. Emil, who'd borne silent witness to the exchange, left in his wake. Alex moved quickly to keep up with them. They took the stairs, always faster for them than an elevator, especially when they didn't have to worry about anyone seeing them almost fly. They hit the main room just as the two boys entered.

"Why didn't you answer my texts sooner?" Val barked out the question as he strode over to them.

"Sorry," Mackie replied. "We were on the T and you know how spotty reception can be." He squeaked as Val grabbed him by the back of the neck and propelled him toward the elevator. "I'm sorry."

"You think so, but you're about to find out how truly sorry you really are." Val's pronouncement ended on an ominous growl.

Quinn trailed behind them, mouth open. Alex rushed to intercept him with what he hoped was an engaging and distracting smile. "I'm glad to see you home safe and sound."

The human stopped and shifted his focus. His lips curved in a shy smile. "Hi. Sorry if we worried you. The T was more crowded than we expected because one of the cars broke or something." He glanced in the direction of the elevator. "We really didn't get the texts until we'd come above ground again."

"Of course." Alex ran his hand down the back of Quinn's head and gave in to the impulse to give him a quick kiss. Quick turned into lengthy because he found that he absolutely lacked control when it came to this boy.

He gulped in a big breath once he'd managed to let go. "We were a touch concerned because there's a murderous lunatic running around out there."

Quinn was equally short-breathed. "Yeah, we know, except come on. What's the chances that the guy would come after us? There's tons of people to choose from out there."

And not one of them warms the beds of two men that Adrian is determined to goad. He didn't say that, of course. Neither Quinn nor Mackie could know what was happening. There might never be a point when they would, but he didn't want to focus on that. What time he had with Quinn would have to be measured for now in small increments and fundamental pleasures such as having dinner together this evening.

He flitted his palm across Quinn's cheek. "I'm afraid Val and I are terribly overprotective."

Quinn frowned as he stared in the direction of the elevator. "Val seemed mad."

"Sometimes that's part of worry."

"I guess."

"He won't hurt him, not in any way that they haven't agreed is permissible. Now, please, let's go have our dinner. Emil has created something wonderful for us."

"Oh." Quinn's smile was back and he allowed Alex the pleasure of escorting him to the elevators.

He kept his hand on the small of the boy's back, needing to keep some amount of proprietary contact. They entered the now-empty elevator and Alex pressed for his private floor. Before he could stop him, Quinn pressed the button for the fourth floor.

"Why did you do that?"

Quinn gazed at him with doe-like eyes. "I need to get cleaned up and dressed."

"You're already dressed and perfectly presentable for my humble table, I assure you."

Quinn stepped back. "No, these are grubby clothes for hanging around in. I have newer and nicer ones."

He frowned at the floor. "This is my first real date. I want to make it special. Okay?" He glanced at Alex.

Alex wanted to argue the point. He wanted to tell Quinn that he intended to divest him of his clothing as soon as possible and lick him up one side and down the other. But, as the elevator chimed for the fourth floor, Alex stuck his hand out to keep the doors open.

He smiled as graciously as he could. "Of course. Forgive me. I understand completely. Please do me the one favor, though, and don't dawdle. I'll be waiting as patiently as I know how, which is to say not very well at all."

Quinn popped onto his toes to give Alex a quick kiss. "I'll be fast. Promise."

Alex let the doors close and leaned against the wall with a heavy sigh. His dick was already hard. He wasn't sure he could make it through dinner. It would be a struggle to stop himself from sweeping all Emil's hard work off the table and fucking Quinn on top of it.

* * * *

"This is all so wonderful. I can't believe you and Emil went to all this trouble."

It wasn't difficult after all to contain his worst impulses. The sheer joy on Quinn's face when he'd seen the meal laid out had made Alex's sacrifice worthwhile. It was rather nice, too, to chat as they ate the chilled gazpacho soup and kale salad and sipped on an excellent Chablis. Quinn had told him about his wandering around Boston and visiting the aquarium. Alex thought it cruel of humans to trap animals in small places for their amusement. Although given how they treated each other, what they did to lower species wasn't a surprise. Quinn had so thoroughly enjoyed himself that he didn't have the heart to argue any point.

They were on to steak, now. His own was barely cooked, a simple way of satisfying the most basic of his blood craving. Quinn's was medium, a guess that Emil had made.

"I hope your steak is cooked to your liking?"

Quinn swallowed his mouthful. "Oh, yes, thanks. It's delicious. Everything is. I don't know how Emil gets his mashed potatoes so creamy. My mother's always has lumps."

The boy's face fell suddenly and Quinn's obvious hurt from even a casual mention of his family infuriated Alex. *Why couldn't a mother who made imperfect food see her son for the blessing that he is?* Quinn stared at this plate, fine tremors running through his lower lip. Alex's keen sight had no trouble detecting them, yet he was at a loss as to what to say. Should he even acknowledge the boy's torment or politely ignore it until he got himself under control again?

"I guess I won't be tasting those anymore." Quinn squared his shoulders and cut another piece of steak. "Their loss." He shoved the food in his mouth and chewed.

Pride rose in Alex over how his boy was able to handle himself with such courage. "Yes, it *is* their loss. You are wonderful, Quinn. I can't tell you how much I enjoy your company."

The human blushed, a pretty pink dotting his high cheek bones. Humans were so expressive. "Thanks. I like yours, too."

After putting his utensils on his plate, he toyed with his wine glass as he watched Quinn eat. "Your new clothes are quite fetching, but I can't wait to take them off you."

Quinn dropped his fork with a clatter and coughed. "You shouldn't say things like that," he admonished in a teasing tone. "You're going to make me choke." He reached for his water.

"Sorry. I'm shameless, I know. Don't you like your wine? I can get you beer if you prefer."

"No, this is fine, thanks. I'm not used to drinking alcohol. I'm technically too young, remember?"

Alex huffed. "An inane law. Where I'm from, drinking isn't given much thought."

"Romania, right?" Quinn cut another piece of steak. "What's it like there?"

He had no trouble coming up with honest answers. He'd spent a great deal of time in that country, having always returned to his point of landing, no matter what journeys he'd taken around the world. The Carpathian Mountains had seemed like home in the wake of not being able to leave the planet—the most familiar place in a foreign land.

"It can be beautiful in the mountains, which is where my family is from. The communist regime made it almost unbearable in the cities. I did a lot of traveling when I could and finally chose to come to the new world."

That was a somewhat inaccurate statement. He'd visited America a few times, once to help counterbalance Dracul when he would have tipped the Revolution to the British and another when he would have made worse mischief during this country's brutal civil war. Always, Alex had returned to his place of origin until Dracul's meddling had almost engulfed the world in flames. The aftermath had left the serene area they'd hid in a dark and dismal place.

"Why Boston?"

The bright, cheerful boy sitting across from him had suffered loss, as well. Instead of wallowing in it, he was forging a new life with an obvious optimism that Alex found infectious.

He sat back and enjoyed watching Quinn eat. "I wanted somewhere near the sea, so unlike the mountains. The perfect change of pace, I suppose. Boston is a small city, far nicer in my opinion than New York or LA. I love living here."

"And you have some family members with you. That must be nice." If there was any self-pity in that question, the boy didn't show it.

"Yes, having Val, Harry and Emil with me is like bringing a bit of home along."

"Do you have family back in Romania? Your parents, siblings?"

"No. I'm an only child and my parents are both dead." That was a lie, although a necessary one that he'd been telling humans for a thousand years. He tried not to think about his siblings and their parents, all likely still alive, yet lost to him forever.

"I'm sorry." Quinn uttered the obligatory words of condolence as if he truly meant them. Then he sat back and gazed at Alex. "I think I'd better stop now. I don't want to get too full."

"No dessert? Emil left a chocolate mousse in my refrigerator."

"Hmm, sounds delicious. Maybe later." A sexy smile played across his lips. "Would you mind terribly if we moved on to the part of this amazing evening where we fuck?"

Alex fumbled his wine glass, the last drops spilling on the table cloth. How was it possible for this untried boy to unnerve him so? "I'd love nothing better." He started to get up. He'd have to buy Quinn some new clothes because he was going to rip the ones he had on. His need had become that strong in seconds.

"Wait!" That single plea rooted Alex to his chair. "I-I'd like to try something, if that's okay?"

Alex made himself relax. "Anything you want, dear boy."

Pushing back, Quinn stood. His movements betrayed his nervousness. It didn't matter. Alex was enthralled by all of it. He watched with hooded lids as the boy approached.

"Can you please turn your chair toward me and spread your legs?"

Alex did as asked and a low moan escaped his lips when Quinn kneeled before him. The human raised his small, delicate hands to lay them on top of Alex's thighs. He slid them toward his crotch, where his dick had already hardened. It had been stiff throughout the dinner. Now it stood erect, pressing against the soft material of his slacks. He hissed when Quinn brushed against the edge of the rigid flesh.

Quinn licked his lips and, leaning in, put his mouth along the length of the rod. The warmth of his mouth seeped through to bathe those few inches of Alex's cock that were being kissed. He cupped the back of Quinn's head and pushed it forward to increase the pressure.

The boy fought the hold and pulled back. "Please. I don't want to do it this way. I want to suck you for real." He glanced up. "Please?"

Alex's answer was another moan. He dropped his hand to his side. "Whatever you want. My body is yours to play with however you wish." The invitation was sincere. He hadn't been anything other than the instigator when it came to sex in forever. He practically quivered in anticipation of what the boy might do.

With somewhat clumsy movements, Quinn first unbuttoned Alex's shirt and shoved it aside to expose his chest. Then he unbuckled Alex's belt and undid his pants, tugging the zipper down with difficulty, given Alex's rampant hard-on. He had to help the boy a bit to wiggle the material past his hips to give his cock the freedom to spring up. As he went commando, there was nothing else to get in their way.

Quinn seemed to like how the dick appeared easily. His mouth rounded into an O in surprise and delight before he brought it close enough to lick at Alex's cockhead. The effort was tentative at first, Quinn exploring with flicks of his tongue along the smooth bulb. It was like being blown by a butterfly. *Maddening.* Alex had to grit his teeth and ball his fingers into fists. He didn't want to rush the boy along.

Soon, the human became bolder, opening his mouth wide to suck. He slid down Alex's dick inch-by-inch. He explored the underside of the shaft with his tongue, tickling that straining bundle of nerves right beneath the head. All the while, Quinn kept his hands on Alex's thighs. He was gripping them for balance, no doubt, but Alex found that simple touch almost as erotic as the cock sucking. He unfurled his fingers to place his hands over the boy's. He needed the contact and squeezed convulsively in response to the exquisite tension building inside his dick.

Quinn couldn't take him in too far. Of course, he couldn't. That human mouth was far too small and tight to accommodate the monster dick Alex housed between his legs. It hardly mattered. The artless blowjob was going to make him come soon with a force that he already knew would outshine others. There was something so intoxicating about being someone's first.

When the boy pulled away, letting Alex's cock slip out, Alex wanted to howl with disappointment. He made an aborted effort to grab that blond head and shove it back where it belonged. Instead, he clutched at Quinn's hands hard enough to hurt, he'd bet.

"Sorry." Quinn looked at him with his shiny, swollen lips. "Is it okay if I don't suck you off? I'd like it if you'd fuck me."

Alex let out a painful breath. "Whatever you want. Remember?"

Quinn smiled shyly. "Right." He stood, drawing his hands free with a tug. Then he attacked the buttons of his nice, new shirt and stripped to the waist. The jeans, socks and loafers came next until, within less than a minute, the boy stood naked before him. His lovely pink skin was flushed with arousal. Those blue eyes were blown wide and his slender cock was standing stiff from his body. Alex had only a few seconds to admire the view before the boy returned to stand between his legs.

He held up a condom. "I hope you don't mind that I bought my own supply."

"Not at all." The damn things were a nuisance, but it was hard to explain why Quinn didn't need to worry about HIV or any other STD. Alex could neither contract nor transmit them. Later, when they'd solidified their relationship, he would convince the boy that bare-backing was fine. For now, it was important that Quinn feel safe.

"Good." He opened the foil packet with some difficulty but managed to roll it down Alex's straining dick. "I got magnums," the boy added with a shy grin. Then he climbed onto Alex's lap. A grunt escaped Alex as Quinn settled with his legs straddling him. Hard cock bumped against hard cock. They both groaned.

Quinn wrapped his arms around Alex's neck. "Is this okay?"

By way of answer, Alex clasped a hand around both dicks, using his natural speed because he had no patience to pretend slowness. "You have to stop asking that question. Everything with you is absolutely perfect."

With that, his control did snap...utterly. He used his free hand to grab Quinn's head and pull him in for a bruising kiss. He plunged his tongue into the same mouth that had so lovingly catered to his cock. He tried to put it where his dick hadn't managed to go, reaching for Quinn's throat and not quite making it. The boy swallowed convulsively from the invasion, yet there was no struggle or resistance. He took that as permission to continue.

While he ravaged the boy's mouth, he ground their cocks together. He pumped his fist, jerking them with only Quinn's pre-cum and some lube already on the condom to grease the way. It wasn't enough, of course. Within seconds, he cupped Quinn's ass. Then he slid two fingers down the crease and circled them around the boy's hole. It quivered at his touch, yet it was too dry to enter. He needed to move them into the bedroom where he kept all the supplies. The idea of moving didn't appeal to him, however.

He growled in frustration before the solution came to him. With reluctance, he let the taut ass go and groped around the table. Things clattered and clinked until he found what he needed. He dug his fingers into the butter dish and scooped a bit of the soft mass. He'd used this before. It was not as helpful as modern lube, but it would do.

Back to the hole he went, rubbing and pressing. Quinn moaned and clenched around the invading fingers. It didn't take long to loosen the boy. At least, he hoped it was enough. He couldn't wait any longer. Breaking the kiss because even he needed some air in his lungs, he used one hand to cup Quinn's ass to lever him up. He let the boy's cock go in order to maneuver his own over. Quinn clutched at Alex's shoulders and helped position himself.

"Look at me." Alex issued the soft order and a thrill shot up his spine when the boy complied. He stared at Alex with sultry eyes. "Are you ready?"

By way of answer, Quinn held his gaze and impaled himself on Alex's dick. He seated himself to the hilt in one long slide. Alex's sight winked out for a second, the pleasure being that intense, then he uttered an oath in Romanian.

"What?" Quinn's expression turned impish. "Did you like that?"

Alex didn't bother to answer. He just kissed Quinn again and rolled his hips to thrust shallowly into the boy's tight heat. Quinn moaned and wrestled with Alex's tongue. Then he began to ride Alex with a languid rhythm. Alex helped by cupping his ass for support, lifting and relaxing as needed. He used his greasy hand to jerk Quinn's trapped dick.

It wasn't going to take long. The climax built in Alex with dizzying speed. The way Quinn's dick twitched within his grasp, he knew the boy was also close. Quinn pulled away suddenly, so he slowed his movements.

"Wait, please." The boy's breath labored. "I want to try something."

Alex had no idea what he meant, but he did as asked and kept his hips stiller than they wanted to be. The only urge he had was to shove his cock in as deeply as possible. He'd promised Quinn he could do what he liked, so he sat and watched. Leaning back, the human reached over to the table and surprised him by grabbing Alex's steak knife. Quinn twisted back to look at him.

"I want to do this for you." Before Alex could fathom the boy's meaning, let alone stop him, Quinn pricked his thumb. A bubble of bright, delicious blood welled up. Quinn tossed the knife onto the table and held up his offering.

It took Alex a millisecond of indecision and attempted self-control before he gave in to his baser instincts. He let go of Quinn's cock and seized his hand instead. He engulfed the thumb with his mouth. The sweet explosion of blood on his tongue sent him flying. He slammed Quinn onto his dick at the same time as he bucked his hips.

From a distance, over the roaring in his ears, he heard the boy cry out. His cock surged in deep as it sent cum shooting into the condom. A splash of something warm hit his stomach. He homed in on all the sensations — the taste of blood, the exhilaration of orgasm and the pride of accomplishment in satisfying his lover.

His human lover who had just offered him the enormous gift of his own life's blood.

* * * *

Quinn woke slowly, becoming aware that his soft, warm covers had been replaced with something harder and cooler that blanketed his body from head to toe. Firm lips pressed against his shoulder while silky hair tickled his face. Something much warmer and unyielding rode the crease of his ass.

Alex. He thought it, then said it on a sigh. "Alex."

"Hmm. Sorry to wake you, love. I simply couldn't resist any longer."

Quinn's own cock would have stiffened at the confession if it hadn't been trapped between his body and the mattress. He wiggled his hips to create a gap, but his movement triggered Alex to press him more firmly. Quinn tried to protest his unfair confinement, except a giggle popped out rather than an admonishment. That silly sound morphed into a gasp when Alex shifted to push his dick inside Quinn's hole.

The rod slid in so easily, like a heated knife through soft butter. That thought reminded him of how he'd instigated this endless night of passion by riding Alex's lap. The makeshift lube had long been replaced by something made for the job. Once they'd both recovered from the explosive orgasm at the table, Alex had carried him into the bedroom. Quinn had no memory of it, though. He thought he'd must have passed out because his climax had been so intense.

The second and the third one had been no less so. *Was it because of the blood?*

Alex humped him with slow, shallow thrusts. His hole whispered mild complaints, having been used so thoroughly in such a short period of time. He ignored it. A little soreness in exchange for such exquisite pleasure was an easy trade to make. Being filled, stretched and claimed by Alex's cock felt more 'right' than anything he'd ever experienced before. He wondered how he could ever live without it now.

All while he kept fucking Quinn, Alex kissed and sucked the ridge of Quinn's shoulder and the base of his throat. The man did so love that part of him. When he scraped his teeth along the tendon of Quinn's neck, the small bite of pain caused him to arch into the body covering his. He clenched his fingers around the sheet beneath him. The pads of two fingers and a thumb protested, mildly. The nicks he'd made to bleed for his lover were closed already. Alex must have given him a salve to help them heal, although Quinn couldn't recall him doing so.

He only remembered how when the man had sucked the blood welling up each time, it had felt as if he was tugging on Quinn's cock instead. He'd understood why Mackie liked this kind of kinky game. It was surprisingly erotic. He'd made the decision to cut himself just to please Alex. Enjoying it himself hadn't figured into it but had been a wonderful surprise.

He shuddered as Alex's cock dragged past his prostate and he clenched his hole to keep the dick inside. Alex chuckled, the sound vibrating against Quinn's neck and down his spine. Then he thrust hard and deep and held still long enough to drive Quinn crazy. He clenched again in an undulating wave to taunt his lover into action. Alex reacted by driving home whatever bit of his cock there was left outside.

"Sweet boy. I set the pace, and I want this time to be slow so that I can savor every moment."

His breath was cool against Quinn's ear. Every inch of him was, except his dick. That hard piece of flesh was as hot as it was heavy—and long and thick. *God*. He loved Alex's cock. But he didn't like this teasingly slow fuck.

He bucked again, a feeble movement given Alex's weight and strength. "Not fair." He sounded petulant to his own ears and didn't care.

Alex chuckled once more. "Who said life is fair?"

Unclenching his fingers, he turned his hand, palm up. "Want another taste?"

"Oh, is that a bribe?"

"Will it work if I say yes?"

In answer, Alex slid his cock out and slammed it home again. Quinn cried out and trembled beneath his lover's weight. His own cock was still trapped and it ached with the need for attention.

"Please!" he begged now, desperate for more. It was as if his three previous orgasms in just a few hours hadn't happened. He craved pleasure, craved release.

With a quick movement that made Quinn's head spin, Alex grabbed his hips and pulled him onto his knees. The man's body split Quinn's legs wide, but at least now his dick was free. Leaning on one arm, he reached for the shaft and pumped.

For all his slowness before, Alex morphed into a frenzy of fucking. He drilled Quinn's ass with brutal thrusts. It was as if they were fucking for the first time that night, not the fourth. Quinn wasn't the only one with an out-of-control need. Alex claimed his body with the kind of fervor he might expect after a long separation, when they hadn't left each other's side for hours. It made him feel not just claimed but cherished.

They finished together—a duet of agonized cries, jerking limbs and a coating of warm, sticky cum over his hand. They ended up tangled, side-by-side, and with Alex's cock still embedded in Quinn's ass.

Alex nuzzled the top of Quinn's head. "Dearest boy, are you all right? I wasn't too rough, was I?"

Quinn snuggled back to lodge the dick firmly inside him. "It was perfect." He sighed.

Alex ghosted his fingers along Quinn's hip. "Oh, the resilience of youth." He pecked a kiss on his head. "I fear you're not to be trusted in this. There will be no more fucking tonight."

Quinn started to make a mewl of protest, but it morphed into a yawn, which only served to amuse Alex. "See? Now I've kept you up past your bedtime," he teased. He wrapped his arm around Quinn's waist. "Go to sleep."

Quinn clasped his hand over the man's larger one. "You didn't take any blood this time. Why not?"

A sigh ruffled his hair. "I don't want to be greedy. You've already sacrificed three fingertips. That's more than I could have hoped for you to do so early in our relationship — or ever, really."

Warmth flooded his insides at the casual mention that they were in a relationship and not simply friends with benefits. "I, um…wanted to do that for you. It was no big deal, not like letting you bite my neck or anything." Even as he said it, he wondered if he could take that next step — and soon.

"And I am touched beyond words. Such a humbling act of trust. I won't ask for more and I don't want you to think you need to give me more." Flexing his hips to drive his still-hard dick farther into Quinn's ass, he added, "I don't need blood to love what we have."

Quinn forced himself to ignore that word 'love' being bandied about. It didn't mean anything. People said it all the time. Loving what they did was no different from loving ice cream. It was just an expression, nothing more.

"I think, though, I enjoyed it, too," he confessed. "It made everything more intense somehow."

Alex drew slow circles around Quinn's navel. "Really? It affected you?" At his nod, Alex hummed. "Interesting. That's not always the case. My hu...my lovers don't always get anything out of it."

Sleep dragged at him and he couldn't quite stifle another yawn. This quiet, cozy talking in the dark was almost as good as the sex. "It felt like you were sucking the cum right out of me, along with the blood."

Alex chuckled. "Keep saying things like that, sweetheart, and I'm going to end up fucking you again."

"Okay." *Sweetheart.* The use of the simple endearment was somehow more intimate than any other pet names Alex had used.

"No." The man stilled his hand and brought it to sit right under Quinn's heart. "Go to sleep."

"Hmm." Quinn couldn't get more than that out, exhaustion dousing him like water.

"You're safe here with me. Nothing and no one can touch you."

As his mind shut down, Quinn had only a second to wonder why Alex felt the need to reassure him on that point. *Still, I do feel safe, so what does it matter?*

Chapter Ten

Wales

Dracul swirled the bottle of amber liquid, impressed despite his fury. "Hiding it in plain sight, pet. And here I thought I'd chosen you for your exquisite beauty and tight hole."

With one last quirk of his lips, he drew back his arm and flung the glass container at the fireplace. It shattered with a satisfying crash that reverberated around the room. Drops of the medicine dripped off the stone into the fire with a hiss. He strolled over to the bed, allowing the naked, kneeling boy tied to the posts to read his future in Dracul's eyes.

It wasn't going to be a good one.

Already that pretty face bore the marks of Dracul's fist. Blood dripped temptingly from the corner of petulant lips. Oh, yes, he'd underestimated the foolhardiness of this human. Dafydd had thought he could deceive him and had succeeded enough to enrage him. It would take all his discipline not to tear the boy limb-from-limb.

Grabbing a handful of the human's hair, he twisted it around his fist to draw the face up. He licked the drying blood with one long lap of his tongue. *Delicious.* The intoxicating taste of near-eternal youth mixed with fear was one reason why he would keep the boy alive. That, and he didn't want to have to turn another. Dafydd had proved fertile and capable of surviving a delivery. Nothing mattered more than increasing his ranks via his own seed.

"You thought you could cheat me of sons," he whispered into the trembling human's ear. "My poor nervous boy, always drinking your silly potion in order to calmly serve your master."

He bit the lobe to taste the blood and to make his point. "Did you think I would never wonder, never test the contents to see if somehow it was interfering with your fertility? Do you think you're clever? That you can outwit me?"

His eyes blurred for a moment as his anger surged. "You've been killing my seed — my sons!"

He roared into the pale face that now dripped with that ridiculous thing humans called tears. His fangs dropped. "I am going to fill your alien womb with as many sons as can fit, year after year. You will never know a moment when my seed isn't growing inside your pathetic body."

He grabbed the human's flaccid cock and balls, squeezing until those tears came faster and the boy screamed. "I will punish you first, of course." He let his tone drop to a more reasonable one, as if they were discussing nothing more than the weather. "Nothing to damage your fertility, just enough to remind you —

again — who owns you. I might cut all this off, finally. You don't need it. You're nothing more than a female now, anyway."

He yanked hard, just to hear another scream pass those swollen, bleeding lips. "You do this to yourself, you know. If only you'd been more accommodating to my needs. I saved your worthless life from the muck and misery you were mired in, gave you untold luxury and nearly endless youth and yet you repay my largess by defying me."

Dafydd stared back at him with a rebelliousness that showed through the fear. Dracul could almost admire him for it. "You are a monster! I would rather be dead and turned to dust than live a life under you. You didn't save me. You kidnapped me and raped me and twisted my body into something to serve you."

Dracul smiled. "You're never so beautiful as when you're angry, my dear. Let's see if I can keep that emotion boiling on the surface, shall I?"

The door to the bed chamber opened after a perfunctory knock, stifling any reply Dafydd might have made. Dracul hissed at the interruption. His irritation abated somewhat at the sight of Petru. That man was wise enough to only bother him with something important.

Petru's gaze flicked to the sight of Dafydd before settling back on Dracul. He bowed slightly. "Forgive the intrusion, sir. I have an update from Adrian."

Oh, yes, business before pleasure. "What is it?"

"He reports that Alexandru seems to have taken a new human to his bed." He licked his top teeth. "At least, the boy is living in his club."

"Hmm. Doesn't really mean anything. That soft-hearted idiot always did like to pick up strays. Still, killing his last pet did take him out of my way for a time. Alex's weakness disgusts me, yet I can't be too bothered by it, given how vulnerable it makes him.

"Tell Adrian to take any opportunity he finds to make the boy one of his victims, although he needn't adjust his timetable to do it. I want him to continue my campaign to bring Alex's new adopted city to its knees. I assume that he's causing havoc already?"

"Yes, sir. As always, it's easy to send the humans into mindless panic. They're calling him the vampire killer. Some who aspire to be like him are even making his latest dumping ground something of a shrine."

Dracul chuckled. "It has ever been so. They do not understand us, but they recognize our superiority." He grabbed Dafydd's chin with a brutal grip. "Some envy us, as they should, and all fear us — again, as they should."

He pressed hard enough to make his dear little pet cry out. "A very foolish few think they can outsmart and defeat us."

He tsked and briefly considered crushing the jawbone in his grasp. But no, he had uses for the boy's mouth, and humans took too long to recover or were too easily killed. Maybe someday, once he had an army of sons behind him, he would allow himself the pleasure of taking this upstart human apart one bit at a time before draining him dry.

"You have your orders," he reminded Petru without taking his eyes off Dafydd. "Now go."

"Yes, sir."

He dismissed the man from his thoughts and concentrated instead on the task at hand. "Where shall I start? Hmm?"

Leaning in, he inhaled deeply, the scent of fear and blood making him hard. "You won't leave this bed until you are breeding. Even then, I won't let you leave this room ever again. And don't think you'll have a chance to cheat me out of my sons by hurting yourself. I won't allow that. If I have to keep you tied up, I will make sure you deliver every brat I get in you."

He could see from the expression that flashed across the human's face that he'd been thinking along those lines.

Dracul shook his head. "Oh, no, my dear. You will not escape me or my plans so easily." He pressed his lips against the pulsing beat at the base of the boy's throat. "Someday, I'll reward all your suffering by ending it — permanently."

With that promise made, he sank his fangs deep into the salty flesh. The scream washed over him, making him smile around the bite. He closed his eyes and drank — and drank and drank.

* * * *

Boston

The opening strains of Beethoven's Fifth Symphony had Quinn jerking awake. He would have slid to his knees if Alex hadn't kept him in place with his hand pressed against Quinn's naked ass. The man was equally nude, his magnificent and pale body visible in the muted light of the bedroom.

"What's wrong, Kitty?" Alex barked into his phone.

At the same time, he lowered his hand to cup Quinn's ass and slid one of his long fingers down the crack to tease the puckered ring. It softened under the gentle assault, ready for more penetration. It didn't seem to matter that it was also a bit sore from the energetic fucking throughout the night. Quinn's dick started to fill. But for it being mashed against the mattress, it would have fully hardened. *God.* He'd never expected to be this responsive to another man's touch.

Alex's grimaced as he listened to whatever the bartender was saying. "Tell them we'll be there in fifteen minutes."

Damn, so much for morning sex.

Alex stilled his fingers. "Then they'll have to continue to be impatient. I don't care if they are the FBI, the CIA or the entire Joint Chiefs of Staff. They have invaded my home at the ungodly hour of — whatever the fuck time it is. They can damn well wait."

He ended the call with a flick of his thumb. "I liked the way telephones used to be. You could slam the receiver to make a point." He tossed his phone on the nightstand. "These tiny computers just aren't the same."

Before Quinn could ask him what was going on, Alex rolled him over, leaned in and planted an enthusiastic kiss on his lips. The man smelled and tasted wonderfully spicy. Quinn doubted very much he was anywhere near as palatable.

Alex pushed the hair away from Quinn's face. "I'm afraid we're going to have to take a very quick and sex-free shower."

"What's going on?"

Alex grimaced. "The FBI is downstairs. They want to interview us about the Crowell murder." He left the bed with the grace of a cat and held out his hand.

Taking it, Quinn said, "I don't understand. The cops already asked us a bunch of questions."

"Yes, well, it seems the murder is now being treated as a serial killer case, so the feds have been brought in."

Quinn followed him into the huge marble bathroom. It was like bathing in the Taj Mahal. "Duncan's off the case?"

Alex went to start the dual shower heads. "It appears so." He turned to smile reassuringly at him. "Don't worry. This is a nuisance, nothing more. I'm sure Emil will have a wonderful breakfast waiting for us."

Quinn returned the look, pretending he wasn't worried. The truth was that this whole thing freaked him out. With Alex by his side, though, he knew he was safe, just like the man had said when he'd drifted off to sleep.

He washed in perfunctory fashion, although Alex's scrubbing his back was a nice touch, despite the situation. Hair still wet and wearing his clothes from the previous night, he went to the first floor with Alex. The man had only bothered to slip on black silk pajama bottoms and nothing more, as if he were entertaining people at an orgy. He'd twisted his own wet hair into a messy man-bun.

He appeared frighteningly sexy, totally unconcerned and rather lethal, given his ginormous proportions and thickly layered muscles, like a gorgeous Frankenstein's monster. Studying the man, Quinn had no trouble imagining how easily he could overpower another with only his bare hands. He worried a bit that the FBI would see the same thing, and unlike the local cops, keep pushing and prodding to find a reason to put the killings on Alex.

When Alex took Quinn's hand in his, however, the press of his cool flesh settled Quinn's nerves. Even if the man was some kind of monster, at least he seemed to be *his*. With Alex standing guard, no one would ever get near him, and knowing he had that kind of support allayed much of his fear. Even while living with his family, he'd never felt quite safe, probably because he'd always known that his true self wouldn't be welcome there.

They took the elevator to the ground floor of the club where the police interrogation over Crowell's murder was being replayed. This time, the two people waiting to question him were harder-edged than the Boston cops. That was the first thing he noticed because of the tableau they set.

Duncan leaned against the bar, nursing a cup of coffee while his partner sat farther down, shoveling in breakfast with intense concentration. Both of the men looked almost at home. The FBI agents, in contrast, sat at the same table as the previous interviews with nothing in front of them other than portfolios. They didn't even have glasses of water, as if accepting any hospitality would compromise their integrity or something.

Kitty ignored everyone, polishing her bar top at the far end with a vicious amount of energy. Val stood near her, clad in his usual T-shirt and jeans, arms crossed. He was still as a statue and gave off an Angel of Death vibe that should have made all these outsiders quake in their shoes.

Alex squeezed Quinn's hand as they stepped off the elevator and that simple gesture reassured him once more that he was not alone. Even though he'd known this man for less than a week, he trusted him completely. Maybe it was naïve of him, or it could have been the sex clouding his mind and judgment, but the feeling was there and strong. Being Alex Stelalux's 'boy' gave him new-found confidence and courage, too. He felt as if he could handle anything. Squaring his shoulders, he headed toward the table, staying by Alex's side.

Alex nodded his head in the direction of the cops as he and Quinn passed the bar. "Gentlemen. Delighted to see you again."

Duncan quirked his lips and took another slug of coffee. Anderson just waved his fork before plowing back into his food. The feds slid out from the booth and held up their badges. The obvious leader was a middle-aged Asian woman. She didn't crack a smile as they approached, nor did her partner, a fresh-faced young man with a brush cut and 'ex-military' written all over him. Normally, they would have intimidated the hell out of Quinn, but knowing they were going up against Alex, he almost felt sorry for them.

"Mr. Stelalux, I'm special agent Cynthia Chin. This is Agent Jacob Kaplan. We'd like to ask you a few questions."

Alex gave the woman the type of smile that would either cause one to melt or freeze, depending on whether Alex was out to seduce or terrorize. Quinn recognized this as being the latter. Alex was not hiding his displeasure. *Did the feds catch the vibe?* The woman's expression hardened, so that would be a *yes*. To her credit, she wasn't showing any signs of being cowed.

Stopping a couple of feet away, Alex dismissed the show of badges with a lazy wave of his free hand. "So I've been told. Please forgive my dishabille. We were asleep when you arrived." Quinn's heart did a slow roll at the casual mention of 'we' and its obvious implication.

Chin stuck her ID back into her pocket. "I'm sorry. I guess club people keep different hours, but we're racing against the clock. There's a vicious serial killer out there and we're trying to catch him before he strikes again. I'm sure you can understand the urgency."

"Of course." Alex gestured toward the booth. "Shall we?"

"Yes, but I'd like to question Mr. Cooper first." She pinned Quinn with an assessing look.

He instinctively moved closer to Alex, who let go of his hand in order to circle his waist and bring him flush against his side.

"I understand." Alex's tone had turned icy. "He needs to eat."

Chin did a poor job of hiding her impatience. "This won't take long, and I don't want a crowd in here during questioning. We really should be speaking to each of you separately."

"No. We stay together, and he *needs to eat*." He pressed his fingers into Quinn's side when he started to open his mouth to reassure him that he wasn't going to pass out from lack of food any time soon. He understood the unspoken message and kept quiet.

Now, Chin did let her irritation show. "Mr. Stelalux…"

"On second thought, perhaps I should call my lawyer before we start answering your questions voluntarily? Given that we've already provided Duncan and Anderson a full account of the incident with Crowell and our whereabouts during both of these unfortunate murders, I can't help but wonder if your renewed interest in us demands a more robust defense."

Oh, wow. The woman clearly didn't like how Alex had just raised the tension level closer to Defcon One. They stood for a few seconds, staring at each other. Quinn could have told the woman she was waging an unwinnable war. He knew Alex that well by now. The man could not be intimidated, and he protected what was his. That included him.

"How about I go get Quinn something to eat from Emil?" This from Duncan, and that simple offer ended the contest of wills.

"Thank you, Sergeant Duncan." Alex turned his head to nod at the man. "I appreciate it."

Without further discussion, Alex led Quinn over to the booth. He slid in first and gently tugged Quinn after him without ever breaking contact. They sat hip-to-hip with Alex's arm draped over Quinn's shoulders. He felt snug, and it would have been wonderful but for the two stern-faced people sitting opposite them. Military boy took notes while his boss made a show of searching through her files.

She gave Quinn a smile that was likely intended to be disarming. It just made him cuddle closer to Alex's strong, cool body. He tried to give her back a neutral expression, but it probably came off as more like a scowl. He wasn't very good at hiding his emotions.

The woman gave up and went back to no-nonsense. "You're Quinn Timothy Cooper of Saginaw, Michigan?"

"Yes, ma'am."

"You're far from home." He didn't respond to that observation because he couldn't imagine what she wanted him to say. It wasn't as if he'd left home because he'd wanted to. "You just turned eighteen recently."

"Yes, ma'am." Alex rubbed his shoulder with a light, soothing touch, reminding Quinn that he was there and that he wasn't alone anymore to face problems like this.

Her gaze slanted briefly to Alex. "You look younger."

He shrugged because again, *so what?* Was her point that Alex must be a child-molester because he was fucking someone who appeared young? And did that mean he must also be a serial killer? If this was any indication of how the interview was to be conducted, he was going to get pissed off pretty fast.

Fortunately, Duncan cut in by bringing him a tall glass of orange juice and a plate of pancakes, sausages and scrambled eggs. "Emil says juice first, then you can have coffee later." The cop delivered the message with a shrug.

Quinn smiled at the man. "Thanks." Then he reached for the juice, suddenly thirsty. The frosty glass felt nice and cool against his sore fingertips. He gulped a third of it before placing it on the table.

Duncan remained standing nearby, staring at Quinn for a few seconds before looking at Alex with a narrowed gaze. Or maybe that was his imagination, because a moment later, the man nodded at them and wandered back to the bar.

Alex nudged him. "Go on and eat, sweetheart. I'm sure Agent Chin won't mind your answering her questions with a full mouth."

Chin gave the impression that she wanted to argue that point, yet merely nodded. "I'd like to go back to the night when Mr. Crowell allegedly assaulted you."

Picking up his fork, Quinn speared some eggs. "Sure, what do you want to know?"

The next fifteen minutes or so were boring. That was all, a steady annoying itch of questions and answers.

He found he didn't mind so much because the food was delicious and Alex never stopped touching him, a constant reminder that he had his back in the literal and figurative sense of the word. Aware of the fact that his lover didn't have any breakfast in front of him, Quinn cut a piece of pancake and held it to Alex's lips. With a smile that left Quinn's insides feeling goopier than the syrup on his plate, Alex inclined his head and accepted the offering. For a second, Chin and everyone else faded into the background as they gazed into each other's eyes.

A loud throat-clearing broke the spell and Quinn returned his attention to the FBI woman, but he continued to offer Alex bits of his food. There was more than he could comfortably eat, and sharing the meal with his lover felt intimate, especially because they were doing it front of others.

Halfway through both the meal and the interview, Duncan returned with an iced mocha latte, courtesy of Emil. Quinn grinned his thanks to the cop, who again lingered a couple of seconds longer than seemed necessary. Poor guy probably felt left out. It couldn't be easy to start an important case only to have someone else come in and trample all over the ground he'd already covered. By the time Chin finished her questions, Quinn and Alex had devoured the food. He sat back nursing his coffee while Alex continued to pet his shoulder.

The federal agent barely paused after thanking Quinn in a tone that conveyed just how little she thought of his help before turning a glacial stare on Alex.

"Mr. Stelalux, you're a Romanian?"

"By birth, yes. I had the great honor of becoming a naturalized American citizen a few years ago."

"Congratulations. You immigrated with Horatiu Stelalux, Valeriu Stelalux and Emil Stelalux, your uncle and cousins?" When Alex gave a curt nod, she continued with a moue of her mouth. "The exact bloodline is a bit murky, record-wise."

Alex stiffened slightly, almost imperceptibly. "Back in the old country, the family tie is all that matters. The specifics, not so much. Anyone older than you are is uncle or aunt, and those who are your contemporaries are cousins if they're not siblings. We don't worry at all about the technicalities of it."

"I see." She made some note in her portfolio. "What part of Romania do you come from?"

"The Carpathians, a small village that you've never heard of, I'm sure."

She parted her lips in what might be considered a smile. "Even so, for the record?"

Out of the corner of his eye, Quinn saw Alex also smile, except his made him look like a shark. "It's already part of the record — my immigration record."

Chin sat staring at Alex, as if she could force him into saying more through her force of will alone. It didn't work. It was never going to, not given how commanding and confident Alex was. They sat in awkward silence for a few seconds — awkward for the woman, that was. Quinn had the impression that Alex would have sat there in silence all day if need be.

Finally, with a huff, Chin moved on. "What did you do there? For work, I mean."

"We were farmers."

"All of you?"

"Yes, our extended family has been farming and raising livestock in that part of the world for centuries."

Chin smiled widely enough to show her straight teeth. "Forgive me, but you don't put one in mind much of a farmer or a shepherd. You're all so unusually tall, for one thing, that it's hard to picture you in such a bucolic setting. I guess I've always thought of the Romanian people as being shorter."

This time, Alex didn't give any indication of annoyance. "You know, I've always believed the same about Chinese people. Then I heard of Shandong Province. Have you? The native population puts out a fair number of basketball players, I believe. Those types of misconceptions make racial profiling inherently problematic, don't you think?"

Chin's smile dropped to a frown, her frustration and annoyance at being called out at her own game clearly written on her face. *What did she expect?* This wasn't some battle of wits. It wasn't a battle at all, more like a slaughter. Alex was going to sit there, batting her questions away as if they were pesky flies before sending them careening right back into this woman's face.

And all the while, a vicious killer stalked the city, likely picking out his next victim. The FBI was wasting its time focusing on Alex and his family. But Quinn wasn't going to worry about any of that. Snuggling back into Alex's warm embrace, he focused on the delightful and new way his body ached. Reliving the memories of his latest all-nighter was far more interesting than what was playing out in front of him.

This was what it meant to be well-fucked and he intended to bask in the pleasure for as long as he could. *Why not?* Alex wanted him, at least for now, and the club was a kind of haven. His family couldn't hurt him here, nor could the crazy killer. Cocooned by Alex's strength, he allowed himself to imagine that nothing could touch him.

He was utterly safe.

* * * *

Chin and her hulking lap dog snapped sunglasses on the moment they stepped outside into the bright, sunny day. Coupled with their severe, dark suits, it was if they were trying to perpetuate a stereotype.

"Well, that was a waste of time," the woman huffed.

Trey didn't even try to hide his smirk. "I did try to warn you, ma'am. These people don't intimidate easily. If you push them, they push back harder. And while they're arrogant assholes, they seem far too smart to dump a body in their own backyard. Plus, their alibis for the second murder checked out."

Chin turned a stony face at him. "Yes, sergeant, I'm well aware of your assessment, but my job doesn't allow me the luxury of taking local law enforcement's views as gospel."

Oh, ouch! He held back a sneer and retort with effort.

Her subordinate turned his stony face in their direction. "You seemed awfully cozy with them." *Ah, the lap dog speaks.* "Making sure the kid was nice and well-fed," he added, as if his comment hadn't been self-evident.

Trey let his irritation show with the pup, because Christ, he had boxers older than this kid. "Stelalux and his whole clan there are very protective of what's theirs. He was like that with Cooper even before they were obviously fucking. Pardon me, ma'am," he added for form's sake. "You weren't going to get anywhere until the boy got some food. That's all."

Chin clucked her tongue. "Cooper is a distraction. The real issue is that family. They are obviously not *farmers*. I suspect they are involved with organized crime in some way, possibly Russian."

"Ma'am, there is no evidence of that, other than the fact they are the biggest, scariest guys I've ever seen in my career."

She turned her hidden eyes in his direction. "They also own a club, the perfect place to launder money." She huffed. "But, I suspect all that has nothing to do with the unsub, not given the second victim and the showcasing of the corpse. Organized crime fares best by keeping a low profile. Now, if you'll excuse us, we have to meet with the coroner."

"Good luck," Karl chimed in. "I think you'll find that the poor bastard died from exsanguination." The feds didn't even bother to respond. They just turned in lockstep and walked away.

"I don't think they like us, Trey."

"Yeah? Well, they know the feeling is fucking mutual," he swore. "If they'd only keep us in the loop. I mean, I get that they have jurisdiction and I'll admit that they are better equipped to handle something like this. But I mean, come on. This is our turf, and coming in hot was never going to be the right approach with Stelalux."

"Yeah, he's the original cool customer, and he all but peed circles around the kid."

"He protects what's his," Trey repeated then paced away. The kernel of worry that had planted itself inside his head early in the interview wouldn't leave him.

"What's eating you?" Karl knew him well.

"It's the kid. Quinn," he clarified. "Although, the redhead, Mackie, is probably also in deep already. He seems better equipped to handle himself."

"Come on. You're not into that 'too young' shtick of Chin's, are you?"

"Kind of, but it's more than that. She's not off-base about the idea of a syndicate. The signs are there, and if it is the Russian mafia, the kid could be in danger just from hanging around his new boyfriend."

Karl shrugged. "Yeah, okay, except we can't save everyone. He's an adult. His first mistake may have been becoming a stripper. That can be a dangerous job."

"Go-go boy."

"Same dif."

"Maybe." Trey shook his head. "It's not only that." He took a deep breath to sort out whether he truly wanted to tell his partner his concerns. *Yeah, what the hell.* "Did you see his fingers?"

"Whose, Stelalux'? Sure, they're weirdly long. Same thing for the whole family. Some kind of genetic thing, I guess. There's probably a lot of inbreeding in the mountains."

Trey shook his head. "No, the boy's."

"Nah, I was too far away to see much of anything."

Trey gave him a wry grin. "Stuffing your face at the bar."

"Sure. Why not? I didn't have anything else to do and that Emil guy is a wizard with food."

"No argument there. When I brought Quinn his breakfast, I saw his hand as he held the glass of juice. I made sure to bring the coffee so I could get another look."

Opening his fist, he tapped the tip of his forefinger, middle finger and thumb. "There were marks in all three places. Not big, maybe the kind of thing that happens to diabetics when they test their blood."

Now, he had Karl's attention. "Maybe he is? Diabetic, I mean."

"Could be." He'd thought of that, and yet he couldn't remember seeing anything like it in the previous interview. "Tough to swing around a pole like that."

"I guess, but what else could it be?" The man paused, made a face, then swore. "Jesus, you're not thinking Stelalux is sucking his blood, are you?"

"It's a fetish club as well as a gay one. We've been operating under the belief that the unsub has a vampire kink."

Hitching up his pants, Karl walked away, shaking his head and muttering. Trey followed him and pulled abreast. "I thought we just agreed Stelalux is too smart to shit where he works, eats, sleeps and fucks?" Karl asked.

"We did. I still believe that. I'm not saying he's the killer. I'm not saying any of them are."

"So, what *are* you saying?"

"I think they might know the killer."

"If they do, then why not rat him out? They don't need us and now the feds breathing down their necks, especially if they are mob-connected."

"Maybe the killer is part of the mob. They could be holding out on us because they're trying to track the guy themselves—silence him before we get our hands on him and start hearing tales we're not supposed to."

"Okay, it plays, I guess. So, what do you suggest?"

This was the tricky part. He stopped and pulled his partner to the side to let a pedestrian pass them. "We keep an eye on them. Let's see if any of the Stelalux boys lead us to the killer."

Karl raised his eyebrows. "We're off the case. You know that, right?"

Shoving his hands in his front pockets, he gave the man a shrug. "Sure. I'm not suggesting we spend department time on this. We both knock off at six today, given that we *are* off the case. Nothing says we can't hang out here afterward."

"You're not planning on telling Chin and her wonder dog?"

"Nope. No point. They don't think we know anything useful. We're just underfoot."

Karl grinned evilly. "I like it."

Trey clasped his hand on his partner's shoulder. "I had a feeling you would."

Chapter Eleven

Alex splashed more Maker's Mark in his glass without looking. His attention was focused on Quinn, as it had been all evening. *Damn.* When had he ever stayed in one spot while his club was in full swing? *Never.* As the owner, he'd always glad-handed about, making newbies feel welcome and chatting with the veterans. It allowed him to keep his finger on the pulse of the place, not unlike what he'd done while captaining a ship.

Now, he was rooted to the spot at the end of the bar closest to Quinn's little stage. Every man who approached him for a bit of conversation was an irritating distraction. Every man who circled the boy, offering him smiles and tips, was someone with a death wish. It took all his well-honed discipline to keep from dropping his fangs, hissing and clawing at any man that got between him and his boy.

My boy.

It had happened, despite his intention to the contrary. He'd become emotionally attached to another human in a way that could not be easily dismissed. He wasn't going to use the word 'love' — such a human emotion. His species didn't even have a word for that one, although with his experience on this planet to guide him, he knew that his people avoided acknowledging something they felt, anyway. Harry would say that it was the ancient hive mentality coloring their views, even with evolution changing their society.

No matter. He lived on this planet now, among humans, and regardless of what he said from time to time to his people, he didn't believe they would ever be rescued. The new queen and her court would have already added hundreds of males to the ranks of soldiers. Would they still be fretting over the loss of a few dozen? *Hardly.*

This was his home now, and with Dracul on a tear again, it scared the ever-loving shit out of Alex to tie himself to someone new that the man could rip from him. Yet living alone with only occasional sex partners and liters of banked blood to keep him company was becoming intolerable. *Had* become so, even though he'd ignored his own feelings. He desperately wanted someone in his life to share everything with, including his bed, including his need for blood. As stupid and as frightening as it was, he'd already come to need Quinn. It was selfish of him to keep the boy close and put him in harm's way. He should toss him out for his own good, and still...

He watched a club member tuck money into Quinn's G-string, the man's hand lingering longer than necessary. It stayed on the boy's slender hip while Quinn undulated in graceful waves that showed how quickly he'd acquired the moves of a go-go boy. The man said something. Quinn bent to hear better, smiled and, with a slight shake of his head, straightened to swing around the pole.

The man walked away in obvious disappointment, but Alex grinned at the sight. He took a long swallow of his bourbon, relishing the burn down his throat. Quinn was refusing to provide lap dances. It was the only explanation of why man after man kept leaving the stage with that look on his face, like his mommy had refused to buy him an ice cream cone. In his own way, Quinn was establishing a type of monogamy that spoke volumes about how the human perceived their burgeoning relationship. It was a risk, keeping him from much-needed money for something Alex had given him little reason to believe was long term.

Alex would have to remedy that tonight. In the face of his lover's courage, he could do no less.

"He's improved rather quickly, hasn't he?" This from Harry, who came to stand by Alex's side. That was strange. The man usually didn't come into the club area, being devoted to his husband and dismissive of the excesses of all vices practiced by the club members.

Alex tore his gaze from Quinn. "Is something wrong?"

"Ah, no," the man replied with a negligent wave. "I could use a drink, though."

Another unusual thing. It made Alex frown with concern as the older man reached behind the bar and snagged a glass for himself. He poured a healthy portion of the bourbon and grimaced around a big swig of it.

"*Harry?*"

"It's nothing." With a sigh, he leaned against the bar. "I simply needed a short break from domestic bliss. Lucien and I have decided to keep Demi inside for the foreseeable future — no leaving the building until this latest nonsense by Dracul has played out. The boy is not happy."

"I wouldn't imagine so, but he should be safe enough during the day, especially if one of you is with him."

"No." Harry's tone brooked no argument. "Lucien would be no match for one of us, and I'm getting too old to go against a young buck like Adrian or any other of Dracul's traitorous men. Demi is too precious to risk. And, of course, for him this ancient war is just that — old, outdated and stupid. He doesn't understand the evil Dracul has perpetrated on this planet. It's all too academic for him, the same way history is for many human teenagers."

Alex studied the contents of his glass. "I'm sure it must be very hard for him being a hybrid — and a secret one at that."

Breeding with humans had been something that he'd prohibited for a long time for his men. He'd harbored hope for centuries that they'd be rescued. There was no reason to complicate their lives with human entanglements and offspring. It meant a whole new group that had to be hidden away and vowed to secrets that could get them all killed. The risk that breeding had presented to the humans was enough of a reason to keep his men in check for a long time. No one on his side of the divide had wanted to join their lives with someone only to kill them with childbirth.

Then Dracul, who held no such compunctions, had shown the way forward. The relatively modern practice of cesarean sections coupled with antibiotics made everything safer. He knew that Harry had agonized over the decision to change his adored Lucien into a breeder, but the human had been sure of his desire from the beginning. Demi was the product of a long and loving relationship. And, while his fathers doted on the boy and never spoke of regrets where Alex could hear them, they did face a daunting task raising their son.

The older Demi got, the more rebellious he'd become and he carried all of Harry's traits compared to Lucien's — too intelligent, too strong and too much in need of blood to be a human. Soon, they would have to accept that he was becoming a full-fledged member of the cadre, a soldier in this fight against Dracul. Risking the boy would be hard for Harry and Alex, as well, which brought him back to thoughts of Quinn.

Can I form a relationship with this human? Could Quinn ever accept what I truly am? And with all that, would Quinn agree to be changed, to become a breeder for my seed? Do I even want him to?

"I guess this is the place where we're all going to brood tonight." With that observation, Val joined them. He already had a glass of clear liquid in his hand. Vodka, no doubt — the man's drink of choice when he was going for the burn and not the taste.

"What's eating you?" Harry asked before taking another swallow.

"Other than my inability to find Adrian?" Val jutted his chin toward the stage opposite Quinn's. "The usual."

Mackie was practically standing on his head, his half-mop of red hair sweeping the floor of the stage. Next to Quinn, he had the largest group of patrons enraptured by his show. Even a human could see from this distance the bruises marring the boy's pert ass.

Alex narrowed his gaze. "You've been playing hard with him."

Val shot back half his drink before answering. "Yeah. I'm frustrated, and frankly, scared about this new front opening in the war. I was just getting comfortable with our lives here and was stupidly hoping we'd heard the last of you-know-who." Grabbing the bottle, Val refilled his glass before it was even empty. "Mackie hasn't safeworded, but I'm beginning to think he's trying to be accommodating past his comfort level."

Alex could well believe that. Mackie worshipped Val, probably because he was the first man to treat the boy with respect and kindness. It would be easy to exploit that devotion. The human had taken to Val's predilection for bondage and discipline as if born to it. He'd readily accepted blood play, as well. Alex suspected that the truth about Val's nature wouldn't faze the boy in the least, if Val ever decided to reveal it.

He hadn't, not yet—perhaps not ever. Val had a strong moral compass. He'd never wavered from his duty to follow Alex's orders, either. Nevertheless, he'd strung this boy along for too much time. Even Alex could tell that Mackie saw 'forever' in his relationship with Val, and yet Alex also understood why Val hesitated to make that life-long commitment. The loyal man had taken a chance once already and the loss had brought him to his knees in a way no physical injury ever would.

Val drained his glass a second time in one long gulp. "I'm thinking now's a good time to cut ties with the boy."

Harry grunted in surprise. "Why? He's perfect for you."

Val grimaced. "Maybe, but I'm not perfect for him. All I can offer him is pain—and not the kind I deliver in the playroom." His grip tightened enough to make Alex worry he'd break the glass.

Wrestling it from Val's fingers, he put it on the bar along with his own. "Now is not the best time to make any major decisions. Our emotions are too heightened."

"Is that why you got involved with that one?" Val asked with a toss of his head in Quinn's direction. "You don't think taking a human to your private bed constitutes a major life decision?" There was more insubordination lacing his words than Alex had heard in over a thousand years.

"Point taken," he replied with more testiness than he'd intended. "I'm obviously not the one to give advice in this arena."

"Sorry, boss." Val was instantly contrite. "I'm just not good with this stuff. I'm better at pounding guys into the ground. I guess I'm looking for reassurance that you'll have my back on what I decide."

Alex also regretted his response. "Of course."

"I want to make sure he's taken care of. You know, money-wise."

"Whatever you want," Alex was quick to reassure him.

Val nodded. "Yeah, well, I haven't quite decided."

Harry sighed and added his glass to the others. "On that note, I suppose I should return to my quarters and the bliss that is my family life. Good night, gentlemen."

They murmured in return, then Val left a second later. He'd schooled his expression back to no-nonsense bouncer. Alone again, Alex leaned against the bar and returned his gaze to Quinn. The large clock hanging on the wall told him that the boy was due for a break in less than fifteen minutes. Given that he'd refused lap dance requests, he'd be available for a little quality time with Alex. Val wasn't the only one who needed to de-stress. As he waited for the minutes to tick by, Alex worked out a nice fantasy that he hoped Quinn would be interested in.

He didn't have to elbow his way through the crowd still lingering around Quinn's stage at the appointed hour. Humans tended to give him a wide berth and the club members were no different. It was moments like this that gave him a glimpse into what drove Dracul in his quest for dominion. Being superior to humans was seductive. It took effort to not feed that beast lurking within him.

Except in a case like this where he was going to claim what he considered his, he didn't even try to bank the power humans instinctively felt and feared. Quinn was in the process of accepting last minute tips and declining last-minute invitations when Alex arrived at the stage. The boy smiled brightly then squeaked in alarm as Alex grabbed him by the waist and carried him away.

"Alex! What are you doing?" Quinn tried to pull away from his embrace. "I'm covered in sweat."

"Yes, I know." He inhaled deeply, savoring the boy's scent—a combination of some kind of body spray and the natural tang humans exuded.

Quinn chuckled. "I'm going to ruin your million-dollar Gucci shirt."

"It's Armani, and I didn't spend nearly that much on it." He took the stairs two at a time, not really caring how much attention he was drawing.

"Oh, I stand corrected, but my point remains." Even as he said it, though, Quinn ceased his squirming and wrapped his arms around Alex's neck. "Where are we headed?"

"You'll see. I know you have time because you seemed to turn away all requests for lap dances."

Quinn snuggled in closer. "How did you know that? Were you watching me?" The tickling of his warm breath against Alex's neck hardened his cock.

He flicked his gaze into those bright blue eyes. "Always."

Quinn's pupils blew open in seconds and his lips parted on quickening breath. A peek at the boy's crotch confirmed that he, too, was aroused. Alex quickened his pace, entered the room he'd reserved and kicked the door shut.

Quinn glanced around. "One of the playrooms?"

"Mmm." Having waited for hours to give in to his urge, he leaned down to kiss the boy. Quinn met his mouth with. By the time they broke for air, Alex had turned the boy vertical. He cupped the naked, sweaty ass and mashed their pelvises together.

Quinn clutched at Alex's biceps. "Do you want to, um, play?"

He showered the human's swollen lips with a few light kisses. "Only a little and only if you want. I mostly want to fuck you, and I'm afraid if I take you upstairs, we'll never leave."

Quinn's grip tightened and he chuckled. "Oh, well…" He swallowed hard and his pulse rate sped up. "Fucking sounds awesome — and maybe a little bondage?"

Alex smiled at him. "My very thought, dearest boy."

He set him on his feet, and hooking his thumbs in the thong, shoved it off. Money went flying all over, but neither of them paid much attention to it. The sight of Quinn's erect dick, so hard and weeping already for him, derailed Alex's plans for a moment. He grabbed the hot shaft, eliciting a satisfying gasp, while he kissed Quinn senseless again. When, once more, they stood gasping for breath, he herded the boy over to the spanking bench dominating the room. It was set particularly high, intended to make it easier for Val to play without having to bend over or squat. It stood at the perfect height for impaling an upturned human ass.

He twirled Quinn around to face it. "I want you to kneel on the lower riser with your legs spread, bend over the top one, and put your hands by your head so that I can cuff them. Do you think you can do that for me?"

The pulse at the base of Quinn's neck beat a rapid tattoo. *Excitement or fear?* Such a fine line, but the boy's response to his request would tell the tale.

Quinn nodded once and pulled away. After only a brief hesitation, he climbed onto the bench, putting himself into position without any noticeable hesitation. He laid his cheek on the padded bench and stared across the room. He looked like the quintessential sacrificial virgin, offering his ass to Alex's gaze and his cock. It was breathtaking in its simple show of trust.

"Good boy," he murmured before tearing off his clothes.

Quinn's gaze shifted to watch him and the boy rolled his hips in a telling way. Alex sauntered to his side and ran a soothing palm down the taut globes of Quinn's ass. He patted it gently in reassurance before grabbing the nearest padded cuff, then he wrapped it around Quinn's wrist.

"I'm going to make this loose enough that you can slip free if you need to, all right?" When Quinn just nodded, Alex walked over to the other side, careful to keep touching the human in a constant show of care. "If I do anything you don't like, you say 'red'. I'll stop immediately, understand?"

Another nod and a sigh. "I trust you, Alex."

You shouldn't.

The stray thought caught him by surprise. He was worried that this boy was too ready to believe the best in him — in anyone, perhaps — even after the betrayal he'd weathered. It scared the shit out of Alex, so much so that his dick started to flag. He stroked it after securing the second cuff and mentally chastised himself for being so easily spooked. He'd promised Quinn a good time and he wasn't going to let worry about Dracul or anything else stop him.

His dick didn't need a lot of coaxing to stiffen. As he went to grab some lube and a condom, he continued with languid strokes until he needed to stop or risk blowing before he got inside Quinn. This was not going to be any kind of slow lovemaking. He'd watched the boy for far too long to do anything other than basic prep followed by a hard fuck.

He rolled the condom onto his cock and slicked it before squirting a healthy dollop on two fingers. Quinn waited patiently for him, his labored breathing assuring Alex that the boy was as eager as he was. He placed the lube on the top bench where Quinn could see it, a reassurance and a clue that things were going to get intense very fast.

With his clean hand, he patted that delightful rump while he pressed his slick fingers against the puckered ring. It opened for him with little effort, additional testament to how aroused the boy already was. Alex easily slid the fingers in and as deep as he could send them. He thrust a few times while scissoring them to loosen the hole. It took very few passes before the channel relaxed. Then he crooked his fingers to stroke Quinn's prostate, and the way the boy jerked and gasped was tremendously satisfying.

So was the whimper that came on the heels of Alex pulling out. He smiled then grabbed the lube to squirt more onto three fingers before sliding those in. Quinn groaned and thrust back to meet the invasion. His hole clenched in silent invitation for Alex to...what? Go faster and deeper or replace them with his cock?

He decided it was the latter — or maybe that was his dick calling the shots. *Whatever.* With the speed of his species, he replaced his fingers with his rod. He was buried to the hilt before Quinn drew his next breath. They both groaned and trembled. Alex's own lack of restraint was both surprising and disturbing. He stood for a few seconds with his fingers grasping Quinn's hips to steady his stance and regain control. If he let go, he could hurt his boy, and that would never do. He was better than that — or at least he'd used to be. Quinn was throwing him off-balance in more ways than one.

Once he felt he could continue safely, he started thrusting, slow and shallow at first with a nice long drag out until all but the head of his cock remained buried inside Quinn's grasping channel. That was followed by a steady balls-deep impalement. He managed to repeat pulling out and driving back in for a few passes before Quinn's ever-needier whining and his own impatience forced him to pick up the pace. Soon, he was drilling that tight ass with fast, hard strokes.

Quinn moaned and writhed with increasing fervor. His fingers were clenched as tightly as his hole and he jerked at the cuffs holding his hands in place. But he didn't safeword, and the way the boy bucked into every thrust confirmed that he was enjoying this little bit of bondage-fucking.

"Please," the boy begged with a stuttering, gasping voice.

Alex tightened his fingers enough to turn the flesh under his tips red. "Please what, baby?"

"H-help me." Quinn bucked as much as Alex's hold would allow. "I need..."

Alex smiled. "Oh, yes, of course. Do forgive me." Leaning over, he moved one hand to clasp the human's dick. One pump was all it took to send ropes of cum spurting out.

Quinn howled with his release. His movements became more frantic and his hole clenched around Alex's rod tight enough to make him grimace. But then it relaxed again, and that was the only opening Alex needed. His climax forced a roar from his lips that blanketed the human's cries. He slammed his dick in as deep as it could go. His balls brushed against Quinn's, and that brief, soft touch was electrifying enough to make them both shudder out more cum.

Panting like an overheated dog, Alex closed his eyes and covered his lover's body with his own. They were both sweaty now, and their skin stuck together, back-to-chest at various points. He came to himself enough to plant appreciative kisses along Quinn's spine, while roaming his hands up and down the boy's flanks.

Quinn lay unmoving, other than a little flutter of his fingers.

"Are you all right?" Alex finally managed to ask, mindful of how bondage was new to the human.

"Hmm." That was all Quinn said, and his boneless repose telegraphed how truly relaxed the boy was.

Alex slid his finger to touch Quinn's femoral artery. The feel of the pulse along with the sound of the boy's heartbeat drove a new hunger within him. All he had to do was place his mouth on the carotid, let his fangs descend, bite and suck, and all that sweetness flowing through his boy would be his. He could taste it already, based on Quinn's generous offerings from the night before. But that had been given, not taken, and there was a big difference between pricks on a finger and bites into a spot that could leave one drained dry.

He pulled away, straightening so that he wasn't so close, so tempted. If and when Quinn ever learned of Alex's true nature and offered that gift of pain and blood, Alex would take it and never drink from another. Now was not that time. It was too soon, and Dracul's antics required more focus than he would be able to give if he became even more entangled with this human than he already was.

He ran his hand slowly down Quinn's spine, counting the vertebrae, enjoying the way Quinn's back rippled with the attention. Even now, he was far too distracted. Adrian had likely already selected his next victim, was probably draining some poor soul's life blood to leave hanging somewhere else in the morning. There was nothing he could do to stop it, but he needed to remember that he had a job to do.

And fucking Quinn was not it.

With a sigh, he pulled his still-hard dick carefully out of Quinn's ass. Then he unbuckled the cuffs, massaging each wrist to make sure they were okay. Quinn watched him with sleepy eyes.

Alex brushed some strands of hair that had fallen across the boy's face. "Come on. Let's get you cleaned and back to work. Break time is over for the both of us, I'm afraid."

"Okay," Quinn replied in soft voice that was laced with satisfaction. He let Alex help him back to his feet and swayed into him briefly. "Can we do this again? The fucking, I mean, after my shift ends?"

Alex kissed his forehead. "Of course. Nothing would give me greater pleasure, my dearest Quinn."

* * * *

"This is so fucking messed up." Mackie put his chin on Quinn's shoulder from behind and watched the television in their dressing room.

Quinn shivered at the images. The police were working to cut down yet another bloodless corpse. This one had been found hanging from the top of the Bunker Hill Monument in Boston's Charlestown area. It was a tall, granite obelisk that looked kind of like a dick and housed an observation room at the top. Thanks to the killer, Quinn was getting a quick lesson on the sites of his adopted city.

"How did the killer even get it there?"

Unlike the bridge, this location didn't seem like anything anyone could access at all during the night, being locked and secure. Somehow, the killer had done exactly that to hang the corpse out of the window. Thank God, the cameras were being manipulated to fuzz out the more gruesome details, although with a huge crowd of people all taking video, it seemed the images would be easily seen on the Internet.

Mackie stood back. "It's like the guy really is a vampire. I mean, who else could climb that thing carrying a body? You'd have to be hella strong."

Like Val – or Emil or Alex. Quinn shook his head against such thoughts. "Maybe he kidnapped the guy, made him walk up, then killed him."

"And yet, the breathless commentary from the reporters indicates that there doesn't even seem to be evidence of a break-in."

"The media always speculates without having all the facts. We don't know anything."

"Except that someone is going around slaughtering guys, like every night now." Mackie paced away and plopped onto the couch underneath where the television hung on the wall. "The family is secluded in Alex's office again. They are clearly getting freaked out, even though all this doesn't seem to have anything to do with the club."

"Yeah, they are. I guess that's because the FBI was here yesterday, making it seem like all of us are suspects." Even as he gave the rationale, he wasn't sure he believed it. Alex and the others seemed too intensely interested in what was going on.

"Did you know Demi is on lockdown?"

"Huh?" Turning off the TV, Quinn joined Mackie on the couch. "You mean he's grounded?"

"No. Grounded implies punishment, and this is more that he has to stay in the building for the foreseeable future because of the murders. Harry and Lucien are being overly cautious, I guess. I mean, it's not like the city is under siege or anything. So far, the killer is only coming out at night, and there's like three million people to choose from. I don't know why he'd go after one annoying teenager."

He would if he's targeting the Stelalux family. Again, the random thought took him by surprise. He wasn't sure why he kept going back to the idea. *Because the first victim was a member dumped outside the club, Alex and Val ran off to the second murder site, and they've given the killer a 'pet' name that is weirdly specific.*

Quinn rested his head against the back of the couch. "This whole thing is freaking me out. It makes me want to ground myself."

"No way." Mackie jumped to his feet and grabbed Quinn's arm. "We aren't going to waste what's left of this beautiful day cooped up in the gloom."

Quinn resisted the tug. "I thought you liked it here?"

"Not twenty-four seven, and Val's acting weird. He's all tense and stuff, no fun at all, and he barely spared me a glance last night, let alone touched me." He pulled up, proving himself stronger than he seemed. "Come on. I know the perfect place to go."

"Not the crime scene?" Quinn asked with alarm.

"Of course not. I mean the Museum of Fine Arts. It's amazing. You'll love it."

That idea piqued his interest. He allowed Mackie to pull him to his feet. "That does sound like fun, actually."

Mackie took his phone out of his pocket. "Great. I'll call for an Uber."

"We should maybe let the guys know we're going out."

Mackie shook his head. "Nah. I told you they're meeting in Alex's office. They don't like being disturbed, and besides, unlike Demi, we're fully-fledged adults and can go out when we want."

Knowing Mackie was right about their independence, he still felt that the situation with the serial killer and the obvious protectiveness of both Alex and Val warranted letting them know their plans. Yet, it was also true that they probably wouldn't like being disturbed. And, if the dominant and submissive roleplaying that Val and Mackie adhered to didn't require that kind of check in, then Quinn needn't worry about it, either. It wasn't as if he and Alex had an official monogamous relationship or anything. Even if they did, he hadn't agreed to any 'daddy' arrangement with the man. He was free to go out anytime he liked.

He worried his lower lip as they left the room. "Let's tell Kitty what we're doing, just in case."

Mackie turned and rolled his eyes at him. "Fine, if it makes you feel better. I promise, though, we'll be perfectly safe. We'll take a car there and back—no T. And no one is going to attack us in the museum, for God's sake."

Kitty gave them a dubious look when they told her on their way out, but she promised to let the men know when they became free. As promised by Mackie, the ride to the museum was uneventful, although all the driver wanted to talk about was the murder. It was a relief when they arrived at the immense building. For a second, Quinn stood staring at it.

"You're right. It is amazing."

Mackie laughed. "Dude, this is only the outside. Come on," he said, linking arms. "Wait until you see what's inside. You'll be majorly impressed."

From his first step inside, Quinn agreed that the guy wasn't wrong about that. He had never been to a museum before—not one like this. It was filled with the kind of art he was used to seeing in books or on the Internet. He'd never expected to see famous paintings, ancient art and even mummified beings this close. Each level, hall and room contained more and more enticing things.

Mackie took him first to all his favorite spots. Not surprisingly, the tour started with the Egyptian exhibit, then onto the Greek and Roman one. He pointed out the pieces he said he kept coming back to explore because each time, he saw something new. Quinn could believe that. It was too much to take in all at once.

"See," the boy said, bumping his shoulder and pointing to a piece of Greek pottery behind glass. "Boys fucking other boys has been around forever."

Quinn's cheeks heated and he looked around to see if anyone could have heard. "I know that," he hissed in a near-whisper before moving on.

They ate a stupidly expensive late lunch in the nicest of the museum's restaurants before taking a final tour of the remaining exhibits. It was hours before they emerged again. The sun was still mostly up because it was summer, after all, but there was a feeling of lateness in the air.

"We need to get back."

"Nervous nelly," Mackie said as he used his phone to call for a car.

Yeah, he kind of was, and maybe that was the residual fear he'd developed for the few weeks when he'd been on his own. A guy like Mackie, who'd spent a lot more time surviving without a safety net, probably didn't spook as easily. Quinn knew he was safe, yet he still felt a measure of relief once they were in the car and heading back to the club. Back *home*.

The sight of it both relaxed him and made his heart beat faster. It already represented security for him and the place where he could find unbelievable pleasure. When he thought back on what he'd done with Alex less than twelve hours ago in that playroom, he both blushed and became aroused. There had been something naughty and thrilling about being cuffed, his ass exposed and vulnerable to another man. He'd trusted Alex to treat him right and he hadn't been disappointed. Maybe the man was free now, and they could play again before dinner and work. He popped out of the ride the moment the tires stopped turning and headed quickly to the club's double front door.

"Thanks, dude," Mackie said to the driver as he followed Quinn out of the car. "Hey, what the fuck?"

Quinn tripped to a stop and turned to see what had upset his friend. A figure loomed, blocking his view. At first he thought it was Val because the guy was so tall and wide and dressed all in black. But when he tipped his head back, he saw that it wasn't. This guy was nothing like the bouncer, except he had the height and coloring of the Stelalux family members — pale skin, dark hair and violet eyes. The man's, though, sneered at him with such obvious menace that Quinn took an involuntary step back.

The guy hissed, like seriously snake-level with air roaring out of his mouth, and struck with the same metaphorical speed to grab the front of Quinn's shirt with a tight fist. "I don't think so, little boy."

"Hey, what do you think you're doing?" Mackie made a grab for the man. "Let him go."

A split second later, the boy was sailing through the air, having been swatted by Quinn's attacker with his free hand as if Mackie were nothing more than a fly.

Mackie landed with a grunt on the sidewalk by the mouth of the alley and lay still. Quinn only had a second to gasp and try to go to his friend before the man hauled him close.

"I only have to keep you alive, not whole. Your choice." He stared into Quinn's eyes, his pupils changing color until they appeared to be dark red. *No, that can't be true. No one has red eyes.* The man licked his tongue across his teeth and his fangs appeared to be incredibly prominent and sharp.

Panic made Quinn struggle. Grabbing the man's hand with both of his, he tried to pry the fingers from his shirt. It was like moving granite — very cold granite. He had no effect. If anything, it egged the guy on. He smiled cruelly and lifted Quinn to the tips of his toes, even as he dragged him away.

"No! Hel—" A big meaty hand covered his mouth, muffling his cries.

Given the hour, this part of Boston had yet to become busy. No one was around that he could see. The man was carrying him away, and Quinn knew that regardless of what he did, he was going to end up dead, the same way the others had, because this had to be the killer. Nothing else made sense, and he realized, too, that this was who he'd caught glimpses of the other days when he'd been out with Mackie. He'd been stalked all along.

Out of the corner of his eye, he could see Mackie struggling to stand, his face a bloody mess. But there was nothing the boy could do except run for help. By the time he got to his feet and into the club, it would be too late. Surely this man was pulling him to some kind of vehicle.

Knowing the moment that happened he was screwed, he fought even harder. He dug his nails into the skin of the man's hands and kicked futilely at his shins. Nothing worked. He was no match for this behemoth. His fate was a foregone conclusion.

Then a cry, like the kind ancient warriors would have made, froze him and the man both. A jarring thud came next, and it was strong enough to rock them. His assailant's grip slackened and Quinn used the chance to jerk forward. He got free and landed on his hands and knees, the pavement making his palms sting.

Gasping for breath, he turned to look over his shoulder just in time to see a dirty, disheveled street person bash the attacker in the head with a board. A bloom of red spurted from the man's head, the sight of it giving Quinn hope for the first time.

He took in a deep, ragged breath and screamed.

Chapter Twelve

Even muffled by the thick walls of the club, the scream shot right through Alex. He was running out of his apartment in a millisecond, his bag of blood lying splattered on his kitchen floor. He headed for the stairs and, punching through the door, he vaulted over the stairwell and thudded onto the ground floor. There was no one to see his inhuman feat and he didn't care in any event.

That had been Quinn screaming. There was no question.

Val beat him to the side door leading to the alley by a half a length. Footsteps behind him told Alex that the others were also coming. Outside, at the mouth of the alley, a scene unfolded that both scared the shit out of him and eased his heart.

Adrian was fighting with the homeless veteran, Logan. It was a David-and-Goliath-type battle, although the human offset her height and weight disadvantage with agility and a wicked two-by-four with nails sticking out of it. Adrian swiped ineffectively at her while she danced away.

Mackie lay sprawled on his back, trying to stand and failing. Blood trickled from his forehead. Val first ran toward him before changing course and landing a flying kick to Adrian's mid-section. Adrian staggered back before hissing his displeasure. With Val engaged in the fight, Logan retreated to help Mackie.

But none of that mattered half so much as seeing Quinn a few feet away from the fray. He crouched on his hands and knees, obviously also trying to stand, yet too winded to do so. An expression of abject fear marred his beautiful face.

Time seemed to slow down — or maybe it was Alex who sped up. He saw Logan bracing Mackie's back to get him to a sitting position. The boy's head lolled like a ragdoll's. Val and Adrian squared off like the warriors they were. Three more people came to flank Alex. Part of him registered Emil, Harry and Kitty ranging across the alley.

Then a tremendous sound reverberated off the brick walls of the alley, a roar like a hurricane-force wind. Everyone stopped. All eyes turned to him. He still only cared about one set. Quinn looked at him, at first startled. His face morphed into such obvious relief that Alex's worst fear — rejection — was abated. The boy's lips moved, but Alex couldn't hear what he said over that deafening sound. *Where the hell is it coming from and how can I stop it?*

It's me. The realization came to him with a jolt. It was coming out of his mouth, and it was a warrior cry to rival all others.

He snapped his lips shut and took off once more. His target was Adrian and the guy was smart enough to realize it. Plus, he was outnumbered by overwhelming odds. He was running away before Alex took two steps. That hardly deterred Alex from pursuing him. He chased Adrian across the street and down another alley. The guy's head start was too great, however, and he'd planned a more pedestrian getaway.

Adrian jumped into an SUV and gunned it just as Alex arrived. He made a swipe at the bumper, yet couldn't gain any purchase to hold the vehicle back. He let out another roar as his quarry sped away. *Damn it all.* He'd liked it better when humans had relied on horses for transportation. As fast as he was, Alex could not catch a car.

He allowed himself one satisfying image of tearing Dracul's lackey limb-from-limb before returning to what mattered most.

Quinn had gotten to his feet, although he wasn't too steady. Val had already picked Mackie up and, stone-faced, held the still, groggy-looking boy against his chest.

"He needs you, Harry," Val said to the older man, his voice oddly flat.

"Of course. Come on." With a grimace shot in Alex's direction, Harry ushered Val and Mackie back into the club through the alley's entrance.

Emil stood next to Logan, his hand on her shoulder. "He should check you out, too."

The woman still held her weapon, and she wiped at a bloody spot on her cheek. "Nah, I'm fine. That asshole barely touched me."

Kitty approached. "Please, come inside and at least take a hot shower. It will help loosen your muscles after a fight like that. Emil will fix you dinner, whatever you want. You've earned it."

Logan stiffened. "I don't need a shower or a meal. I'm fine. Just helping out the boys here. No big deal."

As much as Alex wanted to go to Quinn, he needed to be a leader of his people first. Honor dictated he make sure this ally was cared for. He approached her and stopped a few feet away.

He inclined his head, giving her the courtesy he would have afforded a member of the queen's court. "Madam, what you have done here today for my family will not be forgotten. We owe you a debt that can never be repaid. Please allow us to show our appreciation in these wholly inadequate ways. It's all we have to give."

Logan sniffed and swiped at her face again, leaving a dirty, red streak across her cheek. "I guess I could do with a wash and a meal. I mean...if it makes you happy."

He bowed his head again. "Nothing would please us more," he said in all sincerity. "Thank you."

He shot Emil and Kitty a meaningful look. They needed to keep Logan in the club. She was now a target for Adrian. He wouldn't let the woman's interference go unpunished. Once they were headed back inside, Alex turned to do what he wanted and feared the most.

Quinn stood staring at him with wide eyes. When Alex took a step toward him, the boy did what Alex had been afraid of — stepped back.

Alex planted his feet, even though what he really wanted was to race over and scoop up the boy. "Please don't be afraid of me."

Quinn blinked a few times and shook his head. "I'm not. Not really. Just confused." Putting his hand to his head, he added, "And kind of dizzy."

Now, Alex did give in to his impulse and caught the human in his arms. He was pathetically grateful when the boy didn't struggle against the hold. Then he went all the way and hefted him to cradle him tightly.

Quinn sighed and dropped his head against Alex's chest. That show of trust nearly brought Alex to his knees. Then Quinn's questions were like a bucket of cold water.

"Who was that man? Why were his eyes red? How are you all so fast and did you really roar?"

"Let me get you inside and I'll see if I can answer your questions to your satisfaction."

He treated Quinn like a fragile thing. Alex took care reentering the building and using the elevator back to his apartment. Quinn wasn't fragile, though. He knew better. After all, Quinn had fought back in some manner instead of falling apart in the face of such terror. He was still showing courage and strength in acquiescing to Alex's care, even though he'd witnessed frightening stuff.

He silently cursed himself when he stepped inside his entryway. The direction he held Quinn gave the boy a perfect line of sight to the spilled blood in the kitchen. No hope of him not noticing.

"Is that, um—blood?"

"Yes," Alex answered.

He placed Quinn on the sofa, the same way he'd done not even a week ago. The human curled into a sitting position and stared at him with his hands fisted in his lap.

Alex crouched. "Let me see your palms. They looked scraped and bleeding."

Quinn shrunk back into the cushions. "That's okay. They not that bad, and I really don't want you to—you know—lick them or anything."

Standing, he said, "I wasn't going to." Except, of course, he wanted to—and not only because his first impulse after saving the boy was to reaffirm his survival by tasting his life's blood. His saliva would help with the healing process. Quinn wasn't in a frame of mind to hear that, though. Alex made himself move away and sit on the edge of the nearby chair. He braced his arms on his legs to give a casual appearance. If he kept his cool, maybe Quinn would, as well.

"Ask me whatever questions you have. I promise to answer them fully and truthfully." It was a risk to do so, but Adrian and Alex's own selfish desires had brought them to this point.

Quinn's chest rose and fell on a few harsh breaths and his gaze darted around before landing back at Alex's eyes. "Are you vampires?" The question came blurted out in a rush of air.

Alex smiled. "No. There are no such things as vampires."

The boy shook his head. "No human can move as fast as you, Val and the killer did. It was like watching some superhero movie without CGI enhancing the speed. I saw the man's eyes go from violet to red, the way yours are right now. And that noise you made? Like a hundred lions roaring at the same time." He shook his head again. "Plus, there's...you know, this..." He circled his mouth with his finger.

"What?"

Quinn's eyes widened even more. "You have, ah, fangs."

Alex ran his tongue across his upper teeth and, to his chagrin, felt that his biters had indeed descended. "Oh, sorry." With effort, he retracted them. It wasn't really surprising, given how upset he was. His body craved a fight and blood in equal measure.

"Yeah, like I said, *vampires*." Quinn huffed. "Don't tell me that's normal, because it's not."

Alex dropped his gaze to study his hands dangling between his legs. "I won't. I promised the truth and that's what you'll get. We aren't vampires, but we're also not humans, because we aren't of this world."

Quinn blinked rapidly at him a few times. "You're *aliens*?"

"Yes."

"Oh." He looked away again with furrowed brows. "I guess that is believable. I mean it's the twenty-first century, after all, and an alien invasion is something that even scientists talk about."

"It's not an invasion. We're marooned."

Shifting into a more relaxed pose, Quinn blew out a breath. At least he wasn't freaking out. Hopefully that was a good sign.

"Who are 'we', exactly? I know it must mean you, Val, Harry, Emil and that asshole who attacked me."

"Yes, that's right. There are a few dozen of us who survived the crash and are still living on this planet."

"Not Kitty or Lucien." He bit his lower lip. "Not Mackie?"

Alex shook his head. "None of them. Our species has no variability in skin tone or hair color. And there were no women on the ship. They don't serve on long voyages."

Quinn raised his eyebrows. "So, you're sexist but not homophobic or racist."

Alex had to chuckle over those observations. A band of tension relaxed inside him. Quinn was asking questions and not running screaming from the room.

This might not be so bad after all. Before, when he'd revealed his true nature to others, it had been after a long period of developing a relationship of some kind. Quinn's tolerance for the unexpected and unbelievable was amazing.

"When your species is monochrome, racism never has a chance to take root. Our sexuality is inherently more fluid that the average human's. That's probably due to our evolution. You see, at our biological core, we are more like bees than apes. Our queen is fecund to a degree no human woman could match. In her lifetime, a queen will reproduce more than a thousand times. She also births far more males than females. And while many of her daughters are fertile, we still don't have anything like the equal ratio of male to female that you humans have."

"So, you had an all-male crew because your women are too busy popping out kids?"

Alex winced. "Not exactly. Women do whatever they want. Being pregnant and giving birth doesn't hold them back, but of course, most jobs are filled by males. That's just a statistical issue. They also instinctively stay away from the more dangerous roles because our species can only survive if they produce enough offspring."

"Okay, so you and your crew are marooned here. How did that happen, exactly?"

Alex didn't answer right away. The question itself sent him careening back emotionally to the incident and the nagging feeling that he should have been able to somehow stop it. Unable to sit still with his memories, he rose and paced over to the draped windows. He took a few deep breaths to get himself under control before turning to back to Quinn.

"My people have been exploring space since humans walked Earth. We found and figured out how to exploit wormholes."

Quinn twisted onto his knees, his interest and excitement obvious. "You mean there are wormholes? It's really a thing?"

"Yes." He smiled — or maybe it became a grimace. "They do, and it's tricky to use them. My navigator was young. It was his first voyage and he miscalculated our descent out of it. Instead of coming into your galaxy to explore, we crashed on your planet. Most of my crew were killed on impact."

The boy was silent for a few seconds as he digested the tale. "You were the captain?" he finally asked in a hushed tone.

"Yes, I was responsible."

Quinn shook his head. "No, your navigator screwed up."

"I was the captain. I was responsible," he reiterated, because that was the rule, even on this pitiful planet.

The human rolled his eyes. "Whatever. So, why are you like vampires?"

Alex couldn't hold back the groan. He felt confident enough in his welcome to go back to sit on the couch next to Quinn. "That's humans making up a story to explain what they don't understand and what they fear. You see, we crashed in the Carpathian Mountains in what is now Romania."

"Oh, you mean, like Transylvania?"

"Exactly. I tried to keep my people separate from the indigenous ones in the vain hope that we'd be rescued. Of course, it didn't work. Slowly the natives noticed us and created stories about who and what we were."

Quinn wrinkled his nose and the casualness of the gesture gave Alex even greater hope that the boy would accept him as he was. "You drink blood."

"Part of our natural diet, and human blood is very tasty," he added with a guilty sigh.

Quinn made a disgusted face. "Ick, but go on."

"We're obviously taller, stronger and faster than a human. We climb easily because of our long fingers. Our body temperature is lower, so we're cooler to the touch, making it seem like we're dead. And your planet is closer to your sun. That means we don't tolerate the brightness and the heat of the day very well. We like being out at night better."

"Garlic?" Quinn asked, angling his body closer to Alex's.

"Ask Emil about how much he loves cooking with it. That part of the lore I can't explain."

"Hmm." The boy pursed his lips, making him look adorable. Alex wanted to haul him in for a kiss. It was too soon, though. "I've seen you make the sign of the cross, so that part's bogus, too, huh?"

"Our species has no religion. We adopted Christianity because we were trying to blend into the place where we'd settled. It made no difference. Our 'otherness' was still obvious."

"Yeah, you really do stand out in a crowd. Adrian's been stalking me for a few days."

"What?" Given the attack, he shouldn't have been surprised or alarmed. Knowing that his boy had been close to danger more than once drove him mad, however. He grabbed Quinn's hands and was grateful when the human didn't try to pull away. "Why didn't you tell me?"

"Because I didn't know what was happening." Now, he sounded peeved. "You didn't come clean with me from the beginning. You've always known it was him, didn't you?"

Alex kissed the backs of the boy's hands, ignoring the hint of blood emanating from his palms. "Yes. I'm sorry, dearest boy. I should have done a better job of protecting you."

"It's not your fault—not really. I'm kind of quietly freaking out right now about what you're telling me. And that's even given what just happened out there. I wouldn't have been able to accept any of this a few days ago. But, please tell me this. Why? Why is he killing people and why did he want me?"

He couldn't look at Quinn as he answered, "Because, to my ever-lasting shame, I wasn't able to keep my crew together. Half of them want to take over this world and rule it to their own selfish ends. To them, humans are mere cattle to be controlled and exploited. This thing with Adrian is the latest iteration of a long war we've been waging with humans used as proxies and always as victims."

"You mean like a civil war?"

"Yes."

"How long as this been going on?"

Alex raised his head to gaze into Quinn's eyes as he answered, "Nearly a thousand years."

* * * *

I'm in love with an alien. Quinn couldn't get the thought out of his head. It kept ping-ponging around his thoughts all morning.

After a restless night spent in his own bed at his insistence, he still had a hard time accepting everything Alex had told him the evening before. He couldn't reject it, either, especially after a kind of test. He'd allowed Alex to lick his scraped palms. He could actually see the minor wounds healing before his very eyes, like his own personal special effect. It had freaked him out.

So, yeah, everything fit, and as frightening as the idea of being caught in an alien fight was, the alternatives were worse. If Alex was lying, then either Quinn was losing his mind or Alex and the others were Earth-made monsters. Neither of those possibilities made any more sense or made him feel any better.

"Eat, kiddo," Kitty ordered with a smile. "Everything's going to be okay, but not if you let yourself get weak from hunger."

"Yes, ma'am."

He dutifully shoveled more eggs into his mouth. He'd chosen to eat at the bar instead of the kitchen because knowing that Kitty was both human and in on the truth made him feel relaxed. With the club closed due to the ongoing threat around the city, the place was pretty empty. Most of the staff had been ordered to stay home, with pay, because Alex was a stand-up guy, even if he was an alien. Other than Mackie, Lucien and maybe Logan, Quinn and Kitty were it for the human contingent.

It wasn't that he felt unsafe — quite the contrary. And Quinn understood why Alex wanted him to stay in the building, even while accepting that he needed some space to process all the weird revelations. Still, the club took on an otherworldly vibe, the way it had always done, and it was a little uneasy now that he knew it wasn't his imagination. The bar just felt like a secure zone. That was all.

"How are you feeling this morning?"

He startled, the question coming out of left field. He swiveled to look into Alex's concerned eyes. Alien though they might be, the violet color was still beautiful. Alex was undeniably gorgeous and sexy for any species. Quinn's body reacted with the same needy desire that it had before the big revelations. However else he might take Alex's alien nature, he couldn't regret that they'd become lovers.

Quinn blushed and smiled. "I'm fine, thanks. I'm just—you know—processing everything." He made a circular motion with his hand to vaguely encompass the world then inwardly cringed at his own awkwardness.

"Good. I want you to be comfortable here, Quinn, whatever you may decide to do once we take care of Adrian."

Yeah, they'd put their relationship on hold, something that Alex had raised even before Quinn had thought it through. Right now, Dracul and his minions had their sights on making Boston a terror ground in the first volley of a new round of fighting. Quinn had somehow jumped onto their radar screen and that made Alex vulnerable. The man had said something cryptic in explaining it to Quinn.

Dracul knows how crippling it would be for me to lose you.

Quinn hadn't pressed him on explaining that because profound sadness had crossed Alex's face. They'd both been drained from the encounter with Adrian and hadn't needed to drag out the information dump more than necessary. It had been enough to learn that he meant a lot to Alex. Despite everything that had occurred, Quinn knew he'd fallen for the man, and knowing Alex might feel the same way made him ridiculously happy when he should have been shitting himself six ways to Sunday.

He wasn't sure what to say, however. Even given his burgeoning love for the man, he couldn't say what he intended to do. *Can I make a life with an alien? And what exactly does that entail?* Lucien seemed to be happy with Harry, although Quinn hadn't spoken more than a few words to the guy. Mackie obviously loved Val, but then the kid was cool with the whole blood-sucking thing. Besides, he'd talked to him briefly before going to bed. Mackie had been too out of it from hitting his head to realize all that had happened with Adrian. He hadn't been let in on the truth about Val's nature, according to Alex, and still didn't know.

Before Quinn could think of something to say, a commotion took both of their attentions.

"Val, please. Don't do this!"

Quinn whipped his head around to witness Val and Mackie coming out of the elevator. Actually, Val was dragging the boy out with one hand grasping a biceps and the other carrying a duffel bag.

Mackie was trying to dig in his heels, his fingers scrambling to unlock Val's hold, causing Quinn to flash uneasily on his own fight with Adrian. "I'm sorry. I didn't mean to cause trouble. I was just trying to show Quinn a good time and it was daylight still. How was I supposed to know the killer would come after him?"

Grim-faced and implacable, Val continued to tug the boy across the room and over to the front door.

"Please, Val! Punish me. Beat my ass bloody or use the whip. Anything but this. Please, don't throw me out!" Mackie's obvious panic was heartbreaking.

"No." The word was out of Quinn's mouth and he was on his feet before he even knew what he was doing.

Alex grabbed his arm before he'd taken two steps. "Quinn, stay out of it. Val's only doing what he thinks is best, and Mackie's being taken care of financially."

He tore his gaze from the scene unfolding long enough to scowl at Alex. "You think this is about *money*? Mackie *loves* Val. He deserves to know the truth the same way I do."

"You don't understand. Val can't commit to that boy. Cutting him loose is kinder and safer in the long run."

"Says who?" He shook off the man's hold. "He's sending him out where the killer is. How is that safe for him and not me?"

"Because Adrian targeted you, not Mackie, and Val is about to make sure that if Adrian is watching, he'll know that Val doesn't care about the boy."

"But that's not true. He does care. I've seen how he looks at him."

"It's not the same for us. Our emotions are similar, but you can't judge us by human standards."

"Really? Well, that's good to know. Thanks for setting me straight." With that, he ran after the others, fighting sudden tears because had he just learned that Alex didn't really love him after all. Or worse, never could – not in the way that mattered.

He caught up to Mackie and Val at the curb outside the club. A car waited with its engine running. Val had already tossed the bag in the backseat and was in the process of shoving Mackie in after it.

Tears streamed down the boy's face. "Please, Val, I'm begging you. Give me another chance. I'll take any punishment but this." He hitched a breath. "I'll suck your cock the way you like it and never ask for anything in return."

"Son-of-a-bitch!" Val yelled right in the boy's face. "Stop acting like a whore." The bitter order made Mackie flinch. "Do you think this is a game? That all you have to do is be a good little sub and all is forgiven?"

Mackie whimpered. "Please."

"We're through. I don't *love* you. I don't even like you. You're a whiny, clinging little brat. You were a tight enough hole and decent play partner to amuse me for a while. Now it's over. I have more important things to do and I can't stand the sight of you. Go find some other guy to leach off of."

Mackie reared back his head as if slapped. Then he straightened and dropped his hands from Val's. He turned to get into the car as if in a trance, then he squared his shoulders as if he were trying to retain a tiny shred of dignity.

"Mackie!" Quinn called out and ran over to the boy, shoving Val away. Surprisingly, the guy allowed it, stumbling back as if Quinn had been a tank instead of a small human.

He threw his arms around Mackie. "I'm sorry," he whispered. "This is all my fault."

The boy returned his embrace. "No, it's not." He pulled away and sniffed back his tears. "I'll be fine. I still have my apartment and Val gave me a year's worth of pay."

"You've been fired, too?" Quinn was incredulous. "He can't do that. It's Alex's club."

"He knows. Alex signed the company check."

Quinn glared at Alex, who stood outside the doors. He could see the truth in the man's expression. *How come a break-up means that Mackie has to lose his job? Oh, right, because the aliens are all related, part of being in a hive. And blood is always thicker than water.*

"Then I'm quitting."

Mackie looked alarmed. "No, don't. Please, don't do that for me. It will only make me feel guilty." He offered a watery smile. "Alex is a good guy and I think he really likes you. You don't want to throw away a good thing just because of me." Mackie shrugged. "I'm surprised Val could stand me for so long."

"Don't say that. You're great."

"Thanks." He shrugged again and scrubbed at his tears. "Anyway, I don't know what's going on, but that psycho is after you. You're safer here until they catch him."

Quinn let his arms drop to his side. "I suppose. Text me later tonight to let me know you're okay?"

Mackie gave him a quick hug. "Sure. We'll keep in touch." He got into the car. "Don't worry about me. I always land on my feet."

With that, Mackie shut the door and the car drove off. Quinn watched until it was out of sight. Turning back to the club, he banged into a wall of granite. Alex reached to steady him, but Quinn batted his hands away.

"Don't touch me. I'm mad at you. And I don't know when I'm going to stop being mad at you."

Alex sighed and stepped back. "I understand. Please come back inside. I want you out of harm's way."

"I know." Even as he said it, though, Quinn wondered whether he was safer inside than out. His heart wasn't. That much he knew.

* * * *

Quinn's grandfather had always said that hard work was all the therapy a man needed. Quinn's job now involved dancing around a pole. Even with the club temporarily closed, he still benefited from getting in some practice. It beat lying around, angry at Alex and worried about Mackie, so he folded his clothing on a chair and, wearing only his boxer-briefs, he padded out to one of the stages. Kitty, as usual, was working behind the bar. She seemed to spend an endless amount of time polishing everything within her domain, whether it needed it or not. He supposed his grandfather's adage applied to women, as well.

He shot her a smile that held no happiness. "Would you mind cuing up *Mercy* for me? I feel like dancing to a ballad."

Kitty gave him a nod. "Sure, kid." She switched the sound system from the local alternative rock station to the Shawn Mendes song. Then she went into the back, probably because Kitty only liked the hardcore stuff.

As the first strains began, he wrapped himself around the pole and slowly swayed. Maybe his subconscious mind had picked this particular song more for the lyrics than the music. As he gyrated against the pole, he concentrated on the words and thought they fit his feelings perfectly. Given his growing feelings for Alex the Alien, as he was starting to think of him, the guy had the power to both literally and figuratively drain him of all he was. He wasn't sure he was strong enough to survive that kind of relationship.

Regardless, losing himself in the music and the movement made him feel better. By the time the chorus began, he was confident enough to jump, grab the pole and twirl his way to the bottom again. His movement became more fluid and athletic. He twisted and flipped in tempo with the music, feeling almost carefree for a few minutes. He smiled seductively to his imaginary audience, although in his mind's eye, there was only one man watching him. He showed his imaginary Alex how much—despite perhaps his better judgment—he wanted him still, in the way he undulated and posed his body around the pole.

His concentration was broken halfway through by the sudden appearance of Demi. The boy bounced out of nowhere and jumped onto the neighboring stage. He mimicked Quinn's current contortion then continued to mirror his every move as if they'd been practicing for Olympic-level synchronized pole dancing for years. It was unnerving and distracting at first, but Quinn soon decided it was a disarming and exhilarating way to dance. And, naturally, their routine shifted so that soon it was the younger boy leading the way.

Demi drove Quinn to a new level. They turned upside down and spread their legs into a wide V before shifting upright again and swinging around by one leg. It was scary how well this sixteen-year-old virgin kid knew how to make love to the pole, but when the song and the dancing ended, Quinn felt as if he'd received the best lesson ever.

Hopping off his stage, Demi clapped with genuine-looking appreciation. "That was awesome. Hard to believe you've only being doing this for like a week."

Quinn smiled in response to the praise and grabbed his towel to wipe off. "Thanks, and it's hard to believe you're not a go-go boy at all. Your fathers must have fits when they see you."

Demi made a face and folded his arms. "They don't get me."

"Says every teenager always." He frowned. "Including me, I guess. Don't you have schoolwork?"

"Ugh, you sound like Mackie."

The reminder of the other boy brought back the horrible memory of what had happened only a few hours ago. "I can't believe he's gone."

"Me, neither." The boy came over and sat on the edge of Quinn's stage. "This place is even more boring than usual without him and I'm stuck here for the duration."

Quinn joined him. "Your parents only want you to be safe."

"I know." Demi waved his hands as if in a panic. "Adrian's on the loose. Dracul's restarted the war. Aah!" He folded his arms like the kid he was and pouted. "I don't know why we all have to suffer because of some stupid power grab by dumb aliens."

Quinn hid his smile because, in his own childish way, Demi had expressed Quinn's feelings in a nutshell. "I expect it's weird for you, being half-alien."

"It sucks." He blew out a breath. "Except for the superpowers — you know, brains and strength. Those I like, but I burn like a bitch if I don't slather on the sunscreen — and I'm starting to crave blood. That's a bummer. I was hoping I'd take after my human dad more. I mean, Lucien is really smart and pretty strong for a human of his size without all that 'I want to suck your blood' bullshit."

Quinn chuckled. "Yeah, but you really can't take after someone when you don't share his DNA."

Demi quirked his eyebrows. "What do you mean?"

"You know, you're half your bio mother, not Lucien."

"Um…" Turning more fully toward him, Demi said, "My dad said Alex had told you about us."

"Sure. I know that Alex, your father and the other Stelalux family members are alien. So, you're half-alien." He wasn't sure what the boy was getting at.

Demi nodded. "Right, I'm half-alien because my other dad is human. Harry and Lucien made me — you know, as in the traditional sense of sperm meeting egg. Then Lucien incubated me until Harry cut me out of his womb and ta-da!" He held his arms out wide.

It took a second for Quinn to process what the boy was saying. "Oh, I'm sorry. So, Lucien *is* a transgender man. Mackie said he and Harry had used a surrogate, and I just assumed he knew what he was talking about."

"No," Demi replied with a shake of his head. He opened his mouth to say more, but Quinn's phone ringing interrupted him.

"Sorry." Despite curiosity about what Demi was talking about, Quinn couldn't ignore the call. It might be Mackie, and he didn't want the boy to feel cut off any more than he already did.

Racing back to where he'd left his pants, he saw that it was the other boy and answered it. "Hey, Mackie, how are you?"

"Hi." The voice on the other end sounded watery, as if Mackie had been crying, which he probably had.

"How are you doing?"

A long breath blew across the line. "Oh, hanging in there."

Feeling helpless and stupid, he said, "I'm sorry."

"Yeah, me, too." There was a long pause, then, "I, um, need a favor from you."

"Sure. Anything."

Mackie gave him a brief and bitter-sounding laugh. "You might regret saying that." The boy grunted as if in pain.

"Are you okay?"

"Yeah, sure. You know me. I'm tough."

Only in some ways. "How can I help you, Mackie? Just name it."

"Ah, yeah, so, I need you to come to me."

Aware that Demi was overhearing everything, Quinn walked away from the bar and spoke quietly into the receiver. "Come to you. Why?"

"I've got myself in kind of a jam." He chuckled unconvincingly. "Again. Classic me, huh? I can't really explain it over the phone."

"I'm not supposed to leave the club."

"Right. Alex's orders, I bet."

"He's worried that the psycho killer is going to come after me again."

"Sure. I get it. That idiot serial killer is stupid enough to try it." There was another muted grunt.

"Mackie, are you sure you're all right?"

"Absolutely." This time, his words held an obvious note of pain. "I just need you to trust me. Call for an Uber and I'll text you the address. You go right from building to the car to your destination. Easy, and no way the killer can get at you. Please," he added and the undertone of fear was real.

Quinn tightened his grip. "Okay, I'll come."

"Thanks." Relief laced the one word. "I owe you."

"Not as much as I owe you."

Mackie sniffed. "I was a real asshole to you at first."

"Only at first. We're friends now, right?"

"Right. So, I'll text the address and you'll come right over? It's still light out, for what it's worth."

"That doesn't seem to matter anymore, but I'm coming. No worries."

"Don't tell Alex." Before Quinn could think of a suitable reply, Mackie continued. "Or Val. If he finds out I lured you away from the club, he'll beat my ass for sure. And you know how much I hate that," he added with another sniff. "I can't believe I suffered his sadism for so long."

Quinn's mind practically started smoking as it processed those statements in the millisecond he knew he had to respond. "Yes, I do know…how much you hated his BDSM games."

"I did it for the money. I really am a slut. So, you'll come and not tell anyone?"

"Count on it."

"I am." With that, Mackie ended the call.

The text with an address that he didn't recognized popped up seconds later. Quinn stared at if for long seconds, firming in his mind what he was going to do.

"What's going on?" Demi was suddenly standing right next to him, trying to read his text.

Quinn hugged the phone to his chest. "Nothing you need to worry about."

The boy gave him a pointed look. "Don't do anything stupid."

"I'm not. Go do your homework or something."

The boy responded with a word his fathers probably didn't like him using, but Quinn wasn't listening. He raced to the stairs, his plan solidifying as he took them as fast as he could. Time was not on his side and Mackie needed him. There was really only one path for him to take.

Chapter Thirteen

"This night might not be such another bust after all." Trey sat straighter in his seat behind the wheel, giving his numb ass a much-needed reprieve. Two nights of nothing going on had left him thinking his stakeout plan had been pointless.

Karl was more sluggish. He stilled, leaning against the passenger seat window, a cup of coffee dangling from his fingers. "With much of the city on self-inflicted lockdown, I'm surprised this kid is leaving his sanctuary. I bet the Uber driver is happy to get a fare, though."

The sun hadn't quite set, but that didn't mean it was safe to wander around now that a third body had turned up. And yet, Quinn Cooper had just run out from the alley next to the club and was jumping into a sedan parked at the curb.

"He's sneaking out, like a kid breaking curfew."

"You think Stelalux has that kind of power over him?"

Starting the car, he threw his partner a quick glance. "You've seen the guy. What do you think?"

"I think maybe the boy needs protection if he has to skulk about."

"Maybe, but not our call unless he asks. In the meantime, let's follow him and see where it takes us. This might be a lead and even if it isn't, we got nothing better to do."

"Says the man who has no social life."

Trey started to pull out to follow the car at a discreet distance before the sight of two motorcycles had him hitting the brakes. They tore out of the same alley that Quinn had. The riders were hidden behind huge, full-face helmets and clad all in black leather. Their identities may as well have been written on signs trailing behind them.

"Well, well," Karl drawled. "Looks like the boy hasn't slipped his leash quite as effectively as he thought."

"There's no garage off that alley," he replied, pulling out to now follow the bikes. "He must have seen them parked there, which means he knows they're behind him. It's not an escape attempt."

"Then what is it?"

"I don't know, but I'm keen to find out." With traffic lighter than usual and this not being a chase, it was easy to keep about a block away from the bikes, who were keeping about the same distance from the car carrying Quinn. "Looks like we've got ourselves a convoy."

Karl snickered. "Let's hope it's worth it, otherwise we're idiots. Maybe this is a family outing to escape the hysteria gripping the city."

"Nah, if that were the case, Quinn would be riding bitch behind his boyfriend. The bikes are certainly big enough for two."

"Yeah, those babies are Harley Wide Glides." Karl sighed with obvious envy. "Of course they are. That machine is built for big guys."

"It gives them more flexibility, too. They can separate and sneak through tighter spots. I wonder where this is leading. Probably nowhere."

Even as he said the words, he couldn't squelch the hope that the case might break open that night.

* * * *

"Are you sure about this address, dude?"

The driver had a good point. Mackie had sent him to a spot by the harbor that was both industrial and currently vacant. Quinn checked his phone. "Yeah, this is it."

The guy driving turned to look at him. "There isn't anything here except shipping containers, man. I mean, you do know there's a freaky killer on the loose, ya? Maybe your friend wanted you to meet him at Castle Island or something, not that I'd advise doing any sightseeing right now."

Quinn unbuckled his seatbelt and pulled the handle on his door. "Thanks. I'll be fine. You should probably leave right away, though."

"You got that right." The guy took off the moment Quinn had shut the door again.

The sun was setting and there wasn't anyone or anything stirring that he could tell. He wiped his sweaty palms on the front of his thighs and started moving. Mackie had said to meet him at the end of the pier. The eerie setting had him remembering every stupid horror flick he'd ever seen where multiple dumb teenagers met their inevitable end. Apparently, Adrian hadn't seen those flicks or maybe his species thought he was that gullible.

Regardless, with each step he took, Quinn knew that he was heading into an ambush. He had no doubts about that, but he couldn't abandon Mackie. If he didn't show, the boy would be killed for sure. This way, there was a slim chance that at least Mackie would survive and he hoped they both would. As terrified as he was, though, Quinn would never be able to live with himself if he'd stayed nice and safe at the club while this showdown occurred.

He slowly made his way past shipping containers lined up like colorful dominos. The only sounds he heard were his own tentative steps, the whipping of the wind and the occasional screech of a seagull. When he'd first arrived in Boston, he'd been delighted by the birds. Now they just freaked him the fuck out — like harbingers of doom.

Before he reached the last group, Mackie stepped out from behind it. The fear on the boy's face was visible, even to Quinn's human eyes. "I'm sorry."

Quinn didn't have a chance to reassure him. A tall, dark figure loomed behind Mackie. His hand landed on Mackie's shoulder, making him cry out in obvious pain. The guy shoved the boy to his knees and grabbed a fistful of his hair, pulling his head backward.

"Come here or I'll snap it off."

Quinn had no doubt Adrian could do what he threatened. Despite every fiber of his being telling him to turn and run, he put one foot in front of the other. He kept his pace slow, giving Alex and Val time to do whatever it was they intended. And they would do something to stop this madness and save him and Mackie. He was sure of it, and his confidence in Alex was what had led him to go to the man in the first place. Once Mackie had clued him in to being under duress, the decision to go to Alex had been easy. This wasn't a movie and he wasn't some idiotic teenager running headlong into an obvious trap.

He kept his gaze on Mackie. Tears streamed down the poor kid's face and there was another bruise added to the one from the day before. Quinn realized, too, that Mackie held his right arm awkwardly to his side. His injuries testified to how the boy must have fought his captor before he'd made the call to Quinn. Not that it mattered. In the face of such monstrousness, anyone would have cracked. Quinn could hardly hold this ambush against Mackie. They were both pawns in an alien war.

"It's all right. Everything is going to be fine."

Mackie whimpered and flinched, although whether from Quinn's seemingly hollow words or the grip on his hair, Quinn couldn't tell. He flicked his gaze to Adrian's face because he wanted to know the moment when the guy realized Quinn wasn't alone. He had no idea whether Alex and Val would attack from in front or behind or some combination. He didn't dare take his eyes off Mackie, regardless.

"Police!"

Wait, what? Oh, fuck! That was Duncan's voice. *How the hell did he get here? No way Alex called him.* Quinn stopped in his tracks.

"Let the boy go and put your hands in the air. Now!"

"No, no," Quinn whispered. This was all going to shit.

Adrian's lips curled into a mockery of a smile as he first released Mackie then shoved him to the side. Mackie smacked against the shipping container and fell with a cry. Slowly, Adrian raised his arms and stepped over him. The alien pulled his lips back to expose long, sharp teeth on either side of his upper jaw. His eyes turned a bright shade of red. The look was the Frank Langella version of a vampire with a kind of haunting, dark beauty that must have charmed his victims, even as it paralyzed them with fear.

Where the hell are Alex and Val? Quinn turned to scream out a warning. "Run!"

The cops stood a few feet from each other, their legs firmly planted and their guns held out in a two-handed stance. They undoubtedly thought they were in control. In reality, they didn't stand a chance. This guy wasn't surrendering. He was about to annihilate them.

His warning had barely left his lips before Adrian made his move. His body was a blur of motion that, even knowing it was coming, startled him. Anderson didn't even have a chance to fire before he was sent flying toward the water. His gun dropped from his hand as he hit a nearby loading crane with a terrible ringing sound. Then his body went careening into the water.

Duncan got off one shot. It did him no good. Adrian was on him in a split second, wrenching the gun from his hands and snapping his right arm with a sickening crack that caused bile to rise in Quinn's throat. The cop screamed with the break and went sailing a few yards away to land on a vacant patch of grass.

Quinn had no time to worry about the man because Adrian's gaze became fixated on him. He saw death in those eyes and he couldn't hold back the whimper.

"Alex!" He'd intended to shout the plea, but it came out as barely a squeak.

Adrian laughed and took one step forward. That was as close as he got before a black blur tackled him with a roar. Now, it was Adrian's turn to go flying through the air. A flash of motion in the corner of Quinn's eye took his attention for a second. Another black blur dove into the water where Anderson had gone in.

Alex let out that glass-shattering roar of his, making the hairs on Quinn's arms stand and taking his attention back. For a second he stood mesmerized by the sight of Alex with his fangs descended and murder in his now-red eyes. It was a sense of thrill knowing that all that rage was in his defense.

The resurrection of Adrian, however, got him moving. As the man rose from the ground to go one-on-one with Alex, Quinn ran over to Mackie. He knew he had to stay out of the way so as not to distract Alex. He was also worried about his friend and was relieved to see him awake.

"Here, let me help you. We need to take cover." He tried to raise Mackie to his feet.

The boy stumbled against him and bit back a cry. "He broke my arm."

"I figured. Lean on me." Quinn tried to take the brunt of Mackie's weight and drag him farther behind the nearby shipping container. Realizing that Mackie wasn't going to be able to remain upright, he settled them both in a sitting position on the ground.

They had a clear view of the epic battle that was being waged in the scrubby clearing next to the dock. It was frightening to watch and impossible to turn away from. The two aliens grappled like MMA fighters—a no-holds-barred, vicious battle that involved punches, kicks and the occasional bite. Alex was the taller of the two, yet not as broad as Adrian. They moved so fast that it was hard to tell who was winning. They appeared to be a non-stop twirling ball of black, with arms and legs sticking out.

Mackie clung to him. "You brought Alex?"

"Of course I did. I got what you were trying to say when you mentioned Val. I knew that you were forced to call me. Even if I hadn't believed that, I wouldn't have been dumb enough to leave the club on my own."

Mackie gave an almost hysterical laugh. "He broke into my apartment. I couldn't stop him. He was too strong and he..." His breath hitched. "He's not human. None of them are."

"I know."

Mackie turned his face away from the battle long enough to stare at him. "You *do*?"

"Yeah, I found out after Adrian tried to kidnap me."

Before he could explain further, a commotion by the pier once more caught his attention. Val hoisted himself out of the water with one hand. The other held Anderson in place across his shoulder. The moment he had both feet on the ground, he flipped the man onto his back. Anderson wasn't moving. Val looked up, his gaze homing in on Mackie for a second before he started mouth-to-mouth on the cop.

Quinn returned to watching the fight, and that was when he noticed Duncan crawling. With his injured arm held tight against his side, the cop was dragging himself one-handed over to where his gun had fallen.

No, you idiot. You'll get yourself killed.

He didn't dare shout out a warning to the man, not wanting to draw attention to what he was doing. He also knew that the cop would never get a shot off without Adrian killing him first. And he might even accidently hurt Alex. These aliens weren't bullet-proof.

Alex had told him as much. It took more to kill them than it did a human, but it could be done.

"Stay here," he said to Mackie, propping him against the container.

He didn't allow himself to think too much about what he was doing. Crouching low, he ran over to Duncan and slid next to him like he was heading into home plate. Then he kicked the gun away from the man's reach.

"What the fuck are you doing, kid?" Duncan's voice was strained by more than pain. His eyes darted between Quinn and the men fighting nearby. The man's face was whiter than the aliens' and his fear was palpable.

"Keeping you alive," he shot back in a low voice. "You can't win this fight. Leave it to Alex."

Their interaction had not gone unnoticed, however. Adrian landed a vicious blow to Alex's midsection with his foot, sending the man perilously close to the water. Then Adrian set his sights on Quinn and Duncan, not that he likely cared about the cop. He had Quinn by his neck in the space of a heartbeat. He held him dangling off the ground so far that Quinn's feet couldn't touch it.

His air supply was cut off. Choking and gasping, he scratched at Adrian's hand. That was all the creature needed to hold him in place. It was less than futile, his efforts having no effect. Adrian laughed as he turned Quinn like a prize for Alex to see.

"Let him go, fucker!" Using both feet, Duncan kicked from his position lying on the ground. He hit Adrian's legs enough to jar him.

The distraction caused the grip on Quinn's throat to ease. He was able to draw in a needed breath and almost wiggle free. Adrian hissed at Duncan, all fangs and hot breath. Then he grunted wide-eyed as he flew away by virtue of Alex's newest assault. Quinn landed in the crook of Alex's arm before being pushed down.

"Duncan, keep him out of the way," Alex ordered before racing over to grab Adrian by the throat. "You dare to touch what's mine!" He punctuated his angry accusation by biting off a chunk of Adrian's face.

"Oh." Quinn had to look away from the blood and gore.

Wrapping his uninjured arm around Quinn's shoulders, Duncan pulled him flat on the ground. "You were right, kid. This is nothing for us to get in the middle of. These fuckers are way out of my league for sure, whatever the hell they are."

"Aliens." The word popped out of his mouth before he could stop it.

Duncan sighed. "Of course, they are. Shit! Better than being vampires, I guess. And regardless, I want your boyfriend coming out on top, if only because the other asshole killed my partner."

"I don't think so." Quinn shook his head and pointed a trembling finger in the direction of where he'd last seen Val and Anderson. The cop was lying on his side now. Val had one hand on the man's shoulder in what seemed like a reassuring gesture while he watched Alex and Adrian fight.

"Well, I'll be damned," Duncan breathed. "Thank God." He fumbled around his pocket and pulled out his phone. "I need to call for back-up and an ambulance."

Quinn grabbed his hand. "Not yet. *Please!* Give Alex a chance."

Duncan shook his head. "Sorry, Quinn. This is bigger than any of us."

Alex didn't need to bite Adrian for his killing instinct and strength to come to full force. It had been enough for Adrian to have even tried to lure Quinn into a trap. But drawing first blood gave him the boost to finish things—for good—as had the sight of Quinn being choked.

"You're finished, Adrian. Dracul has sent you to your death."

The guy hissed, bravado in the face of the certain outcome. "Dying for him is a greater honor than serving you ever was."

Alex ignored the taunt and braced for the next assault. He let Adrian run right into him, pivoting at the last moment to slam his leg into the man's midsection. The second Adrian doubled over, Alex wrapped his arm around his neck and sank his fangs into the jugular. The warm, sweet flow gave him power. As he sucked in Adrian's life force, his muscles grew stronger, even as the body within his hold sagged. There was nothing more delicious and energizing than their own species' blood. It had been centuries since he'd last tasted it and he hated how much he loved doing so now.

Adrian reached back to grab Alex by the crotch and squeezed hard enough to remind Alex that everyone was a danger until they drew their last breath. Grunting back his pain, he twisted Adrian's head even farther to one side and tore out a chunk of his neck. Blood spurted out. He toppled them both to the ground and held his opponent there while the man's still-beating heart drained out the rest of his life.

Slowly, Adrian's body went slack. Alex freed his poor genitals from the motionless fingers but didn't let go until there was no more pulse to feel and no more blood to drain. He stood carefully, getting his breath under control and fighting the urge to take the dead body apart anyway.

Something slammed into him. He went to grab it with lethal intent until he realized it was Quinn. The human had his arms wrapped around Alex's waist and his face pressed against his chest.

"Dearest boy." He tried to pry him off. "I'm covered in gore."

Quinn held on even tighter and shook his head. "Don't care."

Alex smiled in spite of himself and hugged the slender, quaking body tightly. "Well, now, this makes it all worthwhile." Quinn was shaking. "Are you crying?" When Quinn didn't answer, he tugged the boy's face to see for himself.

Tears streaked down Quinn's cheeks. "I was afraid he was going to kill you."

Alex swiped at the tears with his thumbs. "I would be affronted at your lack of confidence in me if your concern wasn't so adorable."

A frown settled over Quinn's beautiful face, the only warning he got before the boy smacked him on his chest with sufficient force to sting. "It's not funny." More tears came, then, and a sob.

Alex pulled him back into the hug. "No, you're right. It isn't." He glanced over the boy's head at the man staggering toward him. "Ah, Sergeant Duncan. How are you?"

The cop stopped a few feet away, looking worse for the wear, yet alive. "I've called for back-up, so on the one hand, thanks for saving my life, but on the other hand, you're under arrest."

Quinn gasped and pulled away. "That's not fair! Alex didn't do anything wrong."

Duncan swallowed hard, obviously in pain, and just as obviously scared shitless. Despite both, he held Alex's gaze. "Yeah, I'm not sure about that. Fortunately, aliens are not my jurisdiction. Someone else can figure out guilt and innocence here."

Alex arched his eyebrow at his boy. "Quinn?"

He winced. "Sorry. It came out in the heat of the moment."

"I see. Well" —he smiled to show he wasn't mad— "one way or the other, the cat was out of the bag, shall we say. Unfortunately, unless Quinn and Mackie are willing to testify about all this, you're going to have a very strange and unbelievable tale to tell your fellow cops and the FBI, sergeant."

Sirens sounded in the background, telling him that Duncan had indeed called for reinforcements and time was getting short.

Duncan straightened as much as his injuries would allow. He had to admire the man's guts. "What the fuck, Stelalux? Anderson saw everything, too."

"Alas, I don't think so." He tossed his head toward the pier area. "It appears Val was able to save him. *You're welcome for me saving you.* But he looks to be unconscious. I don't think he saw anything useful. And with his head being hit before he went into the water, his memory would be suspect, regardless."

"Ah, fuck," Duncan swore without much heat. He pointed at Quinn.

The boy shook his head and pressed closer to Alex's side. "Sorry, sir. I'm not saying anything that will get Alex in trouble. He's the good guy here."

The cop closed his eyes briefly. "I have a body. An *alien* one, apparently."

"Hmm, not so much, no." Stepping to one side, he allowed the human a good view of where Adrian had fallen. There was little left other than the guy's clothing, and soon every last trace of his biological material would be so much dust.

Alex wiped Adrian's now-flaky remnants off his own face, then did the same to the parts of Quinn where bits had transferred when he'd pressed against Alex. He flicked the dry particles away, disgusted that any amount of Adrian had touched his boy. The wind did the rest. Duncan stared wide-eyed.

"It's a quirk of our species that we disintegrate in minutes. Our ancient ancestors would have mixed the dust with spit and water and used it as mortar for our dwellings. It was both a good use of resources and a way of keeping our dear departed close."

He gently pried Quinn's arm off and went to kick at the decaying body, sending more particles into the air. "By the time your people arrive, there will be nothing except a pile of clothing and no DNA to analyze."

Bending, he started bunching and tossing everything, as if someone had stripped. Giving Duncan a stern look, he continued, "My story is that a madman kidnapped one of my former employees and lured my lover into an ambush. I was too afraid to call in the FBI because he'd threatened to kill both boys if I did so. I have no idea how you and your partner managed to get here."

Standing, he proceeded to scuff at the remainder of Adrian's dust, scattering it and grinding it into the dirt. "After nearly killing one cop and overpowering another, he tore off his clothing and jumped into the water—in an effort to escape, perhaps. I don't expect the body to be recovered, but as the killings will have stopped, a fair assumption will be that the killer drowned."

"Motherfucker!" Duncan's fury was understandable, yet there was nothing to be done about it. There was really only one loose end.

"Let me go!" Mackie's plaintive demand floated over to them as Val carried the boy in their direction.

"Shut up." Val's tone was dispassionate to human ears, no doubt, but Alex heard the anguish behind it. It had only been rank that had allowed Alex to claim the right to kill Adrian and Val's fury had almost overridden that.

Duncan bared his teeth as the realization dawned on him that he had one more hope. "We do have another witness." The sirens were almost upon them. "Hey, kid, tell me what you saw."

Sniffling, Mackie went from glaring at Val to blinking at Duncan. "I'm sorry, sir, what?"

"The guy who grabbed you… What was he like and what did you see happen here?"

"Um." Mackie bit his lower lip and looked down at the arm he cradled in his lap. "He was scary, and he broke into my apartment and beat me. He broke my arm when I said I wouldn't call Quinn, so I did because I was afraid."

Val made a sharp noise in the back of his throat that caused Mackie to pause and blink at him.

"Sure," Duncan prodded. "I get that. You had no choice. No one's blaming you for that."

"Of course, we're not," Alex agreed. "You are an innocent in all this. Rest assured on that point."

Mackie dropped his gaze. "Thanks, Alex. Anyway, that's all I know."

"No, that can't be all." Duncan was practically tearing his hair out, and now doors were slamming and there was shouting. "You saw this fight, right? I mean, you saw that these guys aren't…"

"Aren't what, sir?"

"*Human.*" Duncan glanced over his shoulder. "Over here. I'm Sergeant Duncan and my partner needs medical attention," he added, pointing to the pier. Then he looked once more at Mackie.

The boy shrugged. "I'm sorry, sir. I don't know what you mean."

"Fuck! God-fucking-damn-it!" Duncan bent over as if his show of temper had hurt him.

Mackie shrunk back from the explosive words, curling closer to Val. Baring his teeth for a second at the cop, Val walked away in the direction of the cluster of people running toward them.

Duncan pointed his finger at Alex. "This isn't over."

"I understand, sergeant." He watched the man stagger toward his fallen partner.

"Is it over, Alex?"

Pressing a kiss on the boy's head, he gave an honest answer instead of the reassurance he knew the boy wanted. "No, my darling boy. This is only the beginning, I'm afraid."

Chapter Fourteen

Wales

"Sir?"

Dracul waved a bored hand in the physician's direction. "Yes, yes, I heard you. You've given my slut IV fluids. I need to fuck him less harshly and drink less of his blood."

"If you want to get more sons from him, yes, sir." The man licked his lips before continuing. "You might also consider letting him get out of bed. A bit of exercise and fresh air would do him some good."

"Hmm. I suppose I could take him out, using his collar and leash. That might be entertaining. Would you like to go walkies, pet?" There was no response from the quivering mass lying on the bed. "No matter. I like the idea and that's all that counts."

The doctor opened his mouth, but a knock on the door made him shut it again.

"Enter," Dracul shouted. "And get out."

Petru and the doctor passed each other with equally hurried steps. The warrior stopped in front of where Dracul lounged by the cold fireplace and gave a curt bow.

"Adrian has failed."

Dracul frowned at the news. "So soon?" He took a noisy breath. "It should have taken him weeks before Alex caught him. What of this new boy of Alex's?"

"Apparently, Adrian took him as bait, but Alex ended up victorious. At least that's what I read from what little the humans have to say about it. They are still looking for his remains."

Dracul hissed. "Fool! He overstepped his bounds by taking Alex on instead of killing the boy as ordered. No redemption, after all." He flopped on one of the large, comfy chairs by the fireplace. "No matter. Partial success will have to do."

He poured a glass of the wine sitting on the table next to him and took a long, glorious swallow. The humans did have some things of value to offer.

"With respect, sir, I don't understand how this helps us."

"You're not a strategist, Petru. Don't try to step outside your comfort zone. This was only meant to be a tap on Alex's shoulder. The real fun will begin soon." He took another sip. "Send me my sons."

With another bow, Petru left without asking further questions. The man did know when to shut up, a useful trait. And this new skirmish had yielded some unexpected ammunition against his enemy — Alex had a new boy, and with him, a new weakness to exploit.

Things were looking much brighter.

* * * *

Boston

The tension from the long, horrible night drained away from Quinn under the onslaught of the hot spray. He groaned as the water pounded over his back. *Thank God for Alex's multi-headed shower.* It was like being massaged by a thousand tiny fingers. He groaned in appreciation.

Alex stepped in and wrapped his arms around him. "You shouldn't make such noises unless you want to issue a different kind of invitation than simply joining you in the shower."

Quinn smiled and melted into the embrace. Alex was already hard and his own dick was making a valiant effort. He didn't want to fuck in the shower, however tempting the thought was. Although he had made the commitment to this man already, saying the words sometime during the interminable night of questioning by the FBI, he still needed answers to his own questions before moving forward with the relationship.

Turning his head, he pressed a kiss to Alex's wet chest right between his pecs. "Can we wash first then talk?"

"Whatever you want."

Alex's easy acquiescence was followed by his lathering a generous amount of soap and rubbing it all over Quinn's body. He started with his shoulders and made his way down. At each point, he massaged Quinn's tight muscles. The touch was both clinical and arousing. By the time Alex had finished, Quinn was equally relaxed and harder than ever.

Alex ran a slick palm up Quinn's shaft, making him moan and reassess his decision. With his eyes closed, he swayed forward, certain that Alex would never let him fall. Their dicks brushed against each other, causing his breath to hitch.

"None of that now," Alex chuckled, before swatting him on his ass. "Out you go. Wait for me on the bed and we'll do that talking, hopefully where we'll fuck afterward."

"Oh." Disappointed, even though he had no one to blame except himself, Quinn reluctantly left the shower.

He gifted himself with drying off inside the steamy room because it allowed him to watch Alex wash. The man's body didn't have a mark on it, despite the epic battle he'd waged less than twelve hours before.

As he soaped his rampant cock, Alex turned to smile at him. He mouthed the word 'go' before getting back to his task.

Quinn dragged his reluctant feet into the bedroom. He found his brush and other toiletries on Alex's bureau, and a quick check of the drawers confirmed that one was stuffed with his minor amount of clothing. He sat heavily on the bed, tending to his hair and absorbing the reality that he was now living with another man.

The decision had been his. Sometime during his separate FBI interview, he'd found himself telling Chin that he and Alex were a couple and that he intended to live with him. It had seemed right, and it reinforced what he'd also said about how Alex had come to his rescue. Sure, Duncan and Anderson had caused the killer to flee, but it didn't change the fact that Alex had come, even knowing that he was walking into a potentially lethal situation.

He loved Alex. He'd said those words to the FBI before he'd had a chance to say them to his lover. He intended to rectify that situation very soon. First, though, he needed answers.

Alex stepped out of the bathroom, his magnificent body now on full display. Quinn's cock jerked in greeting and he had to shove it between his legs to keep it under control. Of course, Alex had seen it already and grinned as he approached and joined him on the bed.

"How's Mackie?" Quinn popped out the question, suddenly nervous.

Alex acted as if it was perfectly fine to procrastinate. "He's comfortably settled in your old room."

Quinn bit his lip. "Is he okay with being back here?"

"He seems to be. With his arm broken and a few bruised ribs, the human doctor said he needs looking after. She was pleased to find out a doctor lives here, too. Harry will take good care of him."

"What about Val?"

Alex sighed and rubbed his towel over his head. "That's not something I can answer. I assured Mackie that he is safe here and that he has his job back with no strings attached. What that means for him and Val is between them."

"He still loves Val. He must or he wouldn't have kept his mouth shut about... You know..."

"Hmm, and Val loves him, in his own way. But, it's not that easy for him to admit or act on his feelings. His past experience with a human partner is painful, as is mine," he added in a quiet voice that didn't sound like the commanding guy he was.

Quinn angled his body to face Alex more. "Tell me. Please. If we're to have a chance together, I need to know everything."

Alex mimicked the posture, keeping his gaze at a point somewhere past Quinn's head. "The first two hundred years or so on this planet, we kept mostly to ourselves." He paused and swallowed visibly. "We held out some hope of our people finding us, and our only plan was to stay unnoticed by the indigenous peoples."

"Humans," Quinn supplied.

Alex nodded his head. "Humans. It wasn't easy because, as I've said, Dracul had other ideas. He kept interacting with them. At first, he claimed it was all accidental. Later, when he started to openly challenge my authority, he dropped that pretense.

"At some point, we just couldn't keep ourselves hidden away completely. The local population was growing and there was nothing for us to do except try to blend in. We adopted human names and began trading with them."

Scrubbing his face with his hand, he stopped for a longer period of time before he continued. His strained expression was hard to see. "We were lonely, as well, for intimate company." He looked into Quinn's eyes. "We're a bisexual species, but we usually find partners of the same sex who are younger than we are. Fucking shipmates is tolerable on long journeys, but not something satisfying for centuries."

"So you formed relationships with humans?"

"Yes, except not knowing if we could breed with your species, I forbade my men from approaching females. No one fought me on that, and eventually, even I found someone that I really wanted. It took me five centuries to let myself go enough to form that relationship."

Quinn's stomach quivered at the confession. In some respects, he felt jealous, even though it was stupid to think that way about some guy who had died centuries ago. "Just the one?" he asked because he had to know.

Alex stared back at him, pain lacing his violet eyes. "Yes, just the one — Antonio. Until you."

"Oh." Well, it made him feel better to know that Alex had only fell for another man once every half-millennium. "Did he stay with you his whole life?"

Alex closed his eyes briefly. "Yes, two wonderful years."

"Two years?"

"Before Dracul killed him. He'd already broken off from my leadership and started his sporadic reign of terror by human proxy. He didn't like it when I took the humans' side and tried to stop him. Killing Antonio was meant to punish me for that sin."

"Oh, Alex."

The knowledge that his lover had been hurt so badly overrode his other questions and concerns. Deciding that they had plenty of time to talk later, he threw himself at the man, much the way he'd done after the battle. And like that time, Alex caught him easily and pulled him in for a hug tight enough to squeeze the breath out of him.

Alex stole the rest by capturing his lips and kissing with an unparalleled hunger. They fell onto their sides, arms and legs entwined and dicks bumping against each other. Alex soon had him on his back, with Alex plunging his tongue down his throat.

Quinn wiggled, moaned and moved his hands around as much of Alex's hard body as he could reach. The coolness of the man's skin no longer surprised him. He understood now why it was so, and although a brief whiff of fear shivered through his body, he stiffened his spine and his resolve.

He loved this man, no matter who or what he was. Unlike his own family, Alex and the other alien males had welcomed him into their orbit with open arms. No one had ever made him feel more cared for or wanted than Alex. There was only one aspect of him that made Quinn's blood run a little cold, which naturally was Alex's desire to suck it.

Alex broke the kiss only to nibble his way to Quinn's chin, then neck. He tossed his head back to give the man better access and scratched him when each lick sent waves of pleasure to his cock. He moaned and rolled his hips.

"Easy." Alex pinned him with a hand pressing flat against Quinn's stomach. "We have all the time in the world and I want to experience every second of it fully."

The import of the man's words became clear as he lavished attention on all the bits between Quinn's head and groin. Using lips, tongue and teeth, Alex played with Quinn's nipples until they were puffy and tender. Quinn repaid the sadistically slow effort by digging his nails into the man's sinewy back muscles.

"Hmm, more," Alex murmured before biting a nipple hard enough to make Quinn's eyes water.

Taking him at his word, he clawed long streaks along the man's flesh. That earned his other nipple some attention that had him yelping. A soothing tongue bath mollified him until Alex continued his journey. It ended, deliciously, with Quinn's cock inside Alex's mouth.

"Shit, yeah." He arched into the blowjob, sending his dick down Alex's throat.

The guy made it seem so easy. Quinn would have happily kept his cock there and come from the intense way it was being milked. Alex, though, had other ideas.

He pulled off it, letting his tongue and teeth slide along the shaft. Then he rolled away entirely.

Quinn whimpered at the loss of contact, even though he knew Alex was only getting lube.

The man chuckled. "Two seconds, impatient boy." He returned and pressed one knee between Quinn's quivering legs to spread them open. "Look at me, Quinn."

It was hard, but he pried open his eyes and gazed into Alex's now-black ones. "They really do change color when you're aroused, don't they?"

"Yes. Black is for passion, while red is for blood lust." He squeezed a dollop of lube onto two fingers, and using his muscular thighs, forced Quinn's to an almost ninety-degree angle. He shoved those greased fingers inside Quinn's hole with a slow, easy motion.

Quinn grunted at the burn and relaxed as much as he could. It didn't take a lot of effort, now, to loosen him. His ability to take something up his ass came easily, especially when Alex rubbed against his prostate with each thrust. He closed his eyes and fisted the bedding, savoring the pleasure consuming him. He even pulled his legs higher to give Alex greater access.

"Do you trust me?"

"Completely," he answered without hesitation.

"Then no condom is necessary. I can't give you any diseases."

Quinn's thoughts scattered as his prostate was goosed by the relentless finger-fucking. "Okay." Some back part of his brain tried to sound an alarm. There was something he was forgetting. He batted it away mentally and concentrated on the exquisite pleasure that was to come.

"Do it now. Please, fill me with your cock."

Alex chuckled again. "So impatient and greedy — and beautiful. My precious boy."

That was all the warning Quinn got before Alex replaced his fingers with his dick. The thick, hard rod slid in almost as easily. It stretched the rim of Quinn's hole wide enough to make him hiss a moment in pain, but Alex mercifully didn't stop. Instead, he kept up the relentless thrust until Quinn's channel was filled to bursting and Alex's balls bounced against his ass.

"I can't take this slow." Alex's voice sounded harsh and strained.

Grabbing the backs of his thighs, Quinn opened himself even more. "I don't want you to."

Alex pushed forward to send his cock even deeper before pulling out and pounding him with a speed and force that sent Quinn bouncing off the mattress. He panted and tossed his head, curled his toes and dug his fingers into his own skin. His unattended dick bobbed against his stomach, weeping and aching with the need to be touched. But he refused to risk the loss of his position. He wanted to give Alex the best ride of his life.

He needn't have worried. The man made him gasp when he grabbed Quinn's cock in a tight-fisted grip. With each flick of his wrist, Alex rubbed his thumb across the head. Pre-cum eased the way and his climax built with predictable speed.

Just as he felt his balls pull in an achy warning of emptying, Alex changed the angle of his body to fall over Quinn. He landed his hand with a thump by Quinn's head, while he used his other one to continue its assault on Quinn's cock.

Alex pressed his lips against the base of his throat. A quick inhale by Alex was the norm by now, except Quinn knew for the first time what the man really wanted — not a sniff, but a taste. The knowledge caused his lungs to freeze and he stiffened before he could stop the reaction.

"This is all I need," Alex whispered. "Nothing more, I promise." He thrust deeply, rasping Quinn's prostate and making him cry out and arch his back.

He almost forgot his thoughts — almost. He knew Alex was lying. Blood was not just a fetish but a staple for the man. If Quinn was going to commit his life to him, he had to do it completely. Otherwise, he would always feel that he was failing his partner on some level.

"No," he breathed out the word, then said it more forcefully. "No. You need blood and I want to give it to you. Bite me, Alex. Please, please, do it. I want it." Feeling the cum boiling up, he yelled, "*Now!*"

The strike hurt more than he'd expected. So much so that he couldn't even breathe at the moment it happened. A second later, he screamed and his body went rigid. It felt suspended like that, hovering over the bed. Then he came crashing down. Cum pulsed out of his dick in the most intense orgasm of his life. It was as if his shaft spasmed in Alex's fingers and his hole squeezed hard enough to make his ass feel as though it were shattering.

He drew in one rasping breath before melting into the mattress. A languid feeling stole over him. The lingering pain where Alex's fangs had sunk into his flesh washed away. In its place there was a rhythmic sucking that matched the snapping of Alex's hips as he continued to fuck him. Quinn could feel the tug of Alex's swallows with each beat of his heart, and when the man's cum flooded his ass, it coated his insides with a hot sensation that somehow spread to the place where teeth met flesh.

Moaning, Alex drew one more mouthful before releasing his hold. Quinn surprisingly missed the connection the moment it was lost. Alex's gentle lapping cooled the spots where the fangs had embedded. He tried to open his eyes to get a look at his lover. He needed to see how much he'd pleased the man. His lids were too heavy to move, however, and quite against his will, he drifted off.

* * * *

Alex couldn't stop staring at his boy, or rather, at the two bruised points where he'd bitten him. Quinn was his now. No matter what happened, that truth could not be denied. More than battling Adrian, claiming Quinn had left Alex wired and bewildered. He couldn't sleep, and he still couldn't believe that the boy had given him his blood after all that had happened.

"Such a brave boy," he murmured, so as not to wake him.

Quinn stirred, anyway, having slept only a few hours, not enough to recover from the all night's misery of interrogation by the tenacious Chin. The woman had known they weren't giving her the entire truth, but unless Duncan had given her the rather tall tale of aliens, he knew there was nothing more the woman could do to them.

Blinking open his eyes, Quinn smiled at him. "You know that technically I'm a man."

Alex smiled and ran his finger down Quinn's nose. "*Technically*. But to me, you are my boy. I'm afraid you need to indulge me in that affection."

Quinn grabbed his finger and bit the tip with an impish smile. "Okay, old man."

Alex laughed. "Touché." Quinn ran his fingers over the bite marks. "Are you all right?"

"Uh-huh. It heals so quickly."

"It's a chemical in my saliva. No regrets?" He actually held his breath waiting for the answer.

Quinn shook his head. "None. It kind of adds to the experience, doesn't it?"

Pleased by the observation, he said, "Yes, it does. At least, it always does for my people. It doesn't always work that way for humans. I'm glad it did for you."

Quinn frowned. "Do you drink other boys' blood?"

"Not now." Bending, he kissed those pouty lips. "Just yours."

"Good, because I'm into monogamy."

"As of today, so am I." He gave in to the temptation to kiss his boy again, then kept on doing it until they were both gasping for air. He cupped Quinn's face. "I promise I will protect you from Dracul. He won't touch you."

"It isn't over. I know. You said as much, and I understand that the guy won't stop until he's dead. I want you to believe me when I say I'm going to stay by your side in this fight."

Quinn was adorable in his fierceness, yet a spike of fear still caused Alex's heart to skip a beat. "I do believe you, and I want you to believe me when I say I'm going to do everything in my power to keep you *out* of this fight."

The boy huffed. "Oh, Alex." He pulled back a bit and frowned. "What's your real name? I mean, you have a name your parents gave you, right?"

"Not exactly. The queen gives a kind of designation to all babies. It's like having a name."

"So, what is it?"

"You don't want to hear it."

Quinn pursed his lips. "Yes, I do."

Alex sighed, seeing his future with his stubborn human. Then he gave his designation, his mother tongue sounding strange to him. They rarely spoke it because of how humans who heard it reacted.

Right on cue, Quinn reared back with an 'ow' and clapped his hands over his ears. "That hurts."

"Like a cat screeching. I know. We don't use the kind of grammar that is common to human languages and use octaves your ears don't like. You couldn't replicate it with your vocal chords, even if you tried."

Quinn blew out a breath. "So much for alien pillow talk."

"It's okay." Sliding down, he pulled Quinn into his chest. "I like human languages anyway."

The boy snuggled into his embrace, that simple show of trust pleasing him more than anything. "How many of them to you speak?"

"All of them."

There was pause before the boy laughed. "Of course, you do. Maybe spending time with you will broaden my knowledge. Oh!" Quinn wiggled out of his arms and curled into a sitting position. "I just remembered what it was I wanted to ask you."

Alex raised his eyebrows. "I thought we'd covered all the ground, but ask away, dear boy."

"What did Demi mean when he said Lucien carried and gave birth to him?"

Oh, shit. He'd hoped to put this one last issue off for a while. A long while. "Umm..."

"And don't say he's a transgender man with working female parts because Demi said no, that's not the case. So, was the kid just pulling my leg or what?"

Shoving up, Alex patted the spot beside him in silent invitation. Once more, Quinn snuggled against him without hesitation. "Okay, this is going to be the strangest thing of all for you to absorb."

"I think we passed strange all the way back with the alien part, but go ahead. I'm ready."

"I told you how my species is hive-based with queens and a few other females reproducing. What I didn't tell you is that over the course of our evolution, we developed the ability for males to convert gender spontaneously. It happens any time our population is threatened by not having enough breeding females. In that situation, males turn into females for other males to breed off of. It only happens to very young males."

Quinn stiffened beside him. "Oh my God, are you saying that by fucking me, you're going to turn me into a woman?" His voice squeaked on the last word of his question, and he bolted to his knees. Surprisingly — and tellingly — he elected to straddle Alex's lap as he did so. He stared back at him with wide eyes.

Alex couldn't help but smile. He tucked strands of hair behind the boy's ears so he could see his beautiful face, as well as the bite marks, more easily. "No, that's not going to happen."

Quinn sighed in obvious relief. "So, how does it work, then?"

"I have to feed you a steady diet of my blood, and it's only effective when the human is younger than twenty-five or so. Your brains, as well as your bodies, are still growing until that point. It also takes months, if not years, for the transformation to occur."

Samantha Cayto

"Oh." He bit his lower lip while he absorbed the information. "Does it turn me fully into a woman? Lucien looks like a guy on the outside."

"That's because he is still male with all his boy bits," he teased to lighten the mood. "The transformation is partial and only on the inside. Even so, you wouldn't be fully female, just enough to produce an egg and gestate it. I don't know all that much about it. Harry can give you more details, if you want."

"Okay, I guess."

"There is something more you should consider that matters to me more than having offspring. Drinking my blood will extend your life."

"For how long?"

"I don't know for sure. Centuries, at least. Given that I have another five hundred or more Earth years to live, it would mean we'd grow old together."

Quinn's expression softened at the idea. "Oh, that would be wonderful. I'll think about it. I have time, I guess."

Pulling him down, Alex kissed his forehead. "Lots, and I won't pressure you. I'm not even sure I want you to take the risk."

"It's risky?"

"It can be. Dracul was the first to figure it out, and he never cared what happened to the boys he tried to turn into breeders."

A shudder ran through Quinn and Alex hugged him into lying on his chest. He ran his palm across his back to sooth him. "Don't worry. My love is not contingent on your giving me sons, and I will be grateful for whatever time we have together."

Another shiver ran through the boy and his dick started pressing against Alex's. "You love me?"

Alex squeezed him tight enough to make him squeak. "Of course, I do."

"You said your species can't love the way we do."

"I misspoke to explain Val's behavior. We do love in our own way, but we also can set it aside when the situation demands it."

"That's like being human, too. And it's a good thing that you do love me because I love you, too."

Alex sighed. "Oh, my darling boy, you make me so very happy."

"That's my plan for the rest of my life." He wiggled his ass. "Do you want to fuck me again?"

Alex laughed and bucked his hips to glide his hard cock against the boy's stomach. "Always."

Before he could follow through on that assertion, his phone rang. He growled his frustration and answered it. "What?"

"Duncan is here to see you," Kitty replied. "He looks like he won't take no for an answer."

"Damn it. I'll be right there."

"I heard," Quinn said, sliding off him. He lay with one arm over his head and ran the other hand up his shaft. "We'll be waiting for you."

"I've created a monster."

Quinn smirked. "Takes one to know one. Maybe we should make another trip to the playroom. You can tie me up and torture me with your tongue." He batted his eyelashes, then ruined the seductive effect by laughing.

Alex leaned down to plant a fierce kiss on the boy's lips. "Be careful what you wish for, darling boy."

He dressed in only loose lounge pants, wanting the cop to know that he was interrupting something. The moment he stepped out of the elevator and saw the man's haunted expression, he felt contrite.

"How is your partner?" he asked, coming to within a few feet of where Duncan leaned against the bar. He didn't want to get within punching distance.

"He's still in the hospital under observation. He got a concussion when he hit the crane but your friend saved his life." Duncan straightened. "I'd like to thank him personally for that. I know he didn't have to go in after him."

"That's where you're wrong, sergeant. By our code, he did. And while I appreciate the sentiment, Val neither needs nor wants your thanks."

The man rubbed his hand across his brow. He looked as if he hadn't slept since the night before. He pinned Alex with sharp eyes nevertheless. "Your code, huh. I guess our species aren't so different. I'd like to think if the situation had been reversed, both Karl and I would have tried to save any of you." He flicked his gaze over to where Kitty was studiously polishing her beer taps. "Is she one?"

"No. We're all male, and we all look like this." He circled a hand around his front. "She does, however, know."

"But she's not talking, like the boys."

"We are fortunate in our friends."

Duncan nodded his head. "Lucky you. I can't say the same. Karl doesn't remember much, as you predicted, and I was too chicken-shit to say anything."

"It takes more courage to employ discretion, sergeant."

The man chuckled, a hollow sound. "Yeah, yeah." He didn't so much as sit on a bar stool as fall onto it. "I guess I could use some coffee, if you don't mind."

"Absolutely." He nodded at Kitty. "And some food, as well."

"Don't go to any trouble."

"I assure you that Emil's love of cooking is genuine."

Placing a big mug in front of the cop, Kitty said, "I'll go get you a cheeseburger and fries."

"Thanks." Duncan grabbed the mug like a drowning man would a preserver. In some respects, the metaphor was very apt. The man had to be swamped by the unbelievable information swirling in his head.

"We're not your enemy," Alex said.

Duncan eyed him over the rim. "Some of you are."

"True. We've split into two factions."

The cop grunted, slurped and eyed him again. "How many of them are you?"

"A few dozen, more or less."

"You don't know the exact count?"

"It varies for complicated reasons. And you should know we are marooned, not some vanguard for an invasion."

"Okay, that's good to know. But you are waging a war."

"Among ourselves. You humans are both pawns and collateral damage, I'm afraid."

"That's reason enough for me to get involved."

Alex was stunned at that declaration. They'd had a lot of human allies over the centuries. Kitty was a prime example. None of them tended to weather the situation well. He liked this cop and hated the idea of him getting killed. It would be hard enough to protect Quinn and even Mackie.

"There is no need. This really isn't your fight."

Duncan's eyes turned to flint. "It became mine the minute they started killing people in my town. You're going to need help. Someone like me with his ear to the ground can only be an asset to your side of the fight."

"You would do that for us?"

Duncan took a long swallow before answering, "No, I'm doing it for Boston and for humanity. Do we have a deal?"

He gave the man the most charming smile he knew how. "Well, I will say that so long as you're willing to keep our secret, I will welcome your help."

Duncan nodded. "That's a deal in my book." He put the mug down. "Do you shake?"

"But, of course." He extended his hand, and yes, sealed the pledge as he'd done many times before.

* * * *

Despite his earlier bravado, Quinn spent the time Alex was away chewing his lip and drumming his fingers on the bed. His erection had flagged, too. The moment he heard the sounds of Alex's return, however, he sat up.

"Is everything okay?"

Alex knelt beside him and running this thumb along Quinn's gnawed-on lip, smiled. "Surprisingly, yes. Our Sergeant Duncan has joined Team Stelalux, as it happens."

Because he knew Alex liked it, Quinn snatched his thumb between his teeth for a second "That's awesome. Having a cop on our side will help."

"So he said."

On a sudden urge of worry, he flung his arms around Alex's neck. "I don't want a war. I just want to be with you."

"I know." Alex's tone was achingly soft and sweet. He rubbed his hands along Quinn's lower back. "I want that, as well. I promise you this much. This won't be the beginning of the next war. It will be the beginning of the last one. I'll finish it. I'll finish Dracul, once and for all."

Alex said it as a vow and Quinn believed him.

Want to see more from this author? Here's a taster for you to enjoy!

Alien Slave Masters

The Captain's Pet

Samantha Cayto

Excerpt

Wid Bryant wrapped his arms around his waist in a futile attempt at warmth. The hangar he stood in was even colder than the transport ship, and without the limits of the confined space, no body heat from others stopped him from shivering. Of course it wasn't the cold alone that made him tremble. Fright contributed to his state. He had been scared for the last forty-eight hours or so, since he and his cohorts had been detained by the Travian security force.

What had he been thinking joining Joel and the others in vandalizing the administrative building of the occupying force? Nothing, except a deep-seated hatred for the aliens who had invaded their colony. His parents had warned him to keep his head down and hope that hostilities between the two races would be settled diplomatically. Seriously? As if there were a prayer of that happening. How did you negotiate with beings who had the superior power to wipe you off the face of any planet and with the certainty they were in the right? The battle between Earth and the Travians for the colony had ended before it began. Conquerors had no incentive to bargain. Harassing them seemed like the best way to go. Irritate them enough and maybe they'd figure the small planet wasn't worth the effort.

Or, they could simply round people up and exterminate them. That's what he had assumed would be his punishment when he'd been caught. Now he wasn't so sure. He couldn't understand why they'd bothered to ship him and eleven other guys up to a battlecruiser. Yet, here they were, standing around, freezing and waiting to learn their fate.

"Do you think they're going to kill us?"

Wid glanced at the trembling red-headed kid next to him — Stuart. He'd been shoved into the transport next to Wid, after being detained for throwing rotten fruit at a Travian convoy — a prank as stupid as the one Wid had tried to pull. The poor guy was only eighteen and more scared than Wid, if that were possible. In fact, all of the other boys that had been brought were no older than Wid's twenty years or so, and most couldn't hide their fear. Thank God there were no girls. Surprisingly the Travians had let the one girl who'd been with them, Joel's girlfriend, go immediately. His mother had scoffed over the Travians being patriarchal, but right now it seemed like a good thing.

"No," Wid finally answered. "What would be the point? I mean, if they wanted us dead, why bring us all the way up here?"

He mostly believed what he'd said. It didn't make sense that they'd be dragged so far when it was easy to blow a laser hole in their foreheads back on the planet. Still, something bad loomed. How could it not? As if in answer to his worst fears, the hangar suddenly filled with a dozen Travians. These males were even more imposing than the security detail that guarded the boys. Each one stood particularly tall, close to seven feet, clad head to toe in red leather. Their shiny black hair fell to their shoulders or below, braided in places to keep it off their harsh faces. He couldn't lie and say that the Travians were an ugly race, but they were unsettling with their pale skin and completely black eyes.

As the aliens filed in and lined up opposite the boys, Stuart let out a little whimper. Wid spared him a glance.

"Don't let them think you're scared," he advised in a low tone.

"Seriously?" Stuart murmured back. "I *am* scared."

Wid suppressed a shudder. "I know, just try not to show it. It's all we have left."

"Quiet!"

One of the guards barked out the order in the guttural language of the Travians. God, he hated being able to understand what they said. Once the occupation had been completed, the aliens had forced every human over the age of five to be implanted with a translation device. The foreign words rattled around his head until they made sense to him. The one word was easy to translate. Longer sentences spoken quickly were harder to get. Not that the Travians were patient when a human struggled to understand.

He shut his mouth, however, his bravado long gone.

The tallest of the males stood a foot in front of the others, staring down the line of human boys. When he got to Wid at the end, his gaze lingered. Wid tried not to squirm under the scrutiny. He felt invaded in the more personal sense of the word by the piercing look. After a few seconds, the male glanced away and gestured to another of them. The tall one said something short and quick that Wid didn't catch. When the other male stepped forward, he headed straight for Wid. Before Wid could even think of recoiling, the taller alien barked out one word.

"No!"

The steps of the second male faltered. His expression turned sour for a second before he changed course a fraction to go to Stuart. His hand shot out and he grabbed Stuart by one arm. The male's eyes took on a feral look as he yanked the boy to his body. Stuart cried out and tried to pull away. The male bared his teeth in what could — in an alternate and ugly reality — be called a grin. Then he turned and dragged a struggling and begging Stuart away.

Silence reigned once they'd cleared the hangar. Wid and the other boys were frozen as they digested what had happened to Stuart and what was going to happen to them. The aliens were quiet too, although that seemed to be more about discipline, waiting for a command. The tallest, who was obviously in charge, gestured to another of them. Once again the boys were perused, and Wid recognized the behavior for what it was — they were shopping, picking out which boy they wanted. He didn't dare think in terms of what they wanted the boys for.

Some of the boys struggled when taken, others acquiesced in silent misery. Joel made Wid smile in grim satisfaction when he punched the male who reached for him. The alien barely reacted, as if he'd been bitten by an insect. The disparity between the races physically meant the humans had no hope of fighting them off. Instead of hitting Joel back, however, the alien simply grabbed the swinging arm on the downstroke and used it as leverage to pick Joel up and toss him over his shoulder. The captured boy howled in outrage all the way out of the hangar.

Minutes later, only Wid and the commanding alien remained. Even the guards filed out. Putting his arms down by his side, Wid straightened to stand as tall as he could. Pride was all he had left and he was determined to hide his fear. The alien approached him with unhurried steps. When he came within a foot of Wid, he stopped and stared down. With an expression of as much defiance as he could muster, Wid stared back. Given the foot or so difference in their heights, he had to crane his neck back.

For a few seconds, they looked each other in the eye. The alien's thoughts and emotions were impossible to read within the endless depths of his black eyes. Wid wondered if the alien could read him, or were the species too different to communicate in subtle ways? Despite the coldness around him, sweat trickled down his back. He suppressed a shudder and silently goaded the male to go ahead and do whatever he intended. The waiting was agony.

Suddenly, as if in response to the unspoken challenge or plea—Wid wasn't sure which it was—the alien lashed out to grab Wid's arm. Instinct made Wid pull away, but it was as futile an effort as it had been for the others. The fingers around his biceps were like a steel vise. Nothing could break that hold. Not wanting to be dragged along, Wid suppressed the urge to struggle and instead picked up his feet to match the long strides of his captor.

They left the hangar and strode down a corridor. The ship held a dark and cold atmosphere. The few aliens they encountered as they wended their way, stared briefly at Wid even as they bowed their heads in quick obeisance of the male who had him. It had to be the captain, or whatever rank they recognized as the one in charge of the ship. Great, just his luck that he had gained the attention of the most powerful and, he assumed, the most ruthless of them all. Then the reason for his destiny popped into his head. Of all the boys standing in that hanger, he'd been the only one with blond hair. A shiver ran up his spine at the implication of why his looks mattered.

Many corridors and one lift ride later, the captain led him through a set of sliding doors into what had to be the male's quarters. Wid only had a second to digest this fact before he was pulled past the first room and into a second one with a large, firm-looking mattress-type thing lying in the middle of the floor. His feet stopped suddenly of their own accord when he realized they'd entered a bedroom. He stared at a bed. What else could it be?

"No!" The word was out of his mouth before his brain thought it. He tried to pull his arm free.

The alien tightened his grip and stared down at Wid with his head cocked to one side. He didn't look any happier than Wid felt, yet instead of letting him go, he reached out with his other hand and ripped Wid's T-shirt from his body. It came apart as if made from tissue paper. In the face of obvious evidence of where things were headed, Wid fought back. Twisting, punching and kicking, he tried to free himself and escape his fate with all the strength he possessed. It was like striking granite — the alien's body so hard and unyielding. If he caused the male any pain, it wasn't evident. The only sounds were coming from Wid and he was the only one showing any sign of strain.

His resistance did him no good. Everything he'd been wearing when captured was torn from his body. As soon as Wid was bare-assed naked, the alien lifted him up by the waist and tossed him onto the bed. Wid bounced a few times while he caught his breath, then tried to stand up to run. There was nowhere to go, of course, because the alien blocked the way back to the other room. But rational thought had abandoned him. Pure instinct made him try to flee. Gaining traction on the mattress proved difficult, and by the time he managed to put one foot on the floor, the alien had moved to catch him and toss him back.

Wid tried again and again, each time failing to get himself more than a step or two from the bed. The Travian said nothing. He merely methodically removed his own clothing and kept snatching Wid up and throwing him down. By the time the alien male was completely nude, Wid lay exhausted and badly winded. It didn't help that he'd been given hardly anything to eat and little water to drink since his capture. The alien, damn him, wasn't even breathing heavily as he approached the bed.

Wid crawled away backward like a crab in a last futile effort to escape. The alien looked somehow bigger without his clothes, his pale skin almost pearlescent in the ambient light of the room. There was no discernable hair on his body other than his head. The massive cock of the being stood out easily with nothing to hide it. Long and thick, it gleamed with wetness that dribbled slowly from the head. With his eyes glued to the weapon coming toward him, Wid shook his head.

"No. Please, don't," he begged in a voice choked with fear. Any bravado he'd ever felt disappeared in the face of being raped.

The alien knelt on the bed and reached for Wid. Grabbing him by the ankle, he dragged him closer. With the last of his energy, Wid kicked out with his free leg. He knew a moment's satisfaction when the Travian grunted from the solid blow that Wid landed on his chest. The creature wasn't immune from pain after all. The gratification was short-lived, however. The alien's fingers clamped down on Wid's arms and hauled him up.

Their gazes locked for a second. "Please," Wid pleaded one more time before he found himself face down on the bed.

A heavy, hot weight pressed him farther into the mattress. Warm breath tickled his ear before a bass voice rumbled, "Lie still! There is no choice for either of us."

It took a second for Wid to realize the alien spoke in English, not Travian. Before he had time to process the meaning of the words, however, something wet and warm and hard slid against his ass. The strange declaration be damned, fear gave him the strength to struggle, albeit futilely. A knee forced its way between his legs, spreading them wide. The blunt head of the alien's cock pressed against his hole, slid up his crack, then returned. Wid couldn't keep the whimper from escaping his lips. He clawed at the slippery cloth he lay on and closed his eyes tight. The alien pushed to gain entrance. Wid squeezed his sphincter tight in a vain attempt to keep him out.

"Don't resist. I'll make it quick."

Again, Wid's mind tried to process the intent behind the alien rapist's version of pillow talk. He sounded almost apologetic, which made no sense. No one hovered over the bed with a weapon to the creature's head, making him do this terrible thing. And did he really believe Wid would just acquiesce to this horror without complaint? Fucker! Wid renewed his effort to keep the alien cock out. He was no match for the creature's strength, however. The thick rod breached his hole. The searing pain of it robbed him of his breath. The cock bore into him, stretching his rectum with relentless pressure. Too stunned to even scream, he could only do as the alien had commanded — lie there and take it.

The alien's copious pre-cum slicked the way, but God, the burning as his body struggled to accept the girth and length brought tears to Wid's eyes. There was no chance to grow accustomed to the invasion. As soon as the alien had sheathed himself fully, he began his thrusting. Hard, long strokes drilled Wid into the bed. Strong fingers held him in place as if the piercing cock was not already enough to do so. He wanted to cry, would have without shame given the brutal assault, if he'd had the breath to do so. Instead, he panted to the rhythm of the pounding and prayed that, as promised, it would be over quickly.

And so it was. With a guttural growl, the alien seated himself deep inside Wid's ass. Wid could feel fluid pulsing into him. Thinking it was over, he bucked up against the heavy male. But the alien didn't get up, rather he rolled over to his side, bringing Wid with him. The cock stayed embedded. Wid tried to expel it with a strong push of his rectal muscles. The damn thing didn't budge. It remained hard and unmovable. The alien's harsh breath wafted onto Wid's head while his arm encircled Wid's chest to hold him close. Wid squirmed to free himself to no effect. Then a heavy leg was thrown over him to anchor him more firmly in place. So much for the bastard's assurances.

He remained trapped and there was nothing he could do about it. The laser shot to the head was looking better to him now. Then he thought of his parents and his sisters and how they must be worried, not knowing where he was or what had happened to him. Better that they not know.

He didn't so much fall asleep lying captured in the alien's arms, as pass out, exhausted by the day's events. He got no rest, however. Plagued by nightmares, he kept twitching awake. Understanding of his plight always came to him quickly and it was like the first time each time it happened. His heart raced with fear and he instinctively struggled to free himself, forgetting that it was pointless. Worse, his captor woke with him, if the creature even slept. His massive cock remained hard and rammed up Wid's ass. He fucked Wid again and again, ignoring Wid's pleas to stop and leave him be.

Eventually Wid's mind simply shut down and went blank.

About the Author

Samantha Cayto is a Boston-area native who practices as a business lawyer by day while writing erotic romance at night—the steamier the better. She likes to push the envelope when it comes to writing about passion and is delighted other women agree that guy-on-guy sex is the hottest ever.

She lives a typical suburban life with her husband, three kids and four dogs. Her children don't understand why they can't read what she writes, but her husband is always willing to lend her a hand—and anything else—when she needs to choreograph a scene.

Samantha loves to hear from readers. You can find her contact information, website details and author profile page at http://www.pride-publishing.com.